Sakura

The Last Blossom

M. K. HIROKAWA

WR Publishing LLC

Contents

Dedication   1

Epigraph   2

Introduction   3

1. Yanaka Village   6

2. The Road To Yokohama   17

3. The Businessman   28

4. A Teapot   39

5. A Kiss   49

6. A Day Like No Other   64

7. By The Light of The Moon   78

8. The Storm   88

9. Unexpected News   101

10. Waialua   111

11. The Best of Friends   120

12. The Pandemic   129

13. The Time Is Now   140

14. The Sting of Transition   149

15. Running From Your Shadow   159

16. Infamy   169

Interlude   181

17. Mad World   185

18. Desperation   193

19. The Triple-V   207

20. Back in The Game   219

21. Letters   230

22. At The Steps of The Palace   240

23. Mud and Rain   251

24. Secrets Told   262

25. Promises in The Fog   276

26. Echoes of The Past   292

27. Bound by Choice   300

28. The Unyielding Path   318

29. Veils of The Unsaid   330

30. The Path to Forgiveness   348

Nonfiction Historical Index   366

Pronunciation Guide   375

Bibliography   383

Dedication

To my father, Dr. Roy Sam K. Hirokawa.

Epigraph

Koko ni sachi ari.

Here lies happiness.

As the Japanese once sang:
Happiness waits beyond the storm—
in love, in hope, in you.

Introduction

The hills of Yanaka are lush, vibrant, and green. Japan is silently basking in peace as the world beyond begins to murmur with change. The small village below, nestled in the folds of the hills, is a haven for skilled artists and dedicated craftsmen. As the mighty sun begins its ascent into the sky, the rice paddies shimmer, reflecting breathtaking hues of pink and orange like polished mirrors of nature. Farmers, weathered yet hopeful, are just beginning to prepare their fields, their hands moving with practiced precision in the hopes of a bounteous season. Beyond the tranquil scene lies a winding road, its dirt path alive with the shuffle of many feet and the creak of handcarts laden with goods—and the unspoken desire to survive another day. It is a grueling twenty-mile journey to the bustling ports of Yokohama.

Friday, April 14th, 1920: The lively streets of Yokohama are brimming with vendors, their voices calling out in eager desperation, hoping to catch the eye of passersby. Wealthy merchant traders, many hailing from generations of esteemed nobility, stroll through the chaos, their sharp eyes inspecting goods with little regard for the laborious hours spent creating them. They do not notice the weathered hands, the patched and tattered clothing, or the gaunt faces etched with hunger and exhaustion. For them, only the lowest price matters, the largest profit their sole concern.

Exotic artifacts from the Orient are wrapped with care and packed meticulously into large wooden crates. These crates are then hoisted onto massive ships, so big they resemble floating mountains silhouetted against the vast ocean. Commands are barked sharply, echoing through the air as workers and sailors move in chaotic harmony, their movements like the flow of a powerful river splashing around unseen rocks and obstacles. Though the air buzzes with a symphony of languages, each person seems to instinctively understand their role, unquestioning and efficient.

Despite Yokohama's embrace of European sophistication and modernity, the deep-rooted traditions of Japan hold steadfast. It is not uncommon to see a Japanese businessman, dressed in a finely tailored double-breasted suit, stepping into an onsen at the end of a long day. Women of high status, adorned in elegant, vividly patterned kimonos, glide through the streets, their laborless white napes artfully exposed in a silent declaration of grace and refinement. Above all, respect for one's class remains an uncompromising pillar of society. Knowing one's place and honoring the family name transcends wealth or personal desire, its value soaring far above even life itself.

CHAPTER 1

Yanaka Village

"Ohayo gozaimasu (Good morning)," Yukie whispered tenderly to her husband, Namio. She knelt on the splintered wooden floor near his futon. Although Namio was only twenty-three years old, his hands were cracked and dry like mud baked under a relentless sun. Namio was a potter. One could tell a lot about a person from their hands. His nails were perpetually filled with clay, and black soot stains traced the deeply etched lines on his face. Yet, as he lay there, exhausted from a late night's work, a quiet sense of kindness radiated with each deep and steady breath.

Yukie and her husband had grown up together in the small village of Yanaka. Although Namio was a few years older, as children, they had lived only a few houses apart. Yukie's family owned a small ryotei that made the most delicious, comforting soups. Namio's father was also a potter, crafting remarkable pottery and sturdy cookware. Namio often brought intricately made bowls and plates from his father's workshop in exchange for hot meals at Yukie's family restaurant. As they grew older, their childhood friendship deepened into a beautiful love affair. After they married, Namio followed in his father's trade, working diligently to master the art of pottery.

Yukie and Namio built a humble, one-room home on a gentle hill near the village cemetery, which was famous for its breathtaking cherry blossom trees. The trees formed a canopy of vibrant pink and white during the season, adding a touch of serenity to the landscape. Namio often referred to Yukie as his beautiful Sakura, comparing her grace and beauty to the delicate blossoms.

"It's time to get up, my love," Yukie said softly, her voice tender.

"Hai (Yes)," Namio groaned, rolling over with a sigh.

Yukie lifted the patched quilt and slowly nestled herself beside Namio. When their feet touched, she felt him shiver slightly at the chill of her cold toes. Gently, Yukie reached her arm across Namio's chest in a warm, protective embrace. She could feel the steady rhythm of his heart through his shirt, and her breath softly reflected off the back of his neck. In that moment, they felt like two parts of the same soul, perfectly united.

Namio whispered, "Sakura, may this moment last as if it were our first. And if not, may I die now so I can leave this life knowing what pure joy is."

"Hai (Yes)," Yukie replied, a concealed tear slipping from her eye. She knew he would remain still, savoring this fleeting moment. Namio lay motionless, as if he were a deer hiding from its predator, unwilling to disturb the peace. After another deep breath, Yukie gave him one final squeeze and rolled him out of bed.

"We cannot live on love alone. Time to get going," she said.

Yukie poured cool water from a ceramic pitcher into a shallow bowl. Namio stretched his stiff limbs, reluctantly walking over before plunging his hands into the refreshing spring water. Instantly, the icy sensation brought his senses to life. He washed the lingering sleep from his eyes, and without a word, a soft towel appeared in his hands. As he dried his face, Yukie helped him dress in his neatly folded robes and well-worn work apron.

On their small wooden table—more like an elevated bench—sat a bowl of warm, fragrant broth and a small rice ball. Looking at the meager meal, Namio realized how close they were to running out of food. The harsh winter had been unforgiving, and the distant summer harvest felt like an eternity away. He sat down quietly as Yukie poured him a steaming cup of tea.

"Yukie, this is too much," Namio said as he broke the rice ball into two halves. "I will only eat half. Please, Yukie, eat."

Yukie smiled faintly, but Namio could see the subtle exhaustion in her face. He noticed how her once-full cheeks had thinned.

"Don't worry about me," Yukie said softly. "You need your strength if you are going to make the journey to Yokohama."

"Hai (Yes)," Namio replied. When Yukie wasn't looking, he carefully wrapped the remaining rice in a small cloth and quietly exited their home to his attached pottery shed outside.

Namio's pottery shed was humble and rustic. Inside, neat stacks of chopped wood lined the walls near his brick stove and kiln. At the center of the space stood a sturdy wooden table covered with half a dozen tools. Many of these had belonged to his father. Although well-worn, they were crafted with precision and care, serving Namio faithfully for years.

As Namio began to gather his items for the journey, he remembered his most prized piece was still in the kiln. Holding his breath, he carefully reached inside, hoping with all his might that it would be in one piece. Slowly, he lifted out a small teapot. It was exquisite, its glaze shimmering with soft hues of pink and white that caught the morning light.

Namio had not told Yukie about the teapot, fearing that the firing process might fail and leave her disappointed. Now, standing motionless, holding the delicate piece in his hands, Namio reflected on its creation and the hope it represented.

Namio added some wood to his stove to warm his stiff hands. The air was crisp and uncomfortably cool, the kind of biting cold that seemed to seep into his very bones, making his joints ache. As the gentle warmth from the stove, feeling began to flow back into his fingers, Namio reached down into a cool wooden box he had carefully stored in the shade. Inside was a small portion of clay wrapped in a damp cloth, its texture soft yet sturdy. This was all the clay he had left. He knew it would be just enough to craft a single teapot.

Aside from this soon-to-be teapot, Namio had crafted eight bowls, six pots, and twelve cups, all of which he planned to sell at the bustling Yokohama ports. These pieces represented their only hope for survival. The weight of this realization pressed down on him, a heavy, unshakable burden. Feeling overwhelmed, he decided to take a walk to clear his mind.

Namio wandered over to the cemetery. Yanaka Cemetery was renowned for its acres of cherry blossom trees, a place of serene beauty. By now, however, all the blossoms had fallen, leaving the bare branches exposed. The season had been breathtaking while it lasted, the delicate pink and white petals creating an almost dreamlike canopy. Walking among those trees with Yukie had always been one of their rare escapes from the harsh reality of their poverty. Hand in hand, surrounded by the fleeting beauty of the blossoms, Namio often thought that if heaven truly existed, it must look like this.

Namio had once heard of Heaven from foreigners who visited Yanaka village. They called themselves Christians and spoke of a merciful God who loved all his children, regardless of their class or status. Their words lingered in his mind as he strolled through the quiet grove of trees.

As these thoughts swirled, Namio wondered if there really was a God. And if there was, now seemed the time to seek his help. Looking around to ensure he was alone, Namio dropped to his knees beneath the skeletal branches and prayed for the first time in his life.

"Dear God, I am a Buddhist. I don't know if you are real. I don't know what I'm doing. My wife and I are starving, and if I cannot sell my pottery, we will die. Please, if you are real, please help us."

Namio clenched his hands together, his eyes tightly shut as he waited, hoping for some kind of sign. A cool breeze brushed against his cheek, soft and almost soothing. Slowly, he opened his eyes. In front of him, resting gently on the ground, was a single sakura flower.

He stared at the delicate blossom in disbelief. Perhaps there wasn't a God, he thought. Or perhaps there was. He couldn't be sure. But it had been worth a try. Namio reached over and picked up the fragile flower. He scanned the surrounding branches, bare and stark against the sky, realizing this must be the very last one.

Carrying the flower carefully, Namio headed back to his shed. The faintly sweet scent of the woodstove lingered in the air, reminding him it was time to work despite the weight of his thoughts.

Back at the shed, Namio sat at his workbench, its surface worn smooth by years of effort, and began to take deep, meditative breaths. He closed his eyes, picturing the teapot in his mind. He envisioned its curves, its proportions, and imagined each step of the process. When his meditation ended, he opened his eyes and let his hands take over.

It was almost as if his soul had stepped aside, allowing his body to work with instinctive precision. His fingers moved purposefully, shaping the clay with practiced skill. Paddles slapped rhythmically, scrapers smoothed the surface, and the teapot slowly began to take form.

It wasn't big, but it was perfect. And therein lay the problem. Nature is not perfect. Nature is alive, full of subtle flaws and unpredictability. A perfect teapot lacked life. Namio glanced around his workbench, searching for a way to infuse vitality into the piece. His eyes fell on a faint flash of pink—the sakura blossom.

He hadn't intended to bring it with him, but its presence felt like an answer. Gently, despite his rough, calloused hands, Namio picked up the delicate flower and pressed it lightly into the soft clay, leaving behind its distinct impression. The imprint added character, a connection to the fleeting beauty of nature. Finally, he inscribed their family's last name, Ikeda, on the bottom of the pot.

A few days later, Namio carefully placed the finished teapot into the kiln. His heart filled with both hope and fear as he silently prayed it would survive the firing process.

This was a memory Namio would never forget. Never had he made a more beautiful piece. Its delicate curves and soft glaze seemed to hold the essence of hope itself. Immediately, he hurried to show it to his wife.

"Yukie," Namio shouted as he opened the door, his voice filled with excitement. Carefully, he placed the small teapot in her hands, cradling it as though it were a treasure.

"It is the most beautiful thing I have ever seen," Yukie replied. As she admired the pot, her fingers traced the intricate imprint of the flower.

Namio saw her gaze linger on the detail and explained, "It was the last blossom."

"But how?" Yukie asked, her brow furrowing slightly, knowing that the season had long since ended.

"I have no idea. But I know this teapot will be the key to our future."

Together, they held the teapot for a moment as if it were made of gold, their hands resting together on its smooth surface.

"This will bring us the money we need," Yukie said. She removed the apron she wore every day and carefully wrapped the teapot in its soft folds. "This will keep it safe. Now, you must hurry if you are to make it to Yokohama by nightfall." Yukie placed the teapot back into Namio's hands, her touch lingering for just a moment. "I will gather your things, and you, please, ready your cart."

"Arigatou gozaimasu (Thank you)."

Yukie scavenged through their cupboards and cold storage, searching for anything she could send with Namio as he began his eight-hour walk to the Yokohama ports. All she could find were a few pieces of dried meat and some hardened mochi. With warm water, the mochi would soften back into edible food. She was unsure what she would eat herself in the days to come, but her love for Namio compelled her to pack the last of their food for his journey.

Namio carefully loaded his handcart with the ceramic pieces he had created. Each item was placed with precision, and the fragile pottery nestled securely. He walked around the cart several times, inspecting its mechanics and testing its balance. Everything needed to be packed perfectly—any crack or break would be a devastating loss for their struggling family. Finally, he was satisfied and ready to leave.

Yukie, noticing his progress, came to meet him at the cart. It was their tradition to remain silent each time Namio departed on this journey. They embraced quietly, their arms entwining as though they could draw strength from one another. In moments like this, they believed their love transcended words.

They did not say goodbye. They lived in hope, each believing they would see the other again soon. Yukie was always the first to break the embrace. She placed the small bundle of food, wrapped in a weathered cloth, into Namio's hands before walking quickly back toward their home. Namio knew where she was going. In the single room of their house stood a small Buddhist shrine, and he knew she would light incense and pray for his safe return.

Namio gripped the handle of his handcart, feeling the familiar grooves worn into the wood by his own hands over countless journeys. Though the road ahead was long and daunting, he reminded himself of the people he might encounter and the sights he would pass along the way. He prepared himself mentally to face the fierce competition of vendors at the bustling docks of Yokohama.

As he began to move forward, he glanced back at their small home. Through the window, he saw Yukie kneeling before the shrine, her head bowed in prayer. At that moment, Namio felt something rubbing against his leg inside his pocket. He stopped and reached in, pulling out the other half of the rice ball from his breakfast that morning.

His thoughts darkened as he hesitated. How much food did they have left? What if Yukie didn't have enough to survive while he was away? A chilling thought struck him: What if she were dead when he returned?

Unable to shake the worry, he quietly walked back to the window. Carefully, he placed the bundle of food Yukie had prepared for him on the counter near the washbowl, along with the remaining piece of rice from his pocket. He would find food along the way, he resolved. Yukie needed this more than he did.

With that, Namio turned and set off down the long, winding road to Yokohama.

CHAPTER 2

The Road To Yokohama

Namio began the long, grueling eight-hour walk to Yokohama. As an artist who meticulously crafted pottery, he was acutely aware of every pothole, every uneven ditch, and every large, protruding rock. Paranoia, knowing the immense value of his fragile cargo, made his journey painfully slow. Walking the winding, narrow streets of Yanaka village caused him to reflect on his childhood. Namio wondered how he had come to this place of relentless poverty.

Growing up, he had always known his family was poor, yet his father never revealed the heavy stress he must have carried each day. As a child, Namio had felt so well cared for, as though their struggles were a distant worry. Now, although he had only been married to Yukie for a short time, he constantly worried about their uncertain future. If a child were to be conceived, how would he provide? Often, Namio would turn away from moments of intimacy. He knew Yukie worried that he had lost the desire to be with her. How could he risk bringing another innocent life into this cruel world, a world that seemed determined to take everything away from them? No, he thought, he must find a way to provide first.

By this time, Namio was exiting the bustling village and entering the sprawling countryside of Yanaka. He envied the farmers standing knee-deep in the rice paddies, their pants rolled to their knees, their toes buried in the cool, wet mud. Their cone-like woven hats shielded them from the relentless sun and sporadic rain. He knew that if he had become a farmer, he would never have to worry about food. At that moment, a sharp pang of hunger gnawed at him, reminding him of how empty his stomach was.

Off in the distance, he spotted another handcart just ahead. Namio thought that if he moved quickly and carefully, he might find an opportunity to barter for some food. Luckily for Namio, he noticed the figure in the distance pause, stopping briefly to catch his breath. As Namio approached, he saw it was an elderly man with a handcart piled high with the most exquisite, colorful fabrics.

Despite the elegance of the finely woven materials, the man's boro kimono was tattered, full of weathered holes. It was clear that this man had traveled to Yokohama many times. His skin was deeply tanned and wrinkled from years under the harsh sun, and although he wore a rice paddy hat, his face was a map of creases and lines, more intricate than cobblestone streets.

"Kon'nichiwa (Hello)," shouted Namio to the old man. Looking up, the old man waved him over, his arm moving slowly with a tired but welcoming gesture.

"Genki desu ka (How are you)?" Namio said as he approached.

The man, without looking directly at him, only replied, "Hai (Yes)." He then went on to say, "Good or bad, it doesn't matter. As long as I can take another step, I know I am still alive."

Namio could now see his face clearly. The man was missing many teeth, and it was astonishing that he could see anything at all with his heavy eyelids sagging almost completely over his eyes. His expression was one of weathered endurance, a life of hardship etched into every line of his face.

"I am Namio, from Yanaka. I am going to Yokohama to sell my pottery. Might I ask, who are you?"

Although the old man did not seem overly eager to engage in conversation, he apparently decided to entertain Namio's words, perhaps as an excuse to rest his tired feet for a moment longer. "I am Takeshi. I come from the north, and as you can see, my wife and I make fabrics to be sold down at the docks.

However, I have seen the sunset many times along this path and feel certain this is my last journey."

Although Takeshi was clearly an old man, it was evident that he was still strong, his frame solid and his movements deliberate. With that, Namio summoned the courage to ask for some food.

"Sumimasen (Excuse me), I see you have brought more than enough provisions for your journey. I am but a poor potter who is in need of some food. Might you have some extra to help me along my way?" he asked, his voice tinged with desperation.

Namio was not of noble birth. However, he knew that by begging, he risked bringing deep shame to his family name. Aware of this, he quickly caught hold of his thoughts and added, "I'm sure there is something in my handcart you could use. Would you be interested in a cup or a bowl?"

Takeshi's eyes slowly scanned what Namio had to offer, his gaze deliberate and discerning. Then he noticed something wrapped in a woman's work apron, the cloth worn but carefully folded.

With a grunt, Takeshi inquired, "What is in that cloth over there?"

"Oh, that is nothing," Namio responded nervously, his hands fidgeting slightly.

"Then I have no food for you. To be honest is the difference between a man and a fool. Be gone with you, for I have no time to deal with a fool," said Takeshi harshly.

"No, please," exclaimed Namio, his voice rising with urgency. "It's just that this item is so very important to me. My wife and I have no food, and if I can sell this…" he stammered, his words trailing off. "If I can sell this teapot, I know we will have enough money to support us till the summer harvest."

After a long, awkward pause that seemed to stretch into eternity, Takeshi started lightly shaking with laughter. The sound grew into a hacking laugh that echoed through the quiet countryside, louder and louder with each breath. After a few moments, Namio found himself laughing too, though he wasn't sure why. Soon, both men were wheezing and wiping tears from their eyes.

Takeshi finally caught his breath and said, "You are neither a man nor a fool. You are a dreamer. I thank you for sharing your optimism. It has been some time now since I've spoken with someone who strives not only to be alive but someone who truly wants to live. Okay then, I will take one of your cups in exchange for a day's worth of food."

"Arigato gozaimasu (Thank you), Takeshi," Namio humbly said as he carefully handed over a simple but well-crafted cup from his cart. "I must go now. Thank you again for your generosity."

Takeshi then sat on a large boulder on the side of the road, his body relaxing into the stone as if it were a familiar friend. "You go ahead. I have come as far as I can go this day. I hope we will see each other again, and remember, don't forget who you are. We have enough men and fools in this world. We can always use more dreamers."

As Namio continued to walk off down the winding road, he could hear Takeshi shouting from behind him, "Ganbatte (Go for it)!" The words carried on the wind, filling Namio with a renewed sense of purpose as he journeyed onward.

At this point, Namio could see the ocean off in the distance. The faint outline of buildings began to take shape, with billows of dark smoke drifting lazily into the air from tall, slender chimney stacks. Resting for a moment, Namio leaned on his handcart, his arms aching but steady, and admired the scene ahead of him. He had never seen England, but in his mind, this is what it might have looked like.

It was as if he were gazing at a watercolor painting. The sun, low in the sky, cast warm hues of orange, pink, and purple across the clouds. The distant water mirrored these colors, rippling with a dreamy brilliance. Below, people moved like ants in organized lines, either on foot or riding in carriages drawn by horses with coats that gleamed in the fading sunlight.

Namio had always been captivated by this very different place. His wife, Yukie, had never been to Yokohama. She always covered her mouth and laughed softly whenever Namio described the city. To Yukie, such a place was almost a fantasy, especially when he spoke of the boats. Namio would tell her that these boats were as big as mountains, large enough for an entire village of people to live on one.

She would laugh and say, "How could something so large and heavy with so many people stay afloat? Truly, it would sink."

Namio thought to himself, One day, she will believe me. A faint smile played on his lips as he gripped his handcart once again. Feeling his fingers settle into the familiar, ever-so-smooth grooves of the wooden handle, he resumed his journey.

By nightfall, he knew he'd find an alley to sleep in. The thought was not comforting, but it was familiar, and for now, it was enough.

The moon was high and full, casting a soft silver glow as Namio entered the city of Yokohama. Many homes were tightly connected to each other, stacked two or three buildings tall, their dark outlines blending into the night. The rich, tantalizing smell of food filled the air, mingling with the sharp, briny scent of the nearby ocean.

As Namio moved forward, the roads underfoot shifted from dirt to gravel and then to stone, each change marked by the subtle crunch of his cart's wheels. The narrow streets were dimly lit, their flickering lanterns casting elongated shadows that danced along the walls. Most of the people bustling about were Japanese, but the occasional sound of English and other foreign languages drifted through the air, a reminder of Yokohama's diversity.

Life on the streets was harsh. Namio saw people who had made the roads their homes, often fighting with alleyway dogs and stray cats for scraps just to survive. Taverns added a chaotic vibrancy to the night, their interiors alive with music that spilled out into the streets, mingled with loud voices, and the sharp, tinkling laughter of women of the night. Gunshots or screams would occasionally punctuate the soundscape, followed by an unnerving silence, a chilling yet familiar rhythm in the city.

Namio worked his way down to the docks, where the air was cooler and carried a hint of salt. The chaos of the streets faded into a peaceful stillness as the ocean came into view. Looking out over the calm, lapping water, he noted how the surface mirrored the pale light of the moon. He knew that by morning, this quiet dock would be bustling with energy and activity.

The boats anchored there were enormous, their lights glowing from the windows like constellations in the darkness. No matter how many times Namio saw these ships, their sheer size and the mechanics of their operation amazed him. He admired the thick, coiled ropes that secured them to the docks. They were so wide he thought if he wrapped his arms around one, his hands would never meet.

Surveying the area, Namio noticed other vendors scattered along the docks. Some were huddled around small barrel fires, the orange flames flickering against their tired faces. Others lay sprawled beneath their carts, fast asleep despite the chill of the night air. A few feet away, Namio spotted a dark alley that looked secluded and relatively safe, a decent place to rest.

Quietly, he guided his cart into the narrow street, his footsteps echoing faintly. The air was heavy with the smell of rotting trash, and the ground beneath him was damp. Carefully, Namio inspected his pottery, ensuring everything was secure and unbroken. Satisfied, he lowered the handle of his cart to the ground and pulled out a small, threadbare blanket. He lay down beneath the elevated side of his cart, using it as a shelter.

Taking a few deep breaths, Namio allowed his aching body to relax. Exhaustion washed over him, and before long, he drifted into a deep, dreamless sleep, surrounded by the faint hum of the restless city.

Everyday life in Yokohama, circa 1908.
From the album of a German tradesman,
Public Domain.

When Namio woke in the morning, the docks were alive with activity. The air was filled with the shouts of men giving orders, the cries of animals confined in wooden crates, and the loud voices of vendors calling out to entice customers to browse their goods. The scene was chaotic, bustling with energy.

Immediately, Namio jumped to his feet, a jolt of panic coursing through him. He had overslept. At that very moment, the most terrifying sound reached his ears: the sharp crunch of breaking glass beneath his sandals. His heart sank as he looked down to see fragments of his pottery scattered across the damp alleyway.

How had he not heard the destruction during the night? Could he have been so exhausted that vandals had come and gone unnoticed? Desperation took hold as he rummaged frantically through his cart. To his astonishment, everything was gone or shattered—everything except two cups and the sakura teapot. They remained unscathed, still resting in the cart.

With trembling hands, Namio carefully picked up the teapot. His gaze fell upon his wife's apron. Overcome with emotion, he dropped to his knees. Tears flowed freely down his face as he clutched the familiar cloth.

Lifting the apron to wipe his eyes, Namio caught the faint scent of Yukie, as though she were there beside him. Her presence seemed to radiate from the fabric, vivid and comforting. The memory of her love, her laughter, and her sacrifices for him brought a deep, aching sorrow. He cried as though she were lost to him forever, his weeping raw and unrestrained.

Despite his despair, Namio knew he still had something to sell. With great effort, he pulled himself together. He gently placed the teapot back into the cart and stood, his shoulders squared against the weight of his misfortune. Determined to make the best of what little remained, Namio walked out toward the bustling docks.

Finding a small space between a chicken stand and a flower stand, Namio positioned his cart. Though he had very little to offer, he believed in the beauty and quality of his work. Taking a deep breath to steady himself, he shouted with all the clarity and strength he could muster, "Teapot for sale!"

CHAPTER 3

The Businessman

"Baka (Stupid)! Get the hell out of my office, you idiots!" shouted Kosuke, his voice echoing against the tall walls of the grand office as he sat, fist-clenched, behind a massive oak desk. The businessmen scrambled to leave the room, their hurried footsteps retreating across the polished wooden floors. The space was imposing, with vaulted ceilings, dark cherry wood walls, and fine leather furniture arranged with deliberate precision.

Frantically, Kosuke dug through the disorganized piles of forms scattered across his desk, his movements sharp and irritated. "Why can I not find the manifest from the last shipment!" he shouted. His frustration mounted as he snatched up a small ceramic cup, took a sip, and immediately spit it out in disgust.

Crash! The cup shattered into countless jagged pieces against the wall as Kosuke hurled it. "Chiyoko!" he shouted.

Moments later, the tall office door creaked open, revealing a beautiful woman dressed in an elegant evening gown. Her hesitant movements betrayed her wariness as she stepped into the room.

"Yes, my husband. Is there something you need?" Chiyoko asked, her voice carefully measured with restrained disdain.

"My sake is cold! Do you expect me to drink cold sake?" Kosuke barked.

"My deepest apologies. I will bring you a new bottle, one that is hot."

"And bring me another cup. The one I have is broken," he added curtly, his attention already shifting back to the chaotic papers spread across his desk.

Kosuke had recently taken over the family business. At almost thirty years old, his hair was already slightly thinning, though he maintained an impeccable appearance. His well-groomed mustache and tailored double-breasted suits projected an image of authority and control. However, Kosuke was a short man with a short temper to match.

Meanwhile, Chiyoko was downstairs in the kitchen. Despite the maids and cooks bustling frantically around her, she moved with an elegant grace, almost floating across the floor like a ghost. Her expression was calm, masking the turmoil beneath. Descending a few more stairs, she entered the cool, shadowy wine cellar.

By the dim light of a lantern, rows of beautiful wine bottles came into view, their glass surfaces reflecting hues like the colors of a stained glass window in a cathedral. In the far corner stood a koshiki rope basket. Nestled within it was her husband's indulgence—sake.

As she reached out and picked up a bottle, Chiyoko paused, gripping it tightly. The solitude of the cellar allowed her mask to falter, her hatred bubbling to the surface. How she despised this drink. Yet, it was nothing compared to her hatred for her husband.

Their marriage had been arranged, a union born of tradition rather than affection. The first time she had seen Kosuke was on their wedding day. Both hailed from high society, families with proud samurai lineage. Like many women of her station, Chiyoko had grown up knowing that marrying for love was not an option. She had accepted it without question, believing her future might mirror her parents' marriage, which was one of mutual respect and eventual happiness.

But reality had been cruel.

Standing in the damp cellar, her chest tightened with emotion. Her life felt like a gilded cage. She longed to trade all her wealth and status for a simpler existence. Even poverty would be a blessing if it meant sharing life with someone kind—someone who genuinely cared for her. Oh, how she envied the merchants and vendors she saw down at the bustling ports.

Living in Yokohama, their home was situated in the shipping district. Often, Chiyoko and her handmaidens strolled along the busy docks, marveling at the endless flow of goods from distant lands. What others might see as a scene of chaos, Chiyoko saw as a world teeming with freedom and possibility—a stark contrast to the stifling constraints of her own life.

Lost in thought, Chiyoko was startled back to the present by a voice calling from above.

"Sumimasen (Excuse me), is anyone down here?" asked a house servant.

Chiyoko composed herself swiftly, her face regaining its practiced calm. "It is I, Chiyoko. I shall be up in just a moment," she replied.

"Forgive me, my lady," said the servant. "I heard a voice and was checking to see if all was well."

Chiyoko ascended the stairs, the sake bottle cradled in her hands. "There is no need to apologize. I am grateful for your service and ask that you please heat this drink for my husband."

"It would be my pleasure," the servant replied, bowing deeply.

"Arigato (Thank you). Please bring it to me quickly with a cup. I will be waiting in the main dining area just beyond those doors," Chiyoko instructed. With that, she turned and left, her footsteps soft but deliberate as she exited the cellar, leaving the weight of her emotions behind—for now.

All the servants loved Chiyoko. She was kind and generous, a rare source of warmth in the otherwise cold and oppressive household. Though most of them lived in constant fear of her husband, Kosuke, they felt a protective pity for Chiyoko and admired her quiet strength.

The servant carrying the sake, whose name was Mei, noticed that Chiyoko's face seemed strained, her eyes slightly red as if she had been crying. Mei couldn't help but wonder if Chiyoko had been struck by her husband. The mere thought of Kosuke sent a chill down Mei's spine.

As a young girl who had only recently begun working for the household, Mei had learned early on how cruel Kosuke could be. She recalled an incident from her first few weeks on the job when she noticed muddy footprints tracked across a beautiful Persian rug near the entryway. Without hesitation, she knelt to clean up the mess. As she worked, she spotted Kosuke's shoes near the stairwell, caked with drying mud.

Moments later, Kosuke descended the stairs. His sharp voice cut through the air as he demanded to know who had dirtied the rug. Mei froze, unsure of how to respond. The longer she remained silent, the louder he yelled, his rage growing with every unanswered question. Finally, out of desperation, she blurted that she had done it.

On her hands and knees, still scrubbing the rug, she felt Kosuke's presence behind her. Without warning, he delivered a sharp kick to her ribs before continuing into the kitchen. The pain had been excruciating, both physically and emotionally. Even now, the memory lingered in her body, the phantom ache reminding her of her powerlessness.

Standing by the stove, waiting for the sake to heat, Mei found herself consumed by anger. She clenched her fists, her chest tight with resentment and helplessness. As her thoughts swirled, an idea crept into her mind—one that startled her. It was reckless, dishonorable, and utterly unlike her. But the more she thought of Kosuke's cruelty, the more her anger demanded an outlet.

Looking around the busy kitchen, Mei realized how invisible she was, just another servant among many. Her heart raced as she cleared her throat, a ball of mucus forming on her tongue. A voice in her mind screamed at her to stop, but she leaned slightly over the bottle of sake. With a quick motion, she spat into it.

It landed perfectly.

A wave of panic immediately overtook her. Her hands trembled, and her thoughts became chaotic. What had she done? Mei considered confessing right then. But before she could act, the door opened, and Chiyoko entered.

"My husband is waiting. I am sure it is warm enough."

"But, but..." Mei stammered, her voice faltering as guilt and fear gripped her.

"Please, I must be going. I'm sure it is fine," Chiyoko interrupted, taking the bottle of sake from Mei's hands and leaving the room before Mei could say another word.

Mei stood frozen, her heart pounding. Despite the dishonor and shame rising within her, she knew there was no turning back now. Interfering at this point could lead to severe consequences—possibly even her death. Kosuke was not only a man of immense wealth but also one with far-reaching power and influence. His dealings stretched from prestigious government circles to the shadowy depths of the underworld.

As Mei stared at the door through which Chiyoko had just exited, she realized the weight of what she had done. The thought of it would haunt her for years—if she even had the luxury of surviving that long.

Chiyoko knocked gently on the office door, her movements precise and measured.

"Hai, enter," shouted Kosuke, his voice carrying the same sharpness that always made her hesitate for a moment before stepping inside.

"I have your sake and a fresh cup," said Chiyoko. She entered quietly but swiftly, her footsteps barely audible against the polished floor. With practiced grace, she placed the bottle and cup neatly on Kosuke's desk, careful not to disturb the scattered papers.

"How long does it take you to do just a simple task? If I ran my business as slow as you move, we'd be as poor as those beggars down below peddling their garbage."

At that moment, Chiyoko silently poured her husband a cup of sake, her hands steady despite the familiar sting of his words. "I hope this is to your pleasure."

Kosuke, having gone some time without a drink, grabbed the cup eagerly and downed the sake in one swift motion, much like a shot of whiskey. "Now that is the way I enjoy sake. Hot and smooth," he muttered to himself, his focus entirely on the drink in his hand.

Noticing his wife was still standing there, he turned his attention to her with irritation. "Why are you still here? Shouldn't you be off spending my money? That's all you're good for," he snapped. Without waiting for a response, he reached for the bottle and poured himself another glass. For a brief moment, he held the cup up to the light, admiring the liquid within as though it were a rare treasure.

Chiyoko bowed slightly, her movements deliberate and respectful, and exited the room. As she crossed the office floor toward the door, a thought formed in her mind. How ironic it was the way her husband admired his drink.

She continued walking, her face calm, though her thoughts grew sharper. To be sake in my husband's eyes would be a miracle.

As she closed the door softly behind her, a faint, fleeting smile tugged at her lips. I hope Kosuke and his drink have a long and happy life together, she mused, but maybe not that long.

Covering her mouth lightly with her hand, she allowed herself one final thought on the matter as a quiet smile lingered. Kosuke and that drink deserve each other.

"Finally, I found it," Kosuke said aloud, his voice echoing slightly in the large office as he scanned the shipping manifest he'd been searching for. At that moment, a firm knock came on the door.

"Enter," he shouted.

A man-servant stepped inside, bowing slightly before announcing, "Mr. Robert Doogan, Commissioner of Trade representing the United States of America, the territory of Hawaii."

"Very good, come on in, Mr. Doogan," said Kosuke, gesturing toward a seat across from his desk with a curt wave of his hand.

As Mr. Doogan entered and settled into the chair, he offered a polite smile. "Please call me Robert. I apologize for arriving unannounced."

"It is of no consequence, as the night is young. May I offer you a drink, Robert? This is some of the best sake you will ever have. Please, it is still warm," Kosuke said. Without waiting for a response, he reached for the bottle and poured a cup of sake, sliding it toward his guest.

"Thank you. Bottoms up," said Robert, lifting the cup and downing the sake in one smooth motion. "Wow, that is smooth," he remarked, placing the empty cup back on the desk. "Again, thank you for visiting with me. I wanted to update you on our contract for laborers in Hawaii. The voyage from Yokohama is approximately thirty-three days. We are willing to pay seventy American dollars for each laborer. We have found that more than half of those contracted decide to stay on the islands and make it their permanent residence. Currently, this is fine, as we find the industry extremely robust. We have a ship ready for sail in the next two weeks and would like to see if you would like to travel with us to inspect operations in person."

"This is fantastic news. I have never traveled to these islands before. I would like to explore new business possibilities."

"Yes, we are making much progress in developing plantations. I assure you that you will be well pleased with your investment."

"We will spread the word seeking new contractors for the upcoming voyage. This calls for a toast," said Kosuke, his tone rising with enthusiasm as he grabbed the bottle. He poured another round of drinks, emptying the remaining sake into their cups. Lifting his glass, he exclaimed, "Bonzai (Victory)!"

The two men tapped glasses and drank down the remainder of that bottle of sake.

Chapter 4

A Teapot

"Ohayo gozaimasu (Good morning)," Mae and two other handmaidens announced as they gracefully bowed and entered the elegant bedroom. Chiyoko squinted as they drew back the heavy drapes, flooding the room with the vibrant morning sunlight. Her quarters featured a large, oversized canopy bed, elegantly draped in vibrant, beautifully colored silks. The walls were adorned with exquisite wallpaper, shimmering in hues of gold and red, with intricate pictures depicting scenes of ancient Japan. In one corner, a crucifix hung above a table adorned with candles bearing the images of patron saints reflected a fashionable trend among the nobility who, towards the end of the Tokugawa period, had converted to Christianity and embraced Presbyterianism. Nonetheless, a Buddhist shrine was discreetly placed, continuing the ancestral customs.

After a long, satisfying stretch, accompanied by a concealed yawn, Chiyoko replied, "Ohayo (Morning)." Quickly, her room became abuzz with activity. Although her servants moved swiftly, they were impeccably trained and not disruptive, their movements as silent as ninjas in the night. Before Chiyoko's feet even touched the ground, Mae was there, presenting sandals for her feet. Another maiden gently draped a fine silk robe over her shoulders as she stood. Though morning baths were uncommon, this indulgence was a necessity for Chiyoko, a mental fortitude to face the day ahead. As Chiyoko stepped into the adjoining room, she observed the steam rising invitingly from a beautiful freestanding porcelain tub, a luxury only the wealthy could afford during this time.

Currently, only Mae was there assisting her, adding sweet-smelling bath salts and herbs to the water. She then began to disrobe Chiyoko. As Chiyoko gracefully entered the bath, Mae observed her with quiet admiration. Her body possessed a rare kind of perfection that seemed sculpted, each curve and contour flowing into the next with seamless beauty. Her skin, milky white and smooth, was devoid of any blemish or flaw. Mae watched as the water embraced Chiyoko, the surface shimmering around her form. She gently scattered a few rose petals, which floated around Chiyoko, accentuating the softness of the scene with a hint of color against her porcelain skin. As Mae stepped back, she couldn't help but feel a deep sense of awe for the flawless figure before her, a living embodiment of elegance.

"Is there anything else you may need, my lady?" Mae inquired.

"It is perfect. Thank you, Mae, that is all."

Chiyoko then closed her eyes, surrendering to the blissful warmth of the bath. She felt her muscles relax deeply as the heat seeped into her, the soothing properties of the bath transforming physical warmth into a mental sanctuary. As she relaxed further, she concentrated on her breathing, inhaling the steam-rich air deeply into her lungs. Breathing slowly transitioned into a form of meditation, and in that moment, her thoughts drifted away.

Chiyoko remembered being eight years old and growing up in the bustling city of Tokyo. It was early spring, a season of delicate blossoms and renewing warmth. Every year around this time, her father would take her for a trip out to the countryside. Chiyoko, an only child, eagerly anticipated this annual adventure. Although her father was a very serious businessman, he transformed into more of an older brother during their excursions, shedding his usual stern demeanor.

She vividly recalled the carriage ride out to the quaint country village just northwest of their home. The journey was just under two hours, but she fondly remembered gazing out the window at the rolling hills, inhaling the crisp, fresh air, and watching the clouds glide gracefully across the sky. During these moments, she thought about how small her hand felt clasped in her father's. She remembered the small tufts of hair on each of his fingers and how she would eventually begin to play with his wedding ring.

Upon entering the country village, they would explore the numerous artisan stands, brimming with local crafts and goods. Often, because the air was still brisk, they would stop at a cozy restaurant to warm up with bowls of steaming soup. However, Chiyoko's favorite part was wandering through the acres of Sakura trees. Gazing up into the blossoming treetops, she'd let her imagination wander, pretending she was a princess in a fairytale. Unbeknownst to her, her life would not follow the fairytale's promise of a happily ever after.

Year after year, she cherished this trip with her father. But when she was fifteen, tragedy struck as Chiyoko's father contracted a severe case of smallpox and succumbed to the illness. Devastated, she found herself adrift in sorrow. Her mother diligently tried to keep the family affairs in order until Chiyoko was old enough to marry. After her marriage to Kosuke, her father's business was seamlessly absorbed into her new family's enterprises, blending her past with her present.

At this point, Chiyoko realized she had lingered in the bath for much too long. She hastily wiped away her tears and summoned Mae back in to assist her in preparing for the day. Since her father's death, Chiyoko had avoided returning to the cherished country village of her childhood. She then briskly readied herself for the day and proceeded to breakfast.

While Chiyoko was finishing her breakfast, she could overhear her husband, Kosuke, loudly issuing commands from his office. Shortly after, she heard the heavy footsteps of her husband as he descended the stairs. With unnecessary force, Kosuke flung the double doors open, dramatically bursting into the dining room.

Under her breath, Chiyoko faintly muttered, "How dramatic."

"Good, wife, you are here—no need to get up. I have important news. In two weeks, we will be traveling to the Hawaiian islands. We will start preparing immediately," he demanded.

Chiyoko, caught off guard, managed to ask, "For what reason might we be embarking on this venture?" She instantly regretted her question upon seeing her husband's face turn from slightly red to a deep maroon.

Kosuke walked slowly over to where Chiyoko was sitting, his presence imposing. He placed his hand firmly on her shoulder, his fingers quivering with barely contained rage. He then leaned down close to her ear and whispered in a tone so low and stern that only she could hear, "How dare you question me, your husband. You should know that I am in a good mood, or else the consequences could be more than you could ever imagine. Never question me again."

"Hai (yes)," Chiyoko whispered back, her voice barely audible, paralyzed by fear.

"We must begin preparing right away. Chiyoko, organize the help. Decide who will accompany us. Also, visit the docks below and purchase items we can use as omiyage (gifts). We have much to do," Kosuke commanded as he exited the room.

Chiyoko then turned to Mae, who was nearby assisting with the breakfast, and instructed her to select two other servants to join them at the docks. Chiyoko always found solace in visiting the bustling vendors, admiring their exquisite craftsmanship.

As they entered the vibrant business district of Yokohama, Chiyoko found a temporary escape from her turbulent life. The streets were alive with music, drama, and the rich tapestry of sounds and smells typical of a busy port city. Muscular men hoisted heavy loads, their bodies glistening with sweat under the sun's gaze, their skin bronzed by the relentless rays. Watching these men work made her cheeks flush with a feverish glow. She mused to herself, "To be married to such a man..." The thought alone was enough to momentarily steal her breath away. Just then, her thought was broken by a vendor's shout, "Teapot for sale!"

A few vendors away, nestled between a flower stand and a chicken stand, stood a young man proudly holding up a small teapot. From a distance, Chiyoko could see subtle hints of pinks and whites reflecting off the delicate ceramic. Intrigued, she decided to have a closer look. As she approached the potter's handcart, which he was using as his vendor stand, she noticed that the man's face was kind, yet carried a sense of desperation.

"Sumimasen (Excuse me), dear lady, I am selling this beautiful teapot with two cups. Would you be interested in such an item?"

Chiyoko took the teapot and examined its fine workmanship. Although small, it was the most exquisite thing she had ever beheld. Soon, her eyes were drawn to a faint imprint of a single sakura blossom. Immediately, memories of her father from her morning bath came flooding back. Absorbed in reflection, she hadn't realized how long she had been standing there when she heard, "I'm sorry, my lady, are you okay?" the potter gently inquired.

"Yes, I'm sorry. Your teapot is so beautiful. It reminded me of someone very dear to my heart."

"I am happy to know that this piece brings you joy," responded the potter. "This is all I have to sell. Last night, vandals came and destroyed the rest of my items."

Hearing this, Chiyoko's heart swelled with compassion. "How much for the teapot and two cups?" she inquired.

The potter paused thoughtfully before answering, "Two silver coins." Mae and the other two servants gasped at the audacity of the vendor asking for so much. Yet, Chiyoko continued to look even deeper into the potter's eyes, sensing there was more to his request.

Although it was personal and out of character, Chiyoko remarked, "She must be a very wonderful woman for you to ask for so much."

Taken aback yet touched, the potter's demeanor softened, and with deep sincerity, he replied, "She is my everything and is worth so much more than two silver coins."

Chiyoko's heart was moved by his words. "Then, I shall pay you one gold coin for your love," she declared, reaching into her purse and placing the money in his hand.

Again, the servants gasped.

The potter was visibly overwhelmed, this being more money than he had ever held at one time. Tears carved clean paths down his dirt-streaked face. Through his sobs, he barely managed to utter, "Arigatou gozaimasu (Thank you very much)."

Chiyoko replied, "Doitashimashite (You're welcome)," and continued on with her shopping. Although she acquired many new and beautiful things to be given as gifts, the teapot would remain in her personal care. It was a treasured gift to herself.

Kosuke, for once, was genuinely excited about a new business venture. That morning, he convened a meeting with editors and artists in his bustling office, orchestrating the design of an advertisement seeking new contractors to work in the plantations in Hawaii.

"Make it sound exciting. Use words like paradise, better living conditions, and opportunities to make money," Kosuke instructed.

Within an hour, a preliminary draft of the advertisement was in his hands. After meticulous revisions to perfect the wording, the advertisement was finalized and ready for print. Kosuke, who owned his own printing shop, mandated that all other projects be put on hold to prioritize this urgent task.

By early evening, Kosuke had his team disseminating advertisements all across the bustling docks. The following day, in front of the ship, the Shinshu Maru, a lengthy line of potential candidates formed. The line was so long that Kosuke could not see its end. Despite this vast turnout, there would only be enough room for six hundred and seventy workers. As Kosuke surveyed the many desperate souls eager for a chance at a new life, a single thought dominated his mind, "I am sure going to make a lot of money."

CHAPTER 5

A Kiss

Namio could not stop staring at the gold coin in his hand. Its polished surface gleamed in the morning sunlight, reflecting flashes of gold onto his face. "Has this really happened?" he thought, his heart pounding with disbelief.

The marketplace buzzed around him, alive with the scents of spices, fresh produce, and the clamor of vendors calling out their wares. At that moment, the chicken vendor to his left, a burly man with sweat staining his shirt, lost hold of the chicken he was swinging around by the legs. The bird burst into a frenzied, chaotic flight, its wings flapping wildly as it darted straight toward Namio's face.

Caught off guard, Namio swatted at the panicked chicken, its feathers brushing harshly against his skin. In his flailing, he dropped the coin.

He fell to his knees immediately, his fingers scrambling over the uneven ground. The cracks between the cobblestones seemed endless as he patted and scoured every crevice. Around him, vendors and customers continued their morning routines, oblivious to his growing desperation. To his great dismay, no matter how hard he searched, he could not find the coin anywhere.

Namio felt deep despair drilling a hole right through his gut when he heard a familiar voice behind him.

"It's good to see you again, Dreamer. I see you have sold all your items. May I have your spot to set up my stand?"

Namio turned to see Takeshi standing with his usual calm demeanor.

"Of course, Takeshi, please take my place," said Namio.

"Why the face? You have won. Your optimism has prevailed."

Namio then shared what had happened—the triumph of selling all his goods, only to lose the precious gold coin he had earned. Takeshi's expression softened, his dark eyes full of sympathy.

"I wish I had an answer for you. To have such luck, only to have it ripped from your hands. If I had more, I would help you."

"I understand," said Namio. "When all is said and done, I am neither a man nor a dreamer. I am a fool."

Takeshi sighed deeply, knowing there were no words that could ease Namio's pain. Head down, Namio wrapped his fingers around the familiar handle of his handcart. The wood was worn smooth by years of use, the indentations a testament to his hard work and perseverance. Yet this time, the cart felt heavier than ever. He'd hoped to return to his wife with a solution to their struggles. Now, he would return with nothing but failure.

At that moment, Namio noticed several men nailing posters onto the walls and wooden posts around the busy market square. One of the workers handed a notice directly to Namio. Takeshi, curious, leaned over.

"Read it out loud," Takeshi requested.

Namio unfolded the crisp piece of paper and began to read. "Seeking contractors to work in the plantations of Hawaii. For a small fee, you can travel with your family. Living accommodations are provided, and wages are paid regularly. Come and experience paradise. To participate, sign up in front of The Shinshu Maru beginning tomorrow, Tuesday, April 16th. Space is limited."

Takeshi, with a wistful smile, replied, "Oh, to be young again. I would be the first in line to escape this desperate place."

Namio sighed, his voice filled with resignation. "Well, I have no dreams. I'm sure there will be many in line for such a great opportunity."

He folded the advertisement and slipped it into the pocket of his apron. As he did, his fingers brushed against something cold and smooth. His breath caught.

"Could it be the coin he'd lost?" Not daring to hope, he reached in carefully. Slowly, he pulled out the object.

"The coin!" he shouted. "Takeshi, I have it. Hope is not lost. I will be the first in line tomorrow."

Takeshi, ever thoughtful, asked, "Should you visit with your wife first?"

Namio's eyes gleamed with determination. "I have no time. I have been given a gift. A chance to have another life. One where I can provide for my family. A life where my wife and I can start a family. No, I will make this decision on my own."

Takeshi nodded. "I once made a decision on my own, too. Well, I'm sure it will be different for you, my young friend. May all your dreams come true."

The two exchanged heartfelt farewells, and as Namio walked away, Takeshi couldn't help but wonder if he would ever see his young friend again.

Moments later, Namio arrived at The Shinshu Maru. The ship loomed above him, its massive hull painted a deep black and adorned with white lettering. The scent of salt water and the creak of dock ropes filled the air. Namio was the first to arrive. As he waited, others began to form a line behind him—farmers, laborers, and families clutching their meager belongings.

He couldn't take his eyes off the enormous vessel. It was larger than he had imagined, a floating city that promised escape and opportunity. Namio's heart raced as he thought about standing on the deck.

"Would it feel just like standing on land?" he wondered. Then his thoughts turned to Yukie, his wife. He would finally be able to show her the boats he had so often described, and more importantly, he could now provide her with the life he had always promised.

Namio's mind buzzed with excitement throughout the night. The line behind him stretched endlessly, illuminated by faint lanterns flickering in the night. Men, women, and children shuffled in quiet anticipation, their faces a mix of hope and desperation. Seeing how far the line extended reassured him. For the first time in years, Namio felt like he had made a decision that could truly change their lives.

*The Japanese landing ship Shinshū Maru,
1937. Vessels like this one once carried Japanese
immigrants to Hawaii, Public Domain.*

The following day, Namio woke just before dawn. A rare sense of optimism stirred within him. As the sun crept over the horizon, its golden rays spilled across the water, casting shimmering reflections on the calm waves. Namio stood still, taking in the moment. With his eyes closed, he let the warmth of the morning sun caress his face, inhaling deeply the briny scent of the sea. For a fleeting moment, the tide seemed to carry away the burdens that had weighed on him for so long.

But his thoughts were abruptly interrupted by a gruff, impatient voice. "Hey! Are you okay? There are so many behind you. Either sign and pay, or off you go," barked a stern businessman who was accompanied by a sailor. The man's sharp tone brought Namio back to reality, the urgency of the moment cutting through his calm like a knife.

Namio didn't hesitate. He reached into his pocket and handed the businessman his gold coin. The man inspected it briefly before sliding it into a pouch. In return, he handed Namio one silver coin and carefully entered his name and Yukie's into a thick ledger.

"Next!" the businessman called out, wasting no time. He then handed Namio two crisp tickets, each marked with the ship's name, The Shinshu Maru, and the date of departure.

Namio stepped away, gripping the tickets tightly in his hands. His heart raced as a surge of excitement washed over him. He could hardly wait to share the news with Yukie. The image of her smile and the life he had promised her filled his mind as he made his way home.

Although the journey back to Yanaka village was eight hours, Namio's excitement spurred him on, and he found himself entering the familiar hills in just under seven. The anticipation of seeing Yukie again filled him with energy, pushing aside the fatigue from his long trek. He could already picture her worried face, especially since he had left without taking the carefully prepared food she had made for him. His heart swelled at the thought of the news he carried.

It was late afternoon when his small home came into view, nestled amidst the soft green hills. The sight of their humble house, with smoke curling faintly from its chimney, brought a deep sense of comfort. At the kitchen window, he spotted Yukie, her figure outlined by the golden glow of the sinking sun. The moment she saw him in the distance, without hesitation, she darted outside, running toward him with all the urgency of someone who had been holding her breath for too long.

Namio, overcome with emotion, set down his cart and ran to meet her. As they collided, her arms wrapped tightly around his neck, and his encircled her waist. Yukie wept softly, her tears soaking into his shoulder. Namio ran his hands gently along her back, his touch lingering over the sharp ridges of her ribs, a painful reminder of their shared hardships. He pressed his face against her neck, inhaling deeply. The faint, earthy scent of her skin soothed him in a way nothing else could. To Namio, Yukie smelled like the essence of home—safe, warm, and irreplaceable.

His hands moved to her face, cupping it tenderly. His rough thumbs brushed away the tears that streamed down her cheeks. Namio's dark eyes locked onto hers, deep pools of longing and affection. He pulled her face closer until their foreheads touched, his breath mingling with hers. His heart hammered in his chest, each beat heavy and insistent, as though it might break free at any moment. He could feel his pulse pounding in his ears, and it felt as though the world itself had disappeared, leaving just the two of them standing there.

Yukie shivered as Namio's warm breath ghosted along her neck, sending waves of anticipation coursing through her body. Her skin prickled, and every nerve seemed to come alive. His hands cradled her head, his fingers tangling gently in her hair as he stared into her eyes with an intensity that made her heart flutter. She suddenly realized she had been holding her breath and exhaled shakily, taking three deep, deliberate breaths to steady herself. Namio seemed different—his gaze was confident, his expression alive with an energy that made her feel as though time itself had rewound. It was as if the weariness of the years had fallen away, leaving the young, vibrant man she had fallen in love with.

As he leaned closer, a tremor passed through her body, soft but unmistakable. Her heart began to race, the rhythm wild and unrestrained, each beat echoing in her chest like a drum calling her back to the past. The golden light of the setting sun spilled across them, flickering against his face, turning his eyes into dark, liquid amber. Her breath hitched as he reached for her, and when his lips finally touched hers, the world seemed to fall away. His kiss was steady at first, then deepened, slow and consuming, like a flame awakening from embers long thought cold. She felt herself yield to it—to him—her fingers curling into the fabric of his shirt as warmth spread through her in waves that blurred the edge between past and present.

Namio's hands moved down the length of her back, the motion unhurried, reverent. His touch left trails of heat that lingered long after, and she pressed closer, feeling the rise and fall of his chest, the pounding of his heart, strong and alive beneath her palms. The scent of him filled her senses—cedar, salt, and something unmistakably his. Her body responded instinctively, remembering every closeness, every moment when love had felt this simple, this certain. The breeze tugged gently at her hair, but even the wind seemed to pause, unwilling to intrude.

The air between them thickened, and she could feel his breath mingling with hers—warm, uneven, alive with all they hadn't said. For a moment, neither moved. The world around them softened to silence: the rustle of grass, the whisper of the evening air, the fading cry of a bird returning to its nest. The last light of day bathed them in gold, and for one suspended instant, it felt as though time itself had bent to witness their reunion.

Yukie's head spun, and she felt lightheaded. Her body melted into his, her lips parting slightly as the kiss deepened, more passionate and unrestrained. The taste of him lingered on her tongue, and every part of her felt electrified, consumed by his touch. She couldn't tell if it was seconds or minutes that passed, but the intensity of the moment made it feel infinite.

She clung to him as though letting go would break the spell, her heart soaring.

When they finally broke apart, Namio's lips hovered near hers, his breath warm and unsteady. His voice was thick with emotion as he whispered, "I am so happy to see you. There is much to tell."

Yukie didn't answer right away. She kept her eyes closed, savoring the warmth of his presence for just a little longer. Slowly, she opened her eyes and met his gaze, her cheeks flushed and her lips still tingling. Smiling softly, she said, "I am glad you are home too. Please put away your cart and come inside."

Namio placed his cart carefully near the work shed. He walked to the well beside their home and drew up a bucket of cold water. As he washed his hands and face, the coolness soothed the lingering fatigue of his journey. The long hours on the road melted away, replaced by the anticipation of sharing his news.

When Namio stepped inside, the comforting warmth of the kitchen greeted him. Yukie was already at the stove, her slender hands busy warming tea. The gentle clink of pottery and the faint aroma of tea leaves filled the small space. Yukie brought over two cups, placed one in front of him, and sat down across from him, her curious eyes fixed on his face.

Namio began recounting his trip, his voice animated. He told her about meeting Takeshi, the fabric vendor, and the vandals who had robbed him. Yukie's brows furrowed as she listened, concern etched into her delicate features. Then Namio described selling their treasured teapot to a wealthy woman in exchange for a gold coin. At the mention of the coin, Yukie's eyes widened with surprise, her lips parting slightly. She had never seen a gold coin before and couldn't resist asking, "May I see it?"

Namio hesitated, his excitement evident, but his answer left her puzzled. "I don't have it," he said.

Though a twinge of disappointment flickered across her face, Yukie encouraged him to continue. Namio explained how he had lost the coin and, through a twist of fortune, found it again. By now, Yukie was leaning forward, her hands gripping the edge of the table. The thought of losing something so valuable was heartbreaking, but then Namio revealed what he had done next. He had spent the coin to purchase tickets for travel to a foreign land.

Yukie's voice trembled as she asked, "Please tell me you still have the coin?"

Namio looked at her, confused by her reaction. "Why are you asking me this? I just told you I used the money to buy us a new future."

"A new future?" Yukie's voice grew louder, her frustration breaking through. "What about our future here, in Yanaka? This is our home."

"What future!" Namio's voice rose, something he had never done before. "What future do we have here in Yanaka? We live as beggars. We have nothing, and I left the food you prepared for me because I worried that you would be dead when I returned. Is that a life? That is not the life I want for you. That is not the life I want for myself. That is not the life I want for our children."

Yukie's sobs broke the silence that followed. Namio's harsh words pierced her heart, and the sound of his raised voice was jarring. Yet, as her tears slowed, one word lingered in her mind. She whispered, almost inaudibly, "Children?"

"Yes, my love. Children." Namio's voice softened, and his face filled with tender resolve. "For years, I've wondered how I could provide for children when I can barely care for you. Please, Yukie, look at this paper." He slid the advertisement across the table toward her.

Yukie's hands trembled as she picked up the paper. Her emotions swirled—anger, confusion, and an overwhelming sense of uncertainty. Namio had never made such a decision without her. She scanned the words: "accommodations, wages, paradise." The promises seemed grand, almost impossible. Yet leaving Yanaka, their home, felt like abandoning a piece of their souls. She thought of the small house they had built together, the life they had envisioned, and the dream of raising a family in the village they both loved.

But perhaps, she realized, this struggle wasn't just about leaving their home. It was about trusting Namio—trusting that this decision, as impulsive as it seemed, was made out of love and hope for a better life.

"I am sorry, my husband, for speaking out against your direction," Yukie said finally, though her voice shook. Each word felt like swallowing a boulder.

At that moment, Namio remembered Takeshi's words: "Should you visit with your wife first? I once made a decision on my own, too. Well, I'm sure it will be different for you, my young friend..."

"Was it different?" Namio wondered bitterly. The weight of his actions pressed heavily on him. Hearing Yukie struggle to speak those words made him realize how wrong he had been. His tone softened, filled with regret. "I realize I have made a terrible mistake. I wanted so badly to escape our poverty and provide for our family that I was blinded by my own obsession. Will you please forgive me?"

Yukie's anger dissolved into guilt. Namio had come home a changed man—confident, hopeful, and full of determination. She had felt it in his embrace, in the way he kissed her. She couldn't let him fall back into despair. As painful as this conversation had been, Yukie realized she needed to have courage. She needed to believe in her husband—the man who had kissed her with devotion, not the one who now sat across from her, defeated.

"Namio, I will go with you to this foreign land. I am sure we will find happiness as long as we are together." With those words, she saw the light return to Namio's face. His posture straightened, and his expression brimmed with renewed hope.

Namio reached into his pocket and gently held Yukie's hand. When he let go, she felt something cool against her palm. Opening her fingers, she found a single silver coin. "This should be enough to help us prepare for our journey ahead," Namio said, smiling at her.

The tension between them eased, and the room felt warmer, filled with a sense of unity. That night, they spoke long into the night, sharing their dreams and imagining the possibilities their new life might hold. For the first time in a long time, they allowed themselves to hope.

CHAPTER 6

A Day Like No Other

It had almost been two weeks since Namio shared the news that they would be moving to Hawaii. Yukie still had many reservations, and for reasons she couldn't fully articulate, she was still deeply upset. She sat quietly in their small, modest home, now eerily empty. The feeling unsettled her. Although their home had never been filled with much due to their poverty, it had never felt as lifeless as it did now. The walls, once filled with their laughter and quiet conversations, now seemed hollow and still.

Yukie reflected on how this house, despite its limitations, had always felt like a home. It was where they shared their dreams and supported each other through hardships. It was where the morning sunlight poured through the kitchen window, casting warm golden rays that never failed to brighten her spirits. Sitting at their humble wooden table, memories overwhelmed her. Tears streamed down her face as she thought of the life they were about to leave behind.

The following day, Yukie felt strongly that they needed to visit their parents to share the news. Namio's father had passed away a few years earlier, leaving his mother to take up work at Yukie's family's restaurant. Despite their dire circumstances, both Namio and Yukie were too proud to burden their parents with their struggles. Sharing their decision to leave for Hawaii would undoubtedly be difficult, but it was necessary.

Their walk to Yukie's family restaurant was only about twenty minutes, but the weight of the conversation ahead made the journey feel much longer. Each step felt heavier as they approached the modest wooden structure with its painted sign gently swinging in the breeze.

As they entered, a familiar voice called out from the back.

"Konichiwa (Hello)," greeted Yukie's mother, her voice cheerful and welcoming.

"Okaasan (Mother), it's us, Yukie and Namio," Yukie replied.

Moments later, Yukie's mother appeared. She was a small woman, barely five feet tall, with a stout, round frame and salt-and-pepper hair tied neatly under a hachimaki (bandana).

She wore her signature homemade apron, its pockets stuffed with various kitchen tools. Despite her plump figure, her legs were fit and strong, a testament to years of tireless work.

The moment Okaasan saw Yukie, she immediately put down what she was doing and rushed to embrace her daughter, just as any loving mother would.

"Yukie, you are so thin. Please, you two sit and have some food," she said with concern in her voice.

"Arigato (Thank you)," Namio replied politely as they both sat down at a well-worn wooden table.

Okaasan moved with a speed and efficiency that spoke to her years of experience in the kitchen. Pots and pans clattered in the back, and in no time, she returned with an astonishing spread of dishes. The aroma of freshly steamed rice, savory miso soup, and grilled fish filled the room. It seemed impossible that she had prepared it all in such a short time.

Trailing behind her was Yukie's father, a man with a strong yet gentle presence. His sun-weathered face was lined with years of hard work, but his dark eyes still sparkled with warmth.

"Hello, Father," Yukie said softly as she rose to embrace him.

The moment her father's arms wrapped around her, the tears she had been holding back fell freely. She felt like a little girl again, safe in the comfort of his protective embrace. The tighter he held her, the harder she cried, her emotions spilling over.

Namio shifted uncomfortably in his seat, feeling like an outsider in the midst of such an intimate moment. The more awkward he felt, the stronger his urge to speak grew. The silence pressed down on him, as delicate as glass, and he feared a single word might shatter the scene. Finally, unable to bear the tension, he broke the silence.

"We are sorry to show up unannounced," Namio began nervously. "Yukie and I have some news to share with you both."

Before Namio could finish, Okaasan interrupted with excitement. "You're pregnant!" she exclaimed, her face lighting up with joy.

At that moment, Namio's mother entered the room, tying her apron as she prepared for her day's work. "Who's pregnant?" she asked.

"It's not me, of course," Okaasan quipped with a laugh.

Yukie's father chimed in enthusiastically, "Namio and Yukie are having a baby!"

Suddenly, the room buzzed with joy and congratulations. Over and over, the parents exclaimed, "Omedetou (Congratulations)!" Their excitement filled the air.

The only ones not speaking were Yukie and Namio, whose silent expressions made the situation all the more awkward.

As the mothers began discussing baby names, Yukie could take no more. Normally soft-spoken, she raised her voice in frustration.

"I am not having a baby!" she shouted, her tone sharp and resolute.

The room fell into stunned silence. Even Namio, who had grown used to Yukie's gentle demeanor, was shocked to hear her raise her voice.

Okaasan, ever quick to recover, broke the silence. "So why did you say you were pregnant?"

Letting out an exasperated sigh, Yukie asked everyone to sit down. She explained the true reason for their visit: she and Namio were leaving soon to live in Hawaii. Namio unfolded the advertisement he had brought with him from Yokohama, but no one seemed eager to look at it. The joy and excitement drained from the room, replaced by a heavy, mournful stillness. The occasional sniffle and quiet tear falling onto the table punctuated the silence.

After what felt like an eternity, Yukie's father finally spoke. "Will we ever see you again?" he asked, his voice low and heavy with emotion.

Hearing those words, Yukie's composure broke. She burst into tears and ran out of the restaurant, unable to face her family's sorrow.

Namio sat frozen, guilt pressing down on him like a mountain. Summoning every ounce of courage, he finally spoke. He explained their poverty-stricken circumstances, their struggles, and their decision to leave in search of a better life.

"I promised you all that I would love and care for Yukie until my dying breath," Namio said, his voice thick with emotion. "I know how difficult it is to hear what we are sharing with you today. Please know that this is the only option I have at this time. I'm sorry we didn't come to you for help. We just needed to see if we could do this on our own."

Namio's words hung heavily in the air. To his surprise, Yukie's father stood and bowed deeply in his direction. Namio was overwhelmed with humility. He felt lower than dirt, undeserving of such a gesture. Yukie's father's face was filled with heartbreak, the kind of look that only a father gives when his soul begins to fracture.

"You are our daughter's husband," Yukie's father said in a grave but steady voice. "And we will trust in your direction. Please let us help you prepare for your journey ahead."

The simple but profound words filled Namio with both gratitude and sorrow. He felt the weight of their sacrifice and trust as if it were etched into his very being. The moment would stay with him forever.

Over the next week, Yukie and Namio's parents had many long, heartfelt conversations with them, often stretching late into the night. The smell of freshly prepared meals filled the air as the families shared their hopes and fears for the journey ahead. Every evening, they gathered around low wooden tables, exchanging memories and advice while the comforting glow of lanterns illuminated their tired but resolute faces. As the week passed, the preparations were completed, and the inevitable day of farewell loomed closer.

When the dreaded moment arrived, both mothers clung tightly to their children, tears streaming down their faces. Their embraces carried the silent plea to stop time, as if holding on longer might somehow delay the departure. Almost in unison, the mothers released their children and turned to each other, seeking solace in a shared grief only they could understand. Together, they retreated into the restaurant's small back room, where a simple Buddhist shrine stood. Kneeling before it, they lit incense, the faint aroma of sandalwood filling the air as smoke curled upward in delicate spirals. Their prayers were silent but fervent, offered with all the love and hope they could muster for their children's uncertain future.

Yukie's father then stepped forward. His voice, though steady, carried the weight of a man trying to hold his composure. He shared words of wisdom, speaking slowly and deliberately, his tone both firm and tender. When he embraced

Yukie, his grip was so tight and full of emotion that no words could convey the depth of his anguish. A large part of his heart seemed to break at that moment, knowing he might never see his daughter again.

When he turned to Namio, he bowed deeply, his expression carrying the gravity of trust and responsibility. Though the bow was not eye to eye, Namio could feel the immense expectations pressing down on him, like an unspoken vow to protect and cherish Yukie. Allowing Yukie's father to rise first, Namio stood in silence, humbled by the gesture.

It was time. Namio reached for his cart, his fingers brushing over the familiar smooth indentations worn into the wooden handle—a testament to years of use. With a deep breath, he and Yukie set off down the road, the weight of their journey heavier than the cart they pulled.

For many hours, Yukie struggled to contain her emotions. The pain of leaving her parents and the life she had known clung to her like a shadow. But as the countryside unfolded before them, dotted with lush green fields and the occasional cluster of trees, a small flicker of curiosity began to stir in her heart. She had never been to Yokohama, nor had she ever seen the ocean. The thought of what lay ahead began to distract her from her sorrow.

Namio, walking beside her, couldn't hide his excitement. He spoke with enthusiasm, describing all the sights and marvels he hoped to share with her. His voice, animated and full of energy, painted vivid pictures of the bustling port city. It warmed Yukie's heart to see him so hopeful. His eagerness was contagious, and for a moment, she allowed herself to imagine the new life he envisioned for them.

About an hour into their journey, Namio noticed several birds of prey circling over the road ahead. Their dark shapes swooped and hovered ominously against the bright sky. At first, they assumed the birds were drawn to an injured or dead animal. However, as they drew closer, the outline of a handcart became visible, overturned on the side of the road. A figure lay motionless nearby, its form partially obscured by the tall grass.

Namio's pulse quickened as he caught sight of the cart's contents—vividly colored fabrics neatly folded in the back. A sinking feeling washed over him. "Please don't let it be Takeshi," he thought, his heart pounding with dread.

Without a word, Namio dropped the handle of his cart and sprinted toward the fallen figure, startling Yukie. She called after him but quickly followed, dragging their cart behind her. By the time she reached him, Namio was already on his knees, cradling the elderly man's head in his lap.

"Yukie! Yukie! Bring water, hurry!" Namio shouted, his voice filled with urgency. Yukie fumbled to grab a damp cloth from their cart and rushed to his side.

"No, no, no..." Namio stammered, his tears falling freely. "Please, Takeshi, please, please be okay."

He carefully wiped the old man's face with the cloth, but his hands trembled as he worked. His gaze darted to the back of Takeshi's head, where a deep gash was visible. A faint trickle of blood seeped from his ear, and Namio noticed a large, jagged boulder nearby, its surface stained red. Takeshi must have tripped and struck his head against the rock.

"Ah, Dreamer," Takeshi whispered faintly, his breath shallow and uneven. "I wondered when I'd see you again."

"Hai (Yes), Takeshi, I am here. Let me help you. You will be okay," Namio replied, his voice cracking with emotion.

"There you go again, my optimist," Takeshi said with a weak, fleeting smile. "I don't think you'll be right this time."

Yukie knelt beside them, her voice gentle but urgent. "Please, Takeshi, save your breath. We will take care of you," she said.

At the sound of Yukie's voice, Takeshi's eyes fluttered open briefly. "Right again, my friend," he murmured. "She did come with you. What a lucky..." His sentence was interrupted by a fit of coughing.

Namio noticed blood on Takeshi's lips. "Takeshi, open your eyes. Please, tell me what to do. You've gotten me this far. I need you," he pleaded, rocking gently as he held the old man's head.

Recognizing the urgency, Yukie leaned closer. "Where do you live, Takeshi? What is the name of your wife?" she asked, her tone calm but insistent.

Takeshi's breathing became ragged, his words slow and strained. "Sendagi... Akiko," he whispered.

With the last of his strength, Takeshi reached for Namio's hand and gripped it tightly. Though his eyes remained closed, his voice carried an unexpected clarity as he spoke his final words: "May all your dreams come true."

His grip loosened, and his chest rose one last time before his breath escaped in a long, slow sigh.

Namio sat frozen, unable to process what had just happened. Slowly, he lowered Takeshi's hand and felt something pressed into his own palm. When he opened his fingers, he found a single gold coin.

He stared at the coin, his heart breaking. He wished he could trade the small fortune just to see Takeshi sitting upright again, perched on the boulder with his familiar toothless grin and sagging eyelids. Instead, he gripped the coin tightly, his tears falling silently as the weight of his friend's passing settled over him.

Takeshi was not a small man. However, Yukie and Namio managed to wrap his body in pieces of fabric taken from the handcart. They worked carefully, their movements slow and deliberate. With steady hands, they gently placed him in the back of his cart, ensuring he rested as peacefully as possible.

Standing on the dirt road, surrounded by the fading light of the afternoon, Yukie and Namio were faced with a difficult decision. The gold coin, glinting faintly in Namio's pocket, represented an opportunity—a chance to return to Yanaka and begin anew. The thought was tempting. But Namio, reflecting on the events of the last few weeks, knew he could no longer make choices for both of them without his wife's voice guiding him. This was a lesson Takeshi had imparted, a truth that would forever stay with him.

Namio turned to Yukie, his voice steady yet filled with emotion. "I've made this decision before on my own," he admitted. "And with all that has happened, I realize that your happiness is what matters most to me."

Reaching into his pocket, Namio pulled out the gold coin. Its polished surface gleamed faintly in the dimming sunlight as he placed it gently in Yukie's hand. His calloused fingers lingered briefly, a silent gesture of trust. "You once told me that you knew we'd be happy as long as we were together," he continued. "I truly believe this, whether it is in Hawaii or back in Yanaka."

Yukie studied her husband's face, seeing the vulnerability and sincerity etched into his expression. She felt the weight of the coin in her hand, a token of not only fortune but of her husband's unwavering devotion. Her heart swelled with both love and resolve.

At that moment, a traveler appeared on the road, pulling an empty cart behind him. The man looked like a laborer, his clothing worn and his face weathered by years of hard work.

Yukie stepped forward, raising her hand to catch his attention. "Sumimasen (Excuse me)," she called out. "A man has died on his way to Sendagi. I will give you this gold coin if you will take him home and seek out his wife, Akiko."

The traveler paused, his sharp eyes glancing at the coin. He approached cautiously, inspecting the gold piece closely. After a moment of silence, he gave a small nod of agreement and took hold of the handcart. Without another word, the man began his solemn journey, pulling Takeshi's body home to his family.

Yukie turned back to Namio, her expression gentle yet resolute. "Let us finish what we've begun," she said softly, her voice unwavering. "You are my home, not Yanaka."

Namio's chest tightened with emotion as he pulled Yukie into his arms. He held her tightly, his heart filled with gratitude and love. As he pressed his face into the curve of her neck, he inhaled deeply, savoring her familiar scent—a scent that, to him, always felt like home. In that moment, he understood that no matter where life took them, he would never be alone as long as Yukie was by his side.

By late that evening, they reached the bustling ports of Yokohama. The city hummed with life as lanterns illuminated the crowded streets and the scent of salt water mixed with the aroma of grilled food from nearby vendors. Laborers shouted to one another as they hauled crates and barrels to and from the towering ships docked along the pier.

When Yukie saw the Shinshu Maru for the first time, she froze. Her eyes widened, and her lips parted in awe. The ship was massive, its dark hull gleaming faintly under the glow of the dock's lanterns. It towered above them like a steel fortress, its smokestacks reaching into the night sky.

Namio watched her reaction, a soft smile spreading across his face. Seeing the wonder and astonishment on Yukie's face made every step of their journey worthwhile. In that moment, he knew that no matter what challenges lay ahead, they would face them together. Their adventure, filled with unknowns, was only just beginning.

CHAPTER 7

By The Light of The Moon

Loading raw silk bales onto a steamer at Yokohama Port, circa 1920. Public Domain, courtesy of Yokohama City Central Library.

The following day, Yukie and Namio awoke beneath their handcart, parked near the Shinshu Maru, a ship of immense size that dwarfed even the largest buildings in their village. The sense of smallness overwhelmed Yukie as she marveled at man's ability to construct such structures. Knowing they could not bring the handcart aboard, they packed their belongings with care and precision. As Yukie fastened the last of their bags, she observed Namio tenderly stroking the handcart that his father had crafted years ago. His voice, low and somber, broke the morning silence.

"Well, my old friend, I cannot take you with me. May you serve another just as you have done for me all these years. I will miss our many conversations. Thank you for always listening to me."

Namio then navigated through the bustling market, passing rows of vendors as he searched for someone to buy the handcart. Yukie watched from a distance as he engaged a portly merchant surrounded by lively children who soon swarmed over the cart. A brief exchange of words and money followed. Namio's return was slow, his head bowed in silent resignation. Yukie sensed that parting with the handcart pained him more than he had anticipated.

The area around the massive ship soon became a hub of activity. Huge walkways thudded into place, and workers shouted commands as they operated large pulleys that swung over the dock. The frenetic environment contrasted sharply with the tranquil life in Yanaka, where villagers' daily routines were synchronized with the rising and setting sun. Suddenly, dizziness overcame Yukie, and the bustling dockyard spun wildly before her eyes. Thankfully, Namio was quick to support her as she lost consciousness.

"Yukie, Yukie, are you okay?" he inquired, cradling her gently in his arms. After she regained consciousness and sipped some water, she expressed her overwhelming distress.

"I don't think I can do this. There is so much happening, and things are just too loud."

"Breathe. Everything will be alright. Once we are on the boat, I'm sure things will slow down," Namio reassured her, though his voice wavered with uncertainty.

Yukie could see the concern etched deeply in Namio's eyes. Despite the chaos, she found strength in his presence and reassured him, "I'm okay. It was just a lot to take in. We will be fine," as she regained her footing.

Soon, the arrival of carriages signaled the boarding of more passengers. Yukie watched as men and women in stark black and white attire maneuvered large luggage onto the ship. Namio explained that these were the upper classes, people who lived lives of luxury, whose daily needs were tended to by a host of servants. The thought made Yukie's stomach churn with a mix of curiosity and mild repugnance. The idea of such dependency was foreign and slightly shameful to her.

"They cannot even open their own doors," Yukie remarked aloud, her tone laced with disbelief, as she observed a servant hurry to assist his master.

Then, the elite of the elite made their entrance. Men in crisp suits and women in flowing dresses that caught the sunlight, making them shimmer as they moved. Their polished appearances and the delicate fragrance of jasmine that seemed to follow them painted a picture of a life so far removed from Yukie's simple existence that she found it unfathomable.

An hour later, Namio nudged her, pointing out a distinguished-looking woman among the crowd. "There she is. That is the lady who purchased our teapot," he whispered.

The woman, regal and poised, with long black hair flowing down her back, was a vision of grace. She glanced their way, locking eyes with Namio briefly. Yukie mimicked her husband's respectful bow, which was met with a nod from the lady as she continued on her way.

With the boarding of the upper classes complete, it was time for Yukie and Namio, along with other contracted workers, to embark. Hand in hand, they began to board, Namio's palm sweaty with apprehension. Yet, this shared moment of vulnerability brought Yukie an unexpected calm.

Their steps onto the ship marked a definitive end to their life on land. As they crossed the threshold, Yukie looked back at the diminishing figures on the dock, feeling a mix of excitement and trepidation. Despite her earlier faintness, she steadied herself, fortified by the resolve that there was no turning back.

Below deck, the atmosphere shifted drastically. The room assigned to them and other contractors was dim and smelled of old grease—a stark contrast to the lively sounds of music and laughter filtering down from the upper decks. Here, the air was thick with whispers and the occasional cough, echoing the uncertainty and subdued hope of those bound for unknown lands. As reality set in, Yukie steeled herself against the rising panic, knowing this cramped, dimly lit space would be their home for the next month.

Japanese immigrants aboard ship bound for Hawaii, early 1900s. Public Domain, courtesy of UBC Library, Rare Books and Special Collections (JCPC_36_004a).

Under a lustrous full moon, Yukie stood at the ship's railing, her eyes closed, surrendering to the caress of the night breeze that moved her hair and whispered secrets of the deep sea. The air was charged with an electric serenity, the kind that only the vast ocean could conjure. She was oblivious to Namio's presence, though he stood just a breath away, utterly transfixed by her beauty as the moonlight danced across her features.

Slowly, with the reverence of a man walking towards his lifelong dream, Namio approached her from behind. His arms encircled her waist, drawing her gently against his chest. Yukie's breath hitched slightly as she felt his warmth envelop her, his touch igniting a thousand tiny fires beneath her skin. Namio's lips found the nape of her neck, grazing her skin so lightly that it sent shivers cascading down her spine. The intimate touch closed the distance between comfort and desire, between sea and shore.

"Are you cold, my love?" he whispered into her ear.

"Ie (No)."

Feeling the steady rhythm of Namio's heartbeat against her back, Yukie let him guide her by the hand, leading her away from the moonlit deck into the shadowed corridors of the ship. They navigated through the narrow passageways to a secluded service door, a portal to a hidden sanctuary known only to Namio. Bending slightly to enter, they found themselves in a compact, closet-like space, illuminated by nothing but the silver glow of the moon through a small tilt-open window.

"This is my quiet place," Namio confessed, kneeling on the wooden bench that served as both seat and bed. The engines stilled, leaving the ship adrift, floating lazily with the current, mirroring the tranquil lull inside the small room. In this secluded haven, lit only by moonlight and filled with the gentle ocean breeze, every breath they took was a shared secret, every glance a stroke of intimacy.

Yukie smiled gently, her eyes reflecting the moonlight and the dark depths of the sea. They kneeled across from each other, the air around them thick with anticipation. Her hands rested lightly in her lap before she slowly, deliberately, let her robes fall away from her shoulders, revealing the soft glow of her skin. Namio followed suit, the fabric whispering to the floor, his eyes never leaving hers.

They lingered there in the hush between breaths, the stillness pulsing with something unspoken. The ship's timbers creaked softly, the sea's rhythm rising and falling just beyond the hull, as if the ocean itself was listening. Yukie's pulse fluttered at the base of her throat, drawing Namio's gaze, and for a moment neither of them moved — held captive by the fragile, perfect tension of being so near.

Namio reached for her, his fingertips brushing a stray lock of hair from her face before tracing down the slope of her neck. The warmth of his touch sent a quiet tremor through her, her breath catching in the small space between them. She lifted her eyes, meeting his with a soft, steady courage. The silence deepened, the air thick with salt and warmth, until even the sound of the sea seemed to fade away.

The ship swayed gently, its motion slow and deliberate, matching the rhythm of their closeness. Yukie's hand rose to his chest, feeling the quick beat beneath her palm. His breath mingled with hers, uneven, then deep, drawing them together until their foreheads touched. For a heartbeat, they simply existed like that — breathing as one, the ship moving beneath them in quiet assent.

When their lips met, the world tilted. The kiss was tender, then fuller — tasting of salt, of moonlight, of everything left unsaid. Namio drew her closer, his hands warm against her back, tracing slow lines that made her shiver. Yukie's fingers found his shoulders, gripping gently as if to steady herself against the motion of the ship. The vessel rocked in time with them, the sea's rhythm blending with their own, carrying them deeper into the stillness.

Moonlight washed over their skin, soft and pale, turning every movement into something fluid and dreamlike. The gentle sway of the ship seemed to follow their breaths — rising, falling, the rhythm of heartbeats and waves. The air between them grew warmer, charged with the quiet hum of desire, each breath shared, each touch deliberate. It was not hurried or wild, but the kind of closeness born from love's ache — patient, knowing, inevitable.

The sea swelled again, lifting the ship higher, and Namio's arms tightened around her. Yukie's breath came shallow, her cheek brushing his as she whispered his name. For a moment, the world felt suspended — the ocean, the stars, their hearts — all moving in one seamless rhythm.

Then the wave eased, the motion softening into calm, and they remained wrapped in that hush, the night folding gently around them. The ship drifted forward, its bow slicing quietly through silver water, carrying them through the dark like a secret.

Afterward, they lay entwined, Yukie resting against Namio's chest, his arm cradling her, both enveloped in the tranquil afterglow. The water lapped softly at the sides of the ship, a soothing lullaby that echoed the calm in their hearts.

"I love you, Yukie," Namio whispered.

"I love you too."

CHAPTER 8

The Storm

It had been two weeks since the Shinshu Maru, a vessel built for wartime now repurposed during peace, set course for Hawaii. For most of the journey, the seas had been serene and accommodating. Although originally designed for conflict, the ship was currently contracted to transport goods and facilitate travel for immigrants seeking new opportunities abroad. Unlike the contracted workers confined below deck, the upper-class passengers enjoyed numerous lavish comforts. The dining area boasted ornate tables and chairs, with a staircase leading to an elevated floor encircled by panoramic windows. This bustling social hub also featured a bar where guests could enjoy a cocktail or two. Additionally, there was an exclusive area on the outer deck for these esteemed passengers, where they could play shuffleboard, breathe in the fresh ocean air, or recline on elegant wicker chairs for afternoon tea. The cabin rooms, a stark contrast to the sparse accommodations below, were appointed with plush beds, expansive wardrobes, and various domestic luxuries.

The ship's attendants, though living in more modest quarters, still enjoyed privileges far beyond those of the laborers below. Frequently, Mae, Chiyoko's devoted handmaiden, compassionately delivered leftover food, extra blankets, and surplus supplies to the workers. Having once survived the harsh realities of street life, Mae empathized deeply with their plight.

Over recent months, Mae had evolved from merely serving Chiyoko to becoming a trusted confidant and cherished friend. Despite their growing bond, Mae never forgot her subordinate role, always treating Chiyoko with profound respect. Chiyoko, fully aware of the social boundaries between them, graciously allowed Mae to cater to her every whim. An attempt by Chiyoko to reduce the formality of their relationship by asking Mae to call her by her first name had only highlighted the discomfort such familiarity caused Mae. Their friendship flourished within the safety of their defined roles, providing a comfortable space for both women to grow closer.

On this particular evening, as the dining hall buzzed with activity, Chiyoko and her husband, Kosuke, made their entrance, followed by Mae and another servant. The room was alive with chatter, and they were greeted by excited voices everywhere. The servants, adhering to Kosuke's precise instructions, managed their coats and found their designated seats. Chiyoko was quickly drawn into a circle of wives who were keenly observing one another and exchanging the latest titbits of gossip. Meanwhile, Kosuke ascended to the upper room, his presence quickly acknowledged as he was handed a drink. Renowned within the circles of the elite, he engaged in subdued conversations peppered with handshakes and the occasional discreet exchange of envelopes. That evening, the culinary highlight was a sumptuously prepared veal dish.

As dusk fell and the ship sailed into the night, the dining area transformed into a vibrant scene of dance, drink, and games of chance. Chiyoko, uncomfortable with the festivities, opted to retreat.

"Sumimasen (Excuse me), I am a bit tired and think I will be off to my room," she said, passing her husband another drink.

"Sleep, sleep, sleep. That is all you do. Why not stay awhile and be my lucky charm tonight?" Kosuke said.

"I am sure I would only be in the way. Please enjoy yourself, and if there is nothing else you need, I shall be off to my quarters."

"Fine, enjoy myself, I will. Who will be my lucky charm tonight?" Kosuke bellowed to the gathering, pulling a reluctant female servant to his side.

The fear in the servant's eyes was palpable, yet she dared not offend someone of such high status. The gaming tables were dominated by poker, where Kosuke's strategy involved aggressive betting to intimidate others into folding. This often gave him an inflated sense of victory, as many were too intimidated to challenge him, even with strong hands. His reputation for being a sore loser was well-known. Rumors circulated of a night when he had lost a substantial amount of money and even an heirloom ring. However, by the next poker game, the ring was conspicuously back on his finger, and the previous night's winner had mysteriously disappeared.

"You cheat!" Kosuke accused loudly across the table.

"Look, a flush beats two pairs every time. It is the cards I have. With all due respect, sir, you have lost," the accused man countered calmly.

"I don't think you heard me correctly. I've won, and you've lost. What say you, my lucky charm?"

The young servant, now uncomfortably seated on Kosuke's lap, averted her gaze in shame.

"How dare you not agree with me. You're nothing but the dirt on my shoe!" Kosuke exclaimed, his anger boiling over as he threw the girl to the ground. Rising to his feet, his hands shook with rage as he snapped his fingers, summoning two imposing servants who promptly seized the shoulders of his adversary.

"Now, let me ask you again. What hand beats a flush?"

In a voice trembling with fear, the man relented, "Two pairs."

"I can't hear you. I want everyone to know that you are a cheater. Who is the winner?"

"You are, sir."

"I said I want everyone to hear!"

"You are, sir!" the man shouted, his voice echoing through the now silent room.

"Get this trash out of my sight," Kosuke commanded, and the servants quickly escorted the man away. The music had ceased, and the attendees were frozen, their attention on the unfolding drama. Kosuke basked, boasting, "What can I say? I'm just that good," followed by a theatrical laugh that, due to his power, drew reluctant participation from the room. The party resumed, but Kosuke's behavior grew increasingly erratic as he continued to demand the presence of his "lucky charm," who was now nowhere to be seen.

"Well, if I can't find my lucky charm, I'm sure a wife will do. Excuse me, gentleman, it has been a pleasure taking your money tonight," Kosuke proclaimed as he staggered to his feet, prompting those at his table to rise and bow respectfully. With Kosuke's departure, the men exhaled collectively, relieved.

That night, the water was rough, the ship heaving violently as it battled the relentless ocean waves. Kosuke, intoxicated and unsteady, stumbled through the narrow walkways of the ship, clutching a smoldering cigar in one hand and a half-drunk bottle of whiskey in the other. He burst into his cabin on his third attempt, his vision blurred and his senses dulled by alcohol. The cabin swayed around him as he squinted to focus on his wife, who lay vulnerably on the bed. His tie hung loosely around his neck, his shirt sloppily half-tucked.

"Chiyoko, Chiyoko! It is I, Kosuke, your husband. I have lost my lucky charm. I could not find her anywhere, so you will do," he slurred, setting down his whiskey with a clatter and biting down on his cigar.

Chiyoko was painfully awake, her heart sinking with each of her husband's heavy footfalls. She had dreaded his return each night, praying he would lose himself in a drunken stupor elsewhere on the ship, or better yet, tumble overboard. But tonight, her worst fears materialized as he invaded their private sanctum.

"Chiyoko, tonight we will make me a son," he demanded aggressively, his voice thick with demand.

Panicking, Chiyoko pleaded, trying to divert his attention. "Please, my husband, please sit and relax. Can I get you another drink?" she suggested, her voice trembling as she edged away from the bed.

"Ie (No)!" Kosuke roared, advancing on her with a predator's intent. He seized her by the shoulders, his grip iron-hard. "How dare you deny me!" In a swift, brutal motion, he backhanded her across the face. The force of his strike sent her sprawling to the floor, the impact sharp against the hard surface. He loomed over her, his shadow monstrous in the dim cabin light. Grabbing her hair in a fierce grip, he yanked her head back, while his other hand savagely tore at her robes, exposing the delicate skin of her back.

Chiyoko's mind recoiled in horror as the reality of her situation set in. Her body began to shut down, shock numbing her senses until darkness mercifully claimed her.

Kosuke, feeling her body go limp beneath him, paused to check her shallow breathing. Releasing her hair, her head thudded against the floor with a sickening sound. "Well, you are no good to me anymore," he muttered coldly, standing to search for his drink. "Now, to find my lucky charm," he said as he exited the room.

The ship shuddered beneath the storm's relentless assault, its timbers groaning as though in shared agony with the sea.

Rain fell in furious torrents, each drop a cold, sharp sting against Mae's skin as she climbed from the lower decks, the empty tray in her hands rattling with each tremor of the vessel. She had been distributing scraps of food—remnants of the upper class's indulgent excess that never ceased to astonish her. Her thin robe, soaked through, clung to her curves like a second skin, offering no shield against the knife-edge wind that lashed at her exposed flesh.

The deck pitched violently, slick and treacherous beneath her feet. She gripped the iron railing, her knuckles white, her fingers numb from cold. Every step toward her quarters was a battle against the chaos of the sea. A fierce gust slapped her face, flinging her dark hair across her eyes, the rain mingling with tears she hadn't realized were falling, salty and warm against her chilled skin. Unaware of the horror unfolding above, Mae pressed on, her body trembling from the cold.

A jagged bolt of lightning split the sky, carving the night in two. In that ghostly flash, the deck flared white, and she saw him—a shadowy figure leaning against the rail, his presence heavy with intent. Thunder roared, a primal sound that shook the world. Kosuke.

The light revealed him: the hard set of his jaw, the glint in his eyes, his body swaying not from the sea but from the whiskey coursing through him. The sharp, bitter scent of liquor cut through the wind. He moved toward her, his steps slow, deliberate, each one closing the distance. Lightning flashed again, illuminating his face—his eyes burned with a volatile mix of malice and desire, his wet hair plastered to his forehead, rain tracing the sharp lines of his features like liquid fire.

Her pulse hammered in her ears. "Sir?" she called, her voice catching, fragile against the storm. "You shouldn't be out—"

The wind stole her words. He spoke her name, low and deliberate, the sound dripping with a dangerous hunger that sent a shiver of fear down her spine. Another flash of lightning framed him, his expression twisted by something darker than anger—a raw, unchecked want. Mae stepped back, her feet slipping on the slick deck. The ship lurched, slamming her against the railing, the cold metal biting into her back. Below, the sea churned, black and endless, whispering escape in its depths.

"Sir, what are you doing? Please, let me by," she pleaded, her voice trembling, her breath misting in the frigid air as she searched his eyes for any trace of reason.

He laughed, a dark, throaty sound that vibrated through the storm. "It's too late for talk," he growled, his voice rough with whiskey and want. "No one stops me tonight, not here." Thunder punctuated his words, the sky amplifying his intent. The storm surged, its fury entwining with the tension on the deck, a wild, untamed force mirroring the menace in his gaze.

Mae's back pressed against the railing. She tried to sidestep, her feet slipping, her body swaying with the ship's violent rhythm. "Please, you don't want to do this," she pleaded, her voice barely audible, her chest heaving with shallow, panicked breaths.

Kosuke closed the distance, his hand shooting out to seize her soaked robe, his fingers curling into the fabric as he pulled her close. The heat of his body clashed with the chill of the rain; his breath was hot and sharp, laced with whiskey, against her cheek. "I decide what I want," he murmured, his voice low and dangerous, his grip now tightening around her arms until it bruised. Mae's body stiffened, every muscle taut with fear, her skin crawling under the weight of his touch.

She struggled, her hands pushing against his chest, fingers slipping on his wet suit jacket, her strength no match for his. Her mind raced, fear and desperation tangling as she fought to break free. "Think of Chiyoko, Chiyoko!" she cried, her voice cracking in a desperate plea to pierce the darkness consuming him.

But Kosuke was lost to it. "Tonight, it's just us," he whispered, his voice a blade, cutting through her words. With a swift, forceful motion, he spun her around, pressing her hard against the railing. The metal dug into her ribs, each jolt of the ship driving it deeper, a sharp counterpoint to the heat of his body pressed against her back. His hands tore at her robe, the fabric ripping with a wet, wrenching sound, exposing her skin to the storm's cruel caress. Her body recoiled at the intrusion, every nerve screaming in protest. The roughness of his hands, the press of his weight, was a violation that seared through her, a brutal claim against her will.

In that moment, the world collapsed into a chaos of terror. The storm's roar fused with the pounding of her heart, the rain lashing her exposed skin, cold against the bruising heat of Kosuke's grip. Her breath came in sharp, ragged gasps, misting in the frigid air, her body trembling with fear. Her mind screamed—*This can't be real*—as disbelief set in, carving a deep wound in her soul.

The act was a blur of violence and storm, the ship's groans and the sea's roars drowning out her silent cries. Her voice broke into silence, swallowed by thunder, her pleas lost to the tempest.

Amid the chaos of the storm, the ship itself groaned and creaked ominously, mirroring the violent conflict unfolding on its deck. This grim scene, set against a backdrop of nature's fury and human cruelty, framed Mae's dire predicament. Each second stretched into an eternity, marked by her desperate struggle and the relentless assault. In the end, Mae was left violated and trembling, a solitary figure on the slick, rain-soaked deck. Kosuke, her assailant, disappeared into the swirling tempest, leaving her abandoned in the aftermath of his brutality.

Chiyoko, emerging from her ordeal, found her way to the deck, her body aching and her spirit shattered. She stumbled upon Mae, curled up and sobbing near the railing. "Mae, Mae, look at me. Who did this to you?"

Mae, too weak to raise her head, managed a faint, "Kosuke."

In that instant, Chiyoko's last hopes dissolved, the brutal truth of the night's events crashing down upon her as surely as the waves had battered their ship. She gently helped Mae up, her own pain forgotten in the face of her friend's suffering. Together, they returned to the cabin.

As Chiyoko cared for Mae, dressing her wounds and brewing tea, a bond formed between them, forged in the crucible of their shared ordeal. They sat in somber silence, the weight of their unspoken pact—a vow of secrecy and mutual protection—solidifying their resolve.

Chiyoko's tears flowed freely as guilt overwhelmed her. "This is all my fault. If I had only given myself to him, none of this would have ever happened."

Mae, her voice stronger, corrected her gently but firmly. "Chiyoko, please do not take upon yourself any responsibility for his actions. Let him own and one day pay for every choice he makes."

Despite Mae's reassurances, Chiyoko was determined to prevent such things from ever dictating their lives again. At any cost, she vowed never to refuse her husband. Her resolve solidified into a somber acceptance of her role as his wife—to bear his child, no matter the sacrifices she would have to endure personally.

CHAPTER 9

Unexpected News

It had been just over two weeks since that devastating night with Kosuke. Chiyoko had kept her word and, since that time, had endured more nights with her husband than she could possibly bear. It was midday, and they stood against the weathered railing of the ship, gazing out at the endless sea. Chiyoko and Mae, bound by shared trauma, comforted each other quietly. Suddenly, a large bell rang, echoing across the deck, and everyone scurried to the bow. Off in the distance, the faint outline of islands began to emerge along the horizon.

"I hope this new land symbolizes a new beginning for us both," said Chiyoko, clasping Mae's hands firmly.

Mae had been part of the household for many years, serving as Chiyoko's personal servant. As such, they shared a unique bond, their monthly cycles as women aligning over time. This made Mae acutely aware of Chiyoko's physical and emotional needs during those delicate days.

"I need to share something with you," Mae said to Chiyoko, her voice tinged with concern. "This might be difficult to hear, so please sit with me." Together, they settled into wicker chairs on the deck, the emerging islands becoming clearer with each passing moment. "I have not had my monthly time as a woman. At first, I hoped I was merely late. However, there's this sense we have as women, a knowing when things are distinctly different," Mae said.

"I understand you more than you know. I am late as well and sense that our lives will be intertwined beyond just our friendship."

"However, I am concerned for our children. To be born of such a vile father. My child will never be accepted and will always be the bastard blemish on your family name. No, I will not let this be our fate. For this reason, when we arrive in Hawaii, I will resign from my employment with your household. I will tell my child that their father was killed in an accident in Japan, and live my life from here on out as a widow. Our children will never know that they are family. Another secret that connects us despite where our paths will go."

Chiyoko now wept with deep, heavy sobs, "No, please, there must be another way," gripping both of Mae's hands. "I cannot face this all alone. You are my sister, my friend, the only pillar I have to lean on. Where will you go? What will you do?"

"I promise you, my sister, that I will always strive to be nearby. Being in the service of your family, I've acquired many valuable skills, such as cooking, cleaning, mending clothing, and other essential trades. I will miss you deeply, and I am terrified to face motherhood alone. However, there is a part of me that is excited to embark on this new chapter in my life."

Chiyoko was still engulfed in sadness. Yet, mixed emotions swirled within her—concern for Mae's well-being mingled with envy at the thought of Mae's impending freedom, a liberty she herself could not imagine.

"You have my blessing. I know we will remain connected till our dying days. Your secret is safe with me," Chiyoko said, embracing Mae and struggling to let go.

Soon, the ship's crew began shouting commands, and the vessel sprang into bustling action. "I must go and finish the final preparations. I love you, my sister. We shall meet again," Mae said with tears streaming down her face, leaving Chiyoko alone on the chair, her eyes fixed on the promising horizon.

"I love you too."

Meanwhile, down in the cramped belly of the boat, news had traveled that the Hawaiian Islands were now visible on the horizon. All the contracted laborers were instructed to stay below deck—they would be the last to disembark. In the dim, confined space without windows, Namio began to feel extremely claustrophobic for the first time. Despite this mounting anxiety, he remained focused on caring for Yukie, who had become alarmingly sick over the past few days.

Holding back Yukie's hair as she vomited into a worn bucket, Namio tried to offer some comfort, "Breathe, my love, we are almost there. From the chatter, I feel as though we have but a few more hours to go." He was puzzled by her sudden illness. Yukie had not shown any signs of seasickness throughout their entire journey. Her complexion was alarmingly pale. Gently, he guided her to a thin futon and pillow. "Please rest. I will go and seek help."

The lower deck was bustling with activity. People were feverishly packing all their belongings, their voices full of excitement and anticipation. Namio navigated through the crowd, searching for anyone with medical experience.

"Sumimasen (Excuse me), my wife is quite ill, and I am seeking out a doctor," he said repeatedly, approaching one person after another. Eventually, an individual directed him to an elderly man standing near the exit. "Please, sir, I am told you are a doctor. Can you please help me? My wife is quite ill, and we need some help."

After some persuasion, and aware that he'd lose his place in line, the doctor reluctantly agreed to follow Namio back to where Yukie lay.

"Please give us a moment," the doctor requested, kneeling beside Yukie.

Due to the overwhelming noise filling the room, Namio couldn't hear their conversation. He watched as the doctor performed a thorough examination: lifting Yukie's eyelids, inspecting her mouth, placing his hands on her chest to monitor her breathing, lifting her feet, and holding her wrist—likely checking her pulse. Once the examination concluded, they spoke for a brief moment before the doctor stood up and walked away. Namio, filled with concern, immediately rushed to Yukie's side.

"Why did he leave? Are you okay? What's going on?" Namio questioned in a panic.

"Namio, please slow down. I asked him to go. I wanted to be the person to tell you."

A wave of dread washed over Namio. If Yukie wanted to be the one to share the news, he feared it must be grave. His stomach churned, and he felt a cold sweat break out as he braced for the worst. The notion of losing his wife just as they were about to start a new life in Hawai'i was unbearable. His thoughts spiraled into despair, only to be halted when he noticed Yukie's smiling face. Puzzled, he thought, "Why was she smiling?"

"Namio, it will be okay. I am not sick," she reassured him gently.

"How can this be? I held your hair while you were throwing up. You do not look well."

Yukie covered her mouth, a light giggle escaping. "I look well enough, my love. I am not sick. I am pregnant."

Stunned into silence, Namio struggled to process her words. Then, as the realization dawned, a broad smile spread across his face. "We are going to have a baby?"

"Yes, we are," Yukie confirmed with a tender smile.

"We are going to have a baby!" Namio shouted out to the entire room. Some clapped in response, others merely stared, and a few couldn't care less.

After a few sips of water, Yukie was feeling a bit more comfortable, reassured by the normality of her condition. Their bags were now packed, and they stood in a long, winding line. They could hear the robust commotion from above as the boat eventually came to a halt. Typically, even when the engines stopped, they would still be drifting slightly. This time, however, they were stationary. Despite the boat being motionless after thirty-three days at sea, it would take some time before their bodies adjusted to the stillness.

Namio could hear the sound of people now exiting the boat, their footsteps echoing down the walkways that were lowered onto the solid land. He could hear bursts of loud talking followed by laughter, then the continuous movement of the crowd. The distinct rumble of carriages on cobblestone roads reached his ears, along with the water gently slapping back and forth between the boat and the pier. Mixed with these familiar sounds was the honk of a horn, coupled with the mechanical noises of what he presumed to be a motor vehicle —a rare sight he had glimpsed a few times back in Yokohama.

Shortly after the sounds above subsided, the door to their chambers swung open. As Yukie and Namio peered out, squinting, Namio immediately felt the dense moisture in the air soaking into his skin. Yukie took a deep breath, inhaling the breeze which carried a unique floral scent—overtones of sugar, vanilla, and honey—an aroma she knew would linger in her memory forever.

Japanese families awaiting inspection aboard ship in the 1920s, during the era of restrictive U.S. immigration laws. Public Domain, courtesy of the U.S. National Archives.

A Japanese man stood in the doorway, a native delegate beside him, poised to address the group. Just before they could speak, a voice erupted from below, filled with frustration.

"This is outrageous. I have brought you six hundred and seventy workers, and now you tell me that you are rejecting all but one hundred and twenty-two because they lack funds," the man bellowed, his words tinged with anger. Namio recognized him as the short, assertive man who appeared to be overseeing the entire operation.

The native delegate then spoke to the group of laborers, his words translated by the Japanese man beside him. "As you know, we will only accept those of you who are able to sustain your families until your first commission. We understand that many of you do not have the necessary funds, and as a result, you will be asked to remain on this vessel and return back to Japan."

The announcement ignited a wave of anger. Voices raised in protest, and many women and children began to cry. Law enforcement officers soon joined the delegate, their presence imposing. A gunshot silenced the crowd instantly.

"Now, when your name is called, please come forward and present your finances. If they are sustainable, you will be allowed off this ship. If not, you will be asked to stay where you are. Any resistance and you will be shot," the translator relayed sternly.

In a desperate act, one man, unable to face another grueling voyage back, charged toward the door. A guard quickly raised his weapon and shot him. A collective gasp filled the room as the man fell, his blood slowly pooling around him.

"Let this be a warning to you all. We will not permit you to exit this ship unless you have the required funds."

The room fell silent, punctuated only by muffled sobs. Namio and Yukie felt a surge of panic as they watched person after person being turned away. Soon, their names were called. Hand in hand, they walked forward to the delegate. They presented the money given to them by their parents for the journey. The official counted the bills carefully, then, with a brief nod to the guards, Yukie and Namio were finally allowed to exit the boat.

CHAPTER 10

Waialua

Yukie and Namio descended the boat ramp onto the bustling pier. The air was filled with the excitement of movement everywhere. Namio had never heard such a medley of different languages and wondered how they would manage without understanding the exchanges around them. They scarcely had time to ponder this as they were briskly ushered onto a flatbed trailer, its two benches flanked along each side, pulled by two sturdy horses. Despite the presence of numerous motorbikes and cars weaving through the traffic, they found themselves sitting among about twenty other Japanese contractors who had embarked on the same journey. The coach driver barked some instructions in brisk English, and promptly, they were on their way, though it was clear that no one truly grasped where they were going.

Amidst the prevailing confusion, Yukie tightly clutched Namio's hand.

"Are you frightened, my love?" Namio asked.

"No, I never imagined such a place could exist in this world. Look, a palace," Yukie remarked as they passed buildings lining the streets. She speculated that this area might be where royalty resided, struck by the sight of many military-like figures patrolling the grounds. While the palace bore an undeniable beauty, it also emitted an aura of sadness.

The trailer's occupants remained silent, and Namio's curiosity piqued. He leaned towards a man who appeared to be traveling solo across the aisle and inquired, "Sumimasen (Excuse me), do you know where they are taking us?"

"Ie (No), I just hope it was worth the journey," the man replied.

While the response was not entirely reassuring, Namio felt a slight relief knowing he wasn't the only one navigating this journey blindly. Back in Yanaka, his home was surrounded by lush landscapes, but this was his first encounter with a tropical environment. To one side of the trailer, dark green mountains ascended majestically into the sky, adorned with cascading waterfalls that carved through numerous crevices. Clouds pushed heavily, jostling to spill over to the other side. Occasionally, the trailer crossed bridges over small streams that fed into fields resembling rice paddies, though these were dotted with other large-leafed plants. Looking towards the opposite side, Namio was captivated by the ocean's vivid blue, pondering its temperature and his own lack of swimming skills, which he now considered acquiring.

The scenery gradually shifted from lush tropics to dryness. The earth was peppered with crops, and Namio observed a train laden with harvested goods. Stilt homes with tin-like roofs clustered near small towns and local stores. After traversing the mountains for about two hours, they encountered cooler, crisp air and rows of trees laden with dark auburn berries. The area bustled with Asian workers and other foreigners harvesting bean-type fruits.

Trying not to distract the driver, Namio ventured, "Is this the work we will be doing?"

To his surprise, the driver responded in halting English, necessitating translation by a fellow Japanese passenger.

"You are not part of this plantation. These are coffee bean workers. You have been contracted to work on the sugar cane plantations in Waialua."

Namio decided against probing further, still puzzled about sugar cane. The trailer soon emerged from the mountainous terrain, revealing a breathtaking view. Below, fields filled with spiky-topped plants and tall, grass-like stalks stretched towards a horizon where the ocean met the sky in shades of profound blue, interspersed with rain-soaked patches.

The translator addressed the group as the driver's aide, announcing, "Welcome to your new home. This place is called Waialua. You are now all employees of the Waialua Agricultural Company, which is owned by the Castle and Cooke families. There are many different jobs for you to do, and assignments will be given when you arrive at camp. You will have this day to get your things in order, and your workday will begin first thing tomorrow."

Waialua Sugar Mill, Oahu, 1930. Public Domain, U.S. National Archives.

As the trailer approached their destination, Namio spotted rows of structured homes near a large building crowned with a towering smokestack. Upon their arrival, Yukie stepped off and immediately vomited, her sickness splattering a by-stander's fine leather shoes.

"What the hell!" the man exclaimed in shock.

Embarrassed, Yukie attempted to wipe his shoes with her apron.

"Get up, woman," the man barked as his words were translated. "Is this woman sick? Do we need a doctor?" he demanded.

"I am so sorry," Namio interjected. "My wife is not sick. She is pregnant."

"Well, I'll be damned, we just got two Japs for the price of one. Let's go ahead and put these people in a joint house. The rest of you go on and report to the office for your living arrangements," said the businessman.

Laborers' homes at Waialua Plantation, Oahu, early 20th century. Public Domain, courtesy of the University of Hawai'i at Mānoa Library.

Namio and Yukie were escorted to a row of connected houses, described by the translator as dual homes, which were on stilts with tin-like roofs. These homes featured a small bedroom, a common living area, and a kitchen, along with an onsen (Bathhouse) and an outdoor toilet. As they settled into their new residence, the contrast between their expectations and reality became starkly evident. Still, to Yukie, their new setup was a miraculous upgrade from anything she could have envisioned, especially the kerosene stove, which fascinated her, having never seen one that operated without wood.

"Namio, this is more than I could ever imagine. I am sorry for ever doubting you," she confessed.

"I know this was difficult, but I can say with confidence that this is where we are supposed to be," Namio reassured her, embracing his wife in their new home, marking the beginning of their new life together.

Within a few hours, the adjoining family had returned to their shared quarters. They were not much older than Namio and Yukie. Both the husband and wife wore traditional hachimaki (Headbands), and the woman tenderly carried a young baby in an onbuhimo (Traditional Japanese baby sling).

"Konichiwa," they all said, offering respectful bows in greeting.

"My name is Namio, and this is my wife, Yukie. We are both from Yanaka."

"Good to meet you. I am Nobu. This is my wife, Emi, and our son Ren. We are both from Sendagi. Have you heard of it?"

"Yes," Namio quickly replied. "A dear friend of ours is from Sendagi. Maybe you know him? His name was Takeshi."

The other couple's eyes widened in surprise. "There are many Takeshis we know. Is there anything else you can tell us about this man?" Nobu inquired.

"I am a potter who would sell my wares down in Yokohama. Takeshi was a fabric vendor whom I met on occasion," Namio explained.

"I think his wife's name was Akiko," Yukie chimed in.

At that moment, Emi's expression changed as tears began to stream down her face. She asked in a choked voice, "Why did you say his name was Takeshi?"

Sensing a deeper connection, Namio invited the other couple to sit down. As they settled into the sparse wooden chairs, he explained in more detail how he'd met Takeshi and the tragic news that he had passed away on his journey back to Sendagi.

Emi was now sobbing heavily, the emotional weight of the conversation overwhelming her. She tried to speak but could not find her voice. Nobu, supporting his wife, took over, "Takeshi was Emi's father."

There was never a greater moment of serendipity than what they experienced at that time. Both couples spoke late into the night, finding solace and unexpected connections in their shared histories. Nobu and Emi expressed a heartfelt desire to mentor and watch over Namio and Yukie as they adjusted to their new lives.

That night, under a clear sky glittered with stars, Yukie and Emi sat outside their makeshift home.

"Emi, I am so glad we are living with you and Nobu. I want to tell you that I am pregnant. Has it been difficult having a baby here on the plantation?" Yukie asked.

"It has been challenging," Emi confessed as she gently rocked Ren in her arms. "There is no one here to help you care for your baby, and we are all required to put in a full day's work. Because of this, Ren always comes with me to the fields."

Yukie began to feel a surge of anxiety about her future responsibilities. At that moment, Emi finished feeding Ren and gently placed him in Yukie's arms. Yukie held Ren with such care. He was serene and did not cry. She was in awe of how perfect he was, and as she touched his tiny fingers, Ren responded by gripping one of hers. A single tear rolled down Yukie's cheek as she experienced a deep connection to the little life in her arms.

"Yukie, Ren has a middle name. It is Takeshi, after my father," Emi shared, her voice filled with a mixture of pride and sadness. "You may have asked me the wrong question. Has it been difficult? No matter what the circumstances are, no matter how little or how much you have been given, as a mother, the answer will always be yes. The better question to ask is, has it been worth it?"

Looking up from Ren, whose eyes sparkled under the starlight, Yukie asked, "Has it been worth it?"

"Hai (Yes)."

CHAPTER 11

The Best of Friends

It was early fall in 1932, eleven years since Chiyoko and her family had left Japan for America, a land once promised to be filled with opportunity. Yet, the gripping reality of the Great Depression had rendered such promises. Her husband, Kosuke, burdened by poor business decisions, saw their chances of returning to Yokohama dwindling as he frequently traveled back to Japan to liquidate assets, desperately trying to salvage their failing enterprise. Despite the grim economic backdrop, Chiyoko found a peculiar contentment. She harbored a deep-seated resentment towards her husband, who was seldom home. When he was, due to exhaustion, there was no interaction between them.

Chiyoko and her son, Peter, resided in a stately plantation home in Haleiwa, a quaint town on the north shore of Oahu. The house boasted polished wood floors and an expansive porch encircling its structure. Despite their financial woes, Chiyoko retained the privileges of upper-class society, living among the haole (white foreigner) landowners and management. While she occasionally mingled at social events, her true joy was spending time with Peter, her son.

In line with their Christian faith—a common choice among Japanese immigrants seeking to assimilate into Western culture—they had given their son a strong Biblical name. Peter, tall for his age, was passionate about baseball and the ocean. Born in the American Territory of Hawaii, he held dual citizenship with Japan. Despite Chiyoko's attempts to sway him, Peter continually sought his father's approval, much to her dismay. This familial rift led Chiyoko towards the very vice she loathed.

"You're drunk again," Mae observed, wiping down the tables at her okazuya (Hawaii Japanese Restaurant).

"I just don't understand how an angel of a son could love a devil of a father more than me," Chiyoko lamented.

"You know, my sister, if all we do is hate, one day, we will become that thing we hate most," Mae cautioned gently.

"What is that supposed to mean?"

"I'm just saying that it was the drink that drove Kosuke to become the man he is today…" Mae trailed off, her voice filled with concern. "Here, have some tea."

"There you go again, still serving me. You know you don't work for me anymore," Chiyoko pointed out.

Despite no longer being employed by Chiyoko's family, Mae remained devoted to her. Her life had taken many turns since disembarking the boat years earlier. After leaving her role with Chiyoko, she had worked various odd jobs to stay close. Eventually, Mae found stable employment with an elderly couple who ran a small restaurant in Haleiwa. The childless couple had taken Mae in, treating her with the kindness and care as if she were their own daughter. Although Mae was pregnant, she remained resilient and helpful. After her son Jason was born, she continued her work at the restaurant. Tragically, within three years, both shop owners passed away, leaving their last will to bestow the shop on Mae and her young son, fulfilling their legacy of generosity.

Just behind the bustling restaurant, Jason pitched the ball to Peter.

"Seriously, that was our last ball. I told you only to hit grounders."

"What can I say? I'm just that good. One day, I'm going to play for the major leagues."

"That sounds great, but now what are we going to do? We have no ball."

"You want to pick lychee?"

In the space behind the restaurant where they were playing, a huge lychee tree stood laden with fruit. Jason and Peter would eat as many as they could until they began to break out in hives.

"So when is your dad coming back?" Jason asked, tossing a lychee up and catching it in his hand.

"I'm not sure. This is the third time this year he's traveled back to Japan. I know we are okay, but I do hear him yelling more than usual," Peter replied.

"I can't imagine what more than usual sounds like. I feel like he is always yelling."

"Hey, don't badmouth my dad. He is just very passionate about his work."

"Well, at least you have a dad."

"I don't mean to pry, but whatever happened to your dad," Peter asked.

"Mom told me that just before she came to Hawaii, he was working on a big ship, and his job was to help load the boat. Mom said that he was very big and strong. However, one day, he was standing under a crate that was being hoisted onto the boat. Something happened, and the crate fell on him, and he died."

Jason started to feel tears welling up in his eyes. Peter could feel the emotional weight, too. In hopes of not even beginning to go there, Peter punched Jason in the arm.

"Hey, why did you do that!"

"Just thought things were getting a bit, you know, emotional. Anyway, you have us. Mom and I were practically family. We see you guys every day. I'm sure I can share my dad with you."

"I'll pass that guy scares me. No offense, but I'm good with just me and my Mom."

The boys heard their moms calling them from inside the shop. They both had martial arts lessons at the local Hongwanji temple, followed by Japanese language school. Although both boys spoke Japanese quite well, their parents were concerned about them losing touch with their culture amid the multicultural environment of Hawaii. Peter, Chiyoko's son, was a very athletic and gifted baseball player. However, Jason, although not as athletic, was very loyal and kind-hearted. Following their lessons on this particular day, they were out playing in the courtyard. Peter and Jason passed a ball back and forth to each other. Soon, a bunch of boys began to crowd around them.

"Let's go play somewhere else," Jason said.

"Why, we were here first," replied Peter.

Soon, the biggest of the boys interjected.

"Eh, give me your ball," he demanded.

The two boys tried to ignore him at first, yet he persisted.

"I don't think you heard me. Give me your ball!"

"Peter, we can find another ball. Why not give him the ball?" said Jason, trying to avoid conflict. Then Jason saw in Peter's eyes a look that he knew he'd regret.

"I'll tell you why, Jason, because maybe this guy is so tall that the air is too thin up there, and it's made him too stupid to find his own ball. Can you hear me up there?" Peter taunted with a defiant glare.

Then, that large boy made a growling sound, and Jason could feel his stomach balling up in knots. At that very moment, he could see Peter's fist also balling up, which resulted in a punch right in the bully's face. Jason thought, "Oh no, not again." Soon, the big boy and his entourage of five other friends were pummeling Jason and Peter. Despite the odds, neither boy backed down. The last thing Jason could remember was looking up through a swollen eye as their ball walked away. Then, a hand reached down to pick him up.

"Thanks, bro, for having my back. We almost had them," said Peter, wiping the blood from off his lip.

"What are best friends for? I'll always have your back."

At that moment, they heard a person clear their throat from behind them.

"Speaking of backs, please turn around," said a Buddhist priest who happened to be standing right behind them.

"I did not see what happened, but I am sure the others do not look any better. I will be informing your parents of this incident when they come to pick you up."

Despite the protest from the boys, they were solemnly escorted into the temple office. Soon, both of their mothers arrived to pick them up. As they waited, neither boy was allowed to speak to the other. Despite this restriction, when asked what had happened, to their surprise, their stories matched except for...

"Please, mother, don't blame Jason. It was all my fault," Peter explained earnestly.

Quickly cutting off Jason, Peter asserted, "No, Peter is full of it. It was entirely my fault."

"I'm sure it was both of your faults," Mae interjected.

"And as for you, Peter, I have had enough of this violent and arrogant behavior. If you keep this up, you'll end up just like your father," Chiyoko shouted.

Peter could feel his anger swelling up inside. Then, under his breath, he mumbled bitterly, "I'd rather be like him than a drunk like you."

Chiyoko immediately raised her hand and slapped her son across the face. At that moment, she caught the look of shock in Mae's eyes. Jason also looked terrified. Most of all, looking down at her son Peter, she did not see sadness, only anger and resentment. There were no tears in his eyes, just teeth clenched and a look that bored a hole directly through her soul. Chiyoko reached up and felt her face. She remembered that night Kosuke had struck her out of rage. She remembered him reeking of alcohol, and she remembered what he had done to Mae.

Mae was right. If we become obsessed with the thing we hate, eventually, we become that. She had become Kosuke, and her son was now the victim.

Tears began to stream down Chiyoko's face. She found herself on her knees in front of her son in that dimly lit office.

"What have I done? What have I become? Please, son, please forgive me."

Mae placed her hand on Peter's shoulder, offering a comforting touch. "It is okay, Peter. I have known your mom for a very long time. No matter what happens in life, she will always be your mother."

"It will be okay, Mom," Peter said as he crouched down near his mother, his voice soft and reassuring.

Together, they held each other in a firm embrace. Peter realized that day that his mother had been through more than he would ever understand. From that time on, he promised himself that he'd never let anyone ever hurt his mother the way he did that day. Peter was now his mother's protector, and

Jason would forever be Peter's. As for Mae, she continued to take care of everyone, just as she had always done.

Chapter 12

The Pandemic

Japanese laborer harvesting sugar cane in Lahaina, Maui, 1932. Public Domain.

"Otousan, Otousan (Father), look what I made," said Kimiko excitedly, as she handed her father a grass doll crafted from the dried leaves of the sugarcane.

"It is beautiful, Kimi. What is her name?" replied Namio warmly. He often called his daughter Kimi, short for Kimiko, as did everyone in their tight-knit plantation community.

"I'm not quite sure. I just pretend that this is my new sister."

"But what if Mama has a boy? Will you be okay with a brother?"

"I guess, but I really think I am going to have a sister."

Suddenly, a boy burst out from a row of sugarcane and snatched Kimi's doll.

"Ren! Give me that back!" Kimi shouted, her voice echoing through the fields as she chased after him.

"Maybe she is right. Maybe they were going to have another girl. Ren is practically her brother. I'm not sure if they hate each other or love each other," Namio said aloud, shaking his head in amusement before returning to his labor.

Often, Nobu and Namio worked side by side. Their primary task was to follow a trailer laden with cane starters. Two men would shovel the starters from the back of the trailer, and workers following behind would firmly press them into the fertile ground, succeeded by another trailer that dispensed water to dampen the soil. The workers, finding a rhythm in their task, spent most of their time hunched over. This was literally back-breaking work. Whenever the trailer with starters returned for more, it signaled a welcomed, albeit brief, break—a break that was always too fleeting.

As Namio and Nobu caught their breath and savored a refreshing drink of water, Nobu inquired, "So, how is Yukie doing? It seems like things are getting close."

"From what the plantation doctor has shared with us, it could be any day now. We are just hoping for a healthy baby. Emi seems to be doing well with your newest child. I can't believe Ren has a brother. Your baby must be almost a year old now."

"Yes, it is hard to believe how quickly our families are growing."

With that, another trailer was pulling out in front of them, and before they knew it, they were bent over, planting stalk after stalk in the rich earth.

Because of strict orders, Yukie was recently excused from her strenuous plantation work. Over the past two weeks, she had taken the time to rest and prepare for the arrival of their second child. As such, she had offered to watch Ren, his new baby brother, and Kimi while the other parents put in a full day's work. However, Ren was a bit of a rascal, always full of energy.

Kimi, on the other hand, was a wonderful daughter who was quickly mastering the many household trades. She loved to help cook, clean, and, most of all, mend clothing. Yukie would often find Kimi's handmade grass dolls scattered around the house, each adorned with meticulously crafted clothing made from scraps of material she gathered throughout the plantation. Kimi also showed a nurturing side, especially when caring for Ren's baby brother. Amid the daily chores, Yukie always found moments to express her deep love for her daughter.

"Kimi, why don't you take a break and go and play with Ren?" Yukie suggested gently.

"Mama, Ren is always teasing me. I don't think he likes me very much."

Yukie found that hard to believe. Ren was only a few months older than Kimi. They were both twelve years old now, and Yukie remembered what it was like growing up with Namio at that age. She knew that the more a boy pestered a girl, the more likely it was that he was struggling to express his fondness. Kimi was a focused, hardworking child and very intelligent, but she often misinterpreted Ren's teasing as dislike.

Yukie and Namio practiced speaking English every night. It was clear that, despite a few Japanese business owners, the majority of the management on the plantation was haole (English-speaking foreigners). The island's plantations, dominated by haole managers, reflected the complex interplay of cultural dynamics. Although they took pride in their culture, Yukie and Namio wanted much more for their children. As a result, they rarely spoke Japanese at home and required Kimi to speak English whenever possible.

Kimi was often asked to translate for many of the plantation supervisors, making her a valuable member of the community. She frequently accepted side jobs whenever they were offered. Namio often told her, "The more you do for the haoles, the more opportunities you'll have in this world." Kimi was often found mending clothing or fixing furniture, tasks she truly loved because they allowed her to work with her hands and express her creativity.

"Kimi, we need your help. Please go with the plantation doctor. Many people are getting sick, and we need you to help us inform the workers," said one of the managers.

Together, Kimi and the plantation doctor visited many homes throughout the crowded camp. Kimi was asked to stay outside while the doctor made his rounds inside each home. She could hear people coughing deeply, and sometimes, she even heard the distressing sounds of vomiting. Although these sounds frightened her, Kimi was deeply interested in helping others and was always fascinated by the medical work on the plantation.

"Kimi, these people have a sickness called Influenza. I will paint this symbol on the door, letting people know they need to stay away for a little while. Can you paint a Japanese symbol that will let people know the same?"

Kimi thought about it for a minute and used the kanji characters for "sick" and "stay out." Over the next few weeks, Kimi diligently helped the doctor go from home to home. One day, Kimi helped file papers at the office near the tall chimney stack. She loved the way the sugar smelled as they extracted the sticky sap from the cane. She breathed in deeply and savored the scent, finding solace in feeling useful. Kimi felt as though she didn't have a care in the world.

"Kimi, come quick!" Ren burst into the office.

"What is going on? Seriously, Ren, I'm busy. I don't have time for your childish games," Kimi responded, her voice tinged with irritation.

Trying to catch his breath, Ren stammered out the words, "Your mom, I think she is sick."

Kimi did not respond. She immediately placed the papers on the nearby desk and ran home. Ren could barely keep up as she sprinted down the dirt road to the work camp. When she approached the house, her heart sank. The doctor had just exited and painted the symbol that meant someone in this house had influenza.

"I'm sorry, Kimi. Can you please paint the Japanese words?" said the doctor, who was now walking over to the house just next door.

Kimi felt the tears streaming down her face as she painted the Japanese characters. Just beyond the doors, she heard her mother coughing heavily. Ren had no idea what to do. He walked up the porch and slowly sat down near Kimi. She then placed the paintbrush back into the bucket, put her head on his lap, and cried. Ren gently placed his hand on Kimi's back and lightly patted her. Although he did his best to be strong, he could feel tears welling up in his eyes. He also loved Aunty Yukie and was worried. Neither of them spoke. It was a moment that seemed to stretch on for hours.

Kimi knew that she would not be able to visit with her father until he came home from his long day at the plantation. Even if she were able to share with him all that had transpired, he would still be required to complete a full day's work. Sitting on the porch, waiting for her father, felt like an eternity. Despite everything, Ren did not leave her side. For a moment, she wondered if this was the same boy who bothered her every day. Why was he being so unusually kind? Nevertheless, she was grateful for his comforting presence.

As the sun began to set, casting long shadows across the dusty plantation grounds, Kimi knew her father would be returning soon. She spotted him in the distance, walking alongside Uncle Nobu, approaching their home. At that moment, she jumped up and ran towards him.

"Daddy, Mama is sick," she announced breathlessly.

Namio enveloped his daughter in a reassuring embrace, doing his best to comfort her. "There, there, child. I know these things already. Aunty Emi picked up her baby and heard Mama coughing. She sent for the doctor. Once Aunty Emi knew what was going on, she came and told me."

"Is Mama going to be okay? Is the baby going to be okay?"

As much as Namio wanted to reassure his daughter with certainty, he couldn't. Looking down into Kimi's anxious eyes, he felt compelled to instill hope in the grim situation. "Yes, my child, I'm sure everything will be just fine."

Namio asked Kimi to stay outside. He then removed his hatchimaki (headband) and wrapped it around his face as a makeshift mask. As he entered the home, he noticed that the room where Yukie lay was isolated with sheets, creating a makeshift quarantine from the rest of the house. There, on a futon, lay his precious wife, looking unusually pale and visibly exhausted. She was dripping with sweat, a clear sign of her discomfort, especially challenging in her ninth month of pregnancy. Namio's heart ached with sorrow. He had never felt so powerless. Yukie's eyes were closed, and she moaned softly in discomfort. He knelt beside her, his presence a silent pillar of support. Touching her forehead, he felt the scorching heat of her fever. Gently, he took a cool, damp cloth from a bowl beside the bed and placed it on her brow, hoping to offer some relief.

"Yukie, I am here," he whispered.

"Namio, I wondered when you'd come. I'm so sorry. I don't know how this happened. I am worried about our baby. How are you feeling? Is Kimi okay?"

"Please rest. We are all doing fine. No one else is sick right now," he reassured her gently.

Yukie, ever selfless, continued to worry about everyone else. "That is good. Is there anything you need, my love?" she asked, her voice weak and breath ragged.

"Of course not. Please find a way to relax and sleep," Namio responded, continuing to tenderly wipe her forehead with the cool cloth.

After a few hours, Yukie's fever finally broke, and she drifted into a deep sleep, exhausted from the ordeal. Emi and Nobu took care of Kimi, preparing dinner and allowing her to rest on their side of the house. Despite the overwhelming stress of the day, Kimi fell into a deep sleep almost immediately. Her young body, overcome by the day's events, desperately needed the rest. That night, Namio stayed awake, his silhouette just visible through the sheets, illuminated by a dim lantern. Like a vigilant sentinel, he remained still, kneeling by Yukie's side until the dawn.

Although exhausted from being up all night, Namio stood and methodically changed his clothes. Kimi was also awake, her eyes wide with concern.

"Okay, my child, please do not go in there. If Mama needs anything, you must wear this hachimaki (headband) around your face. Only enter the room if you absolutely have to," Namio instructed firmly, his voice carrying a mixture of caution and care.

Kimi did not respond verbally. Instead, she just held her father tightly around his waist, silently hoping he would not leave.

"I'm sorry. I have to go to work. Aunty Emi will stay home today. If you need anything, she can help. I must go," replied Namio. Leaving that day took all the strength he could muster.

As Namio and Nobu worked in the fields, Nobu noticed how unusually quiet Namio was. He understood that although Namio was physically present, his heart and mind were with Yukie. Nobu had never met a couple who loved each other as deeply as they did, a testament to their enduring partnership.

As the day wore on, the effects of a sleepless night began to manifest in Namio. He found himself grappling not only with physical fatigue but also with a mental strain that felt heavier than ever before. As the sun began to dip below the horizon, marking the end of the laborious day, he saw a young child sprinting towards him. Initially, he mistook the figure for Kimi until he heard Nobu's voice cut through the evening air.

"Ren, what are you doing out here?" Nobu called out.

The young boy, panting from his run, managed to stammer out, "Aunty Yukie."

Immediately alert, Namio pressed for more information. "Aunty Yukie, what?"

Breathing heavily, Ren delivered his message: "Mother sent me to tell you that Aunty Yukie is going to have her baby!"

CHAPTER 13

The Time Is Now

Namio dropped everything and sprinted, his mind racing as fast as his feet moved across the dirt path leading to his small wooden home. He was acutely aware that his wife was due to give birth to their baby at any moment. However, her illness added a layer of complexity and urgency to the situation. As he approached, he noticed the plantation doctor's buggy parked outside, a sign that the situation was already serious. Disregarding traditional customs in his haste, Namio left his shoes on and burst through the doorway to be by his wife's side.

Inside, the air was tense with worry. "Kimi, stay with Ren and help watch his brother. I need to go in and assist," said Emi, her voice steady as she handed the infant to Kimi.

"I'm sure it will be okay," Ren reassured, placing his hand gently on Kimi's lap to comfort her. Together, they sat on the creaking wooden stairs of the porch. Every few minutes, the children could hear Aunty Yukie's screams piercing through the thin walls. With each cry, Ren felt Kimi's body stiffen next to him. Tears soon began to stream down both of their faces.

Inside the modest, dimly-lit house, Namio knelt beside his wife, gripping her hand with a blend of tenderness and firmness, radiating reassurance amidst the chaos.

"Namio, this does not feel right," Yukie gasped between contractions, her voice laced with distress.

Feeling her forehead, Namio's hand met the unsettling heat of her fever. "Doctor, what do we do? She is still so very sick?"

"There is very little we can do. We do not want to hurt the baby," the doctor replied.

"Please, my love, whatever happens, do not hurt our baby. Promise me you will do everything to save our child?" Yukie pleaded, locking her gaze with Namio's, her eyes brimming with desperation.

"I will."

Another contraction seized Yukie, causing her to arch her back and release a scream that filled the room with fear. Namio had never felt so powerless in his life.

"It looks like the baby is ready," the doctor announced.

Following that intense contraction, Yukie's breathing slowed to a shallow, uneven rhythm. Her eyes fluttered and then rolled back, her lids closing as she lost consciousness.

"What is happening!" Namio shouted, panic rising in his throat. The doctor quickly checked her pulse and called out for smelling salts.

"She's fainted. Her blood pressure is dropping," he informed the nurse.

After inhaling the salts, Yukie's eyes snapped open with urgency. "You need to push now!" the doctor shouted.

Yukie complied instantly, mustering her remaining strength. Namio, overwhelmed by the rapid developments, felt his own stability wavering.

"I can see the head. Just one more push," the doctor urged firmly.

At that critical moment, Yukie's eyes shut once more, her breaths becoming faint and sporadic. Namio shook her shoulders gently.

"Yukie, Yukie! Please open your eyes. We are almost there."

"Namio, the baby is suffocating. You have to choose. We can inject your wife with adrenaline, but she will probably not live much longer after the birth. If we don't act quickly, your child will die. Maybe they will both die," the doctor presented the grim options.

"I don't know. I don't know," Namio repeated, his voice breaking as the weight of the decision crashed down on him.

"Pull yourself together, man! You have but seconds to decide," the doctor pressed.

Then, as if time itself had paused, Namio's mind vividly flashed back to that serene and unforgettable night aboard the boat in his quiet sanctuary with Yukie. He remembered kneeling before his wife, their hands intertwined, as they gazed deeply into each other's eyes. A single tear traced a path down his cheek.

"Why so sad?" Yukie inquired softly.

"It is just that I love you so much. I can't lose you," Namio confessed, his voice thick with emotion.

"You will never lose me. Even when you would travel for days on end to Yokohama, I was always with you."

"Please don't make me choose. You mean everything to me," Namio pleaded.

"You don't have to choose, my love. Remember, you promised me you'd do everything to save our baby."

"I can't. I won't."

"You will."

Then, Yukie leaned over and kissed Namio tenderly. Instantly, he was transported back to the present moment.

The doctor's voice cut sharply through the air, "This is it. You are out of time!"

"Do it. Give her the adrenaline!" Namio commanded.

Swiftly, the doctor administered the adrenaline injection to Yukie. Her eyes flew open immediately, wide with startled awareness.

"Push now!" the doctor barked, and with that final command, the baby was born. After a brief, tense moment, Namio heard the newborn's cry.

"It's a girl," announced the doctor, handing the tiny infant to Emi. She and the nurse quickly busied themselves with cleaning and swaddling the new little life.

Overcome with a tumult of emotions, Namio turned back to his wife and exclaimed, "Yukie, we have another daughter."

Still clasping her hand firmly, Yukie could not speak, but a single tear escaped her eye. She offered a brave smile to her worried husband.

"You're okay. We'll be okay. Yukie, don't go," Namio implored, his voice cracking with fear and hope intertwined.

It was but a fleeting moment. She then closed her eyes, her grip loosening. She was no longer holding onto Namio's hand.

Kimi was still perched on the wooden porch when she heard her mother's anguished cry, followed by the distinct wail of a newborn, and then her father's voice joining the chorus of cries. Soon, the door creaked open slowly. Her father stood in the threshold for a moment, his eyes shut tight as he took a deep, labored breath.

"Daddy, is Mama okay?" He did not reply. "Daddy, is Mama okay?" He still didn't respond or even glance in her direction. Now driven by panic, Kimi's voice escalated, "Daddy, is Mama okay?" As tears streamed down his face, he found himself unable to meet his daughter's eyes. Namio slowly descended the stairs, each step heavy and deliberate, and soon his slow descent turned into a sprint.

Kimi was bewildered, unable to grasp the unfolding events. She could still hear the baby's cries echoing from inside the house, while her father was sprinting away in the opposite direction. He was nearly out of sight when she witnessed him collapse to his knees. Now just a distant silhouette against the fading light, his hands thrust skyward, Kimi would forever remember the scream he let out that day — a heart-wrenching sound that seemed to encapsulate the shattering of a thousand hearts, broken.

Namio then stood and, without a backward glance, continued to run until he reached the ocean. He removed his shoes and methodically waded into the cool water. Standing motionless, he felt his feet sink into the soft sand with each gentle ebb and flow of the ocean's waves. Soon, he was waist-deep, and as the waves splashed against his face, he could feel his tears merging with the salty mist of each swell.

He then shouted out to the horizon, "I cannot do this! She was my everything. I am nothing without her." Namio took a few more steps forward. The water became deeper and noticeably cooler. He struggled to keep his head above the water. Soon, he was pushing off from the sandy bottom of the ocean floor. Each time he dipped below the water's surface, Namio instinctively held his breath, finding a somber peace in the quiet depths.

Becoming physically exhausted, Namio felt the ocean's current tugging him further out to sea. Now submerged, he envisioned Yukie's face looking down at him with serene beauty. He felt his body begin to sink deeper into the ocean's embrace. The mental struggle to cling to life faded away. Looking up towards the water's surface, he could see the last rays of sunlight piercing through. Yukie seemed to be still gazing down at him from above.

In his mind, he reached out to her, "I am coming, my love. We will be together again soon."

She replied gently, "Not yet. I will be here waiting for you. Remember your promise and know that I will always be with you, no matter what."

Namio then perceived Yukie extending her hand. As he reached towards her, the world around him began to darken.

At that crucial moment, he was forcefully pulled upwards, he gasped for air, his lungs burning as he expelled the salt water. Eagerly anticipating Yukie's hand in his, as his vision cleared, he instead saw small fingers, the nails caked with dirt, and a face overwhelmed with panic and worry.

Kimi had chased after her father, her small legs pumping as fast as they could. He was much faster than her. She watched helplessly as he walked steadily into the ocean. She yelled with all her might to get his attention, but no matter how hard she tried, he continued his relentless march forward. Her heart sank with heavy dread, knowing that her father did not know how to swim. Although Kimi was a very good swimmer, she knew she was still too small to save him on her own. When she reached the shore, she saw a small homemade dock crafted from old wood and empty water barrels. She pushed against it with all her might, trying to get the dock into the water. Despite her determined efforts, the dock would not budge. Soon, she saw her father's head go under the water.

In a surge of desperation, she cried out, "Mama, please help me." She had no idea why she called out for her mother. It didn't matter. She leaned into the dock with all her might, and to her surprise, it moved. She then grabbed a long bamboo pole lying on the sand, which she presumed was used to steer and move the dock in the water. She wasn't very far offshore when she saw her father reaching up to the surface. Quickly, she plunged her hand into the water. Feeling his strong grip, she pulled with all her might. He was now sprawled over the floating dock, gasping for air and coughing up water. He clung to her hand tightly.

"Yukie, Yukie, you've come back to me," he said.

"Daddy, it's me, Kimi. Mama is still at the house with the new baby."

A bit confused and disoriented, Namio replied, "I'm sorry, Kimi, she's not."

CHAPTER 14

The Sting of Transition

That night, Kimi and her father walked in heavy silence back to their home. She could distinctly feel the trade winds blowing offshore against her damp shirt. As they neared their house, a wooden wagon, drawn by a sturdy mule, was parked near the stairs of their weathered porch. She wondered what someone had brought them. Whatever it was, it lay hidden beneath a pristine white sheet. As they approached, her father's gaze remained fixed straight ahead, and his steady pace did not falter until he crossed the threshold of their home. Kimi slowed down, her curiosity piqued about the contents of the cart. Aunty Emi and Uncle Nobu stood solemnly on the porch. As Kimi drew closer, she noticed Uncle Nobu embracing Aunty

Emi, offering her comfort. What had transpired? Was the baby alright, she thought?

Distracted by Namio entering the home without acknowledgment, Nobu and Emi did not notice Kimi nearing the cart. It was in that precise moment that they realized it was too late.

"No, no, no, this can't be," Kimi cried out.

Quickly, Aunty Emi rushed to her side. "Come away, my child. Don't look anymore."

Kimi resisted fiercely. "Mama! This can't be happening," she protested, reaching and tugging at the sheet in the back of the cart. Kimi seized the sheet and released it instantly as she saw her mother there, lifeless and motionless in the cart. She screamed and immediately lost consciousness.

Uncle Nobu lifted Kimi gently as Emi delicately replaced the sheet over Yukie.

"Where is Namio?" Nobu inquired.

Nobu then carried Kimi into the house. He laid her down on the same futon where she had slept the night before. Exhaustion overwhelmed her. Nobu cherished Kimi deeply. Having only sons, he often wondered what it would have been like to have a daughter.

Just inside, Namio sat at his kitchen table, his face bare, devoid of any covering. The assistants of the plantation doctor were methodically moving through the house, gathering all of

Yukie's personal effects to be incinerated in hopes of controlling the influenza outbreak.

"Please, sir, please put this face covering on," implored one of the workers to Namio.

"Ie (No)!" Namio shouted as he strode over to a cabinet beneath the sink. He retrieved an old bottle of alcohol. "What does it matter? Either way, we all die someday." He then settled at the table and poured himself a drink.

The workers were nearly finished evacuating all of Yukie's possessions when Namio spotted her apron.

"You will not take this!" he bellowed.

"But, sir, all these items have been contaminated and must be destroyed."

"How dare you? This is my wife's apron. She needs it!" With that, Namio struck the worker, who collapsed to the ground. Quickly, Nobu intervened, pulling Namio away.

"What is wrong with you?" the worker demanded.

"More than you will ever know," Namio muttered to himself, now sitting and pouring another drink. After gulping down another glass, he pressed his face into Yukie's apron, inhaling deeply. He cherished the scent of his wife. To Namio, Yukie always smelled like home.

Friday, December 5th, 1941 – two days before the attack on Pearl Harbor.

Waikīkī Inn and Tavern, circa 1940s. Public Domain, courtesy of Bishop Museum Archives.

"Okay, my brother, it's time to celebrate. Drinking alone is no fun. Let me be the first to buy you a drink," said Peter as they entered the bustling Waikiki Tavern. "Ladies and gentlemen, and to be honest, we're mostly talking to the ladies—how about a round of applause for my boy Jason on his twenty-first birthday, bartender, drinks on me for everyone."

The crowd cheered, and the band kicked up the lively music. It was a regular sight to see Peter and Jason out on the town each weekend. Although Jason did not come from wealth, he was considered hanai (informally adopted) by Aunty Chiyoko and her household. She treated him like her own cherished son.

As the night progressed, the tavern became increasingly crowded. For some time now, the world had plunged back into war. Japan was now allied with Germany, and America was actively resisting. However, at this time, Hawaii served as a haven where American soldiers serving in Asia found solace on their way back to the States.

"Come on, Jason, this place is getting packed with G.I.s. Let's head down to Hotel Street. I guarantee we can find some ladies there," Peter suggested eagerly.

As they were navigating their way to the exit, a soldier stuck out his leg, causing Peter to trip and crash onto the table right in front of him. Drinks flew everywhere.

"What the hell!" bellowed the large G.I. from behind the table. "Watch where you're going, you stupid Jap!"

For some inexplicable reason, Peter, usually fearless and bold, was terrified of the military.

"I'm sorry, it was a mistake. I tripped," he stammered apologetically.

"Here I am, serving my country. I'm doing my best to fight against people like you. I just can't escape. You Japs are everywhere," the soldier ranted angrily.

Jason interrupted firmly, "If you say 'Jap' one more time, you'll be sorry, soldier boy. We're Americans just like you."

"Really, you think you're just like me?" The soldier now stood menacingly inches from Jason's face.

Despite Peter's fear, he stood resolutely by Jason's side. At that moment, four more soldiers stood up, and the room fell quiet.

"Stupid Jap."

Without a moment's hesitation, and before the soldier could react, Jason unleashed. First, a fist straight into his nose, followed by an uppercut to his chin, then a kick to his gut, finished with a knee to the groin. Trained in martial arts since he was a child, the soldier went down hard and fast. The entire confrontation lasted less than ten seconds. To Peter's surprise, the other soldiers quickly scooped up their fallen comrade, and that was it.

As they dragged the man across the ground to a nearby table, Jason declared, "I'm an American, not a Jap."

"Me too!" shouted Peter, his voice echoing in the now silent tavern.

"I'm so sick and tired of all this bullcrap racism," said Jason as they drove down the vibrant Kalakaua Avenue towards Hotel Street.

Peter replied thoughtfully, "I don't know. Seriously, sometimes, it gets kind of confusing for me. Am I Japanese or American? It's hard to know. I love Japan—the food, the sports, the people."

"Well, I've never been to Japan, and you have. Hawaii is my home, and I'm grateful for everything we have because we are Americans."

"Check out those ladies," Peter said, swiftly changing the subject.

"Hey, boys, looking for a good time?" called out a few prostitutes working the corner as their car rolled to a stop.

Out jumped the boys from their polished green 1940 Chevy Special Deluxe convertible—complete with a sleek tan interior and gleaming whitewall tires. They rarely used the doors. With a girl in each arm, they strutted into Smith's Union Bar.

"See, Jason, you worry too much. Who cares if we're American or Japanese? Ladies, do you care?" Peter asked, attempting to lighten the mood.

"Honey, we only care if we get paid by the end of the night."

That night, the boys reveled in dancing and drinking. This turned out to be the best birthday ever, thought Jason.

"Okay, okay," said Jason, his voice filled with resolve, "Let's make a pact, American or Japanese, no matter what happens, we'll always have each other's backs."

"Of course, you know that. Hey, look at the time. I have an early practice first thing in the morning. Ladies, it's time to say goodnight," said Peter, finishing his drink and tipping the women.

"Honey, the night is young. I give you a good price. We can go next door to Aloha Café, and I can take care of you all night long."

"As tempting as this may sound, our boy here is going to be a famous baseball player someday and needs his beauty rest," Jason interjected.

"You heard the man, ladies. I'm off to become more beautiful—if that's possible," Peter quipped, his laughter echoing as they departed.

Peter played on the Japanese plantation baseball teams in Waialua. It was just past midnight when the boys returned home. Peter's mother, Chiyoko, was fast asleep. It was part of his routine to check on her each night. There always seemed to be a lingering sadness that loomed behind her eyes. As he navigated his way to his room, he noticed his father's light on in the office. Careful not to be caught arriving home late, Peter walked slowly and deliberately. Despite his efforts, the old wooden floors of plantation homes were notorious for creaking at just the wrong time.

"Eh! Peter, is that you?" called Kosuke from his office.

"Hai (Yes), Father, it is me. Forgive me for coming home at such a late hour."

"Fine, fine. Come in here. I would like to talk with you."

Peter loved his father. He looked up to him and, at the same time, feared him. He knew his dad was a powerful man. Every time he walked into his office, he enjoyed the rich smell of his fine leather furniture. Looking in, he saw a desk made entirely of koa wood with matching dark timber used as trim along the roof, floor, and around the windows. There, behind the desk, with a bottle of whiskey and papers scattered, sat his father. Peter knew it was best not to speak and wait to be spoken to.

"So, what do you think about this war?"

"To be honest, I'm a bit confused. I want to stay true to our Japanese heritage, but I enjoy the freedom I have as an American."

"Do you love this country enough to fight for it? To die for it?"

Peter did not know how to respond. Was this a test, he wondered. Feeling torn, especially with all that had happened that night, he truly wasn't sure. He knew that if this were asked of Jason, there would be absolutely no question. Jason would defend America. Peter wondered if his dad was testing to see if he was a coward.

After a long, tense moment, Peter responded, "Father, I am not afraid to die for something I believe in. However, I don't think I could fight for this country yet."

"I understand. You are a man now, and it is decisions like this you must be able to make. Realize that either way, there will always be consequences. Good or bad, you must live with them."

Peter noticed a baseball on his father's desk. Instinctively, he picked it up and started fumbling with it.

"Listen, son, with this war, as an American, who knows if you will be asked to fight. This is something that I do not want you to do. I have a contact in Japan who is part of the Japanese Professional Baseball League. In the next month, I have some business to do back in Yokohama. My contact has agreed to meet you and see if you'd like to try out to be on one of the teams. This could ensure your safety."

"What about mother? What about Jason?"

"I learned early in my life that there comes a time when the only person worth looking out for is yourself. This is what my father taught me, and now I am teaching you. Take some time to think about it. You are of royal heritage and status that could live or die with you. That is your responsibility."

Peter graciously thanked his father and wished him good-night. To play professional baseball was a dream come true. Still holding the ball in his hand, he thought, then why did he feel so terrible?

CHAPTER 15

Running From Your Shadow

Saturday, December 6th, 1941 — one day before the attack on Pearl Harbor.

"Kimi, go ahead and clean up this wound. Let me know when you are finished and prep the tools so we can stitch this fella up."

"Right away. Now, hold still. This is going to burn a bit."

"Yikes, that hurts!"

"Oh, relax, you big baby. What is this? Is this your third time this month I'm putting you back together?"

"Nope. It's my fourth time. Remember, you attached the tip of my pinky finger just last week. Seriously, Kimi, how many times does a guy have to hurt himself to get a date with you?"

"Ren, you are exhausting. The idea of you and me isn't even a thought. You're practically my brother. You know, deep down inside, you are still the same mischievous kid who used to take my dolls and tease me relentlessly."

Ren sat up and took Kimi's hand in his. "Seriously, will there ever come a time when you will see me not as that little kid running through the cane fields?"

"Nope. Doctor, the patient is ready for his stitches."

"But you haven't numbed me up yet."

"I know," Kimi said with a smile as she walked away to prep the next injured person. As she did so, she said out loud, "What can I say? Love hurts."

Kimi would never forget the day her mother died. It had been nine years since that harrowing moment in time. Her father, Namio, had never been the same since. She often worried about her dad and did her best to take care of him. Despite her efforts, he would stay up until the late hours of the night, often with a drink in his hand. When he was drunk enough, he could even be heard having somber conversations with Yukie. Although Namio blamed himself for the death of his wife, there was a part of him that also blamed his youngest daughter.

Namio did not want anything to do with his newest child. He rarely looked at or spoke to Kimi, and often, when he did, he would slip and call her Yukie. Namio had transformed into a completely different man.

Uncle Nobu and Aunty Emi took on the care of Kimi and her little sister as best they could. They were now hanai (informally adopted) into their family. Because Emi was still breastfeeding their youngest son at the time, she took on the responsibility of nourishing Kimi's sister as well. Namio did not give his new daughter a name. For the first few years, this child responded only to "Hey, you." Most thought that this was her name and wondered if it was of Asian origin. Because plantation life was too busy, this child was often overlooked, and as such, she grew up slightly feral. Hey-You loved playing games with Ren. She thought Ren was the most incredible person she had ever met. Her favorite thing was to pull pranks with him on Kimi. She loved how exasperated her older sister would get when they would tease her.

Mary Kawena Pukui with her daughter Pele and a Japanese hānai (adopted) child, Patience Namaka Wiggin, circa 1938. Public Domain, courtesy of Bishop Museum Archives.

Soon, the time came when Ren was old enough to start working on the plantation. He was now seventeen years old, and she was just nine. Hey-You was the type of kid who seemed to belong to no one. One day, while roaming around the different plantation homes, an old Hawaiian lady sitting on a rocking chair on her porch called out to her.

"Little girl, where are your parents?"

"I have no parents," Hey-You replied.

"No parents. Well, who takes care of you?"

"I live with Aunty Emi and Uncle Nobu. My mother died, and my father..." she stammered off. "My father is no longer here too."

"Come closer," the old lady beckoned. "Yes, it is clear there is no one taking care of you. You are absolutely filthy. What is your name, child?"

"People call me, Hey-You. But I don't really think I have a name."

"Huh, I see. You can call me Aunty Haunani. I once had a sister who died when she was about your age. Her name was Lynette. We just called her Lyn. It would be a shame to let such a nice name go to waste. So, I will call you by her name if that is okay?"

Hey-You thought about it for a moment. She thought the name Lynette was the most beautiful name she had ever heard. "I like it," she responded.

"Maika'i (Great). Then it is settled," said the old Hawaiian lady. "I am a kupuna, which means I am quite old. I need some help around my home. I cannot pay you, but if you come over every day, I will feed you lunch and make sure you have the things you need, like a bath and clean clothes."

Lyn agreed. From that point on, she never missed a day visiting with Aunty Haunani. Often, she would go to her home and wash the dishes and do other chores. She would then help prepare lunch. Although Hawaiian food was vastly different from Japanese food, she grew to love it. More than the food itself, she cherished hearing all of Aunty Haunani's stories.

On this particular day, Lyn was just finishing the lunch dishes, her hands immersed in soapy water. Her older sister Kimi was diligently training to become a nurse and working closely with the experienced plantation doctor.

"So, my dear," Aunty Haunani inquired gently, "you'll be turning ten in just a few days. Is there anything in particular you want?"

Lyn thought for a moment, her mind wandering to Ren, for whom she had secretly developed a fond affection. She so desperately wanted to say, "I just want him to notice me." However, what came out was, "I'm good, Aunty. Just getting the chance to spend time with you is all I want."

"You're sweet. I don't know what I would do without you, Lyn."

Although she had heard Aunty's stories countless times, she asked again, "Aunty, tell me the story about the time you caught over a hundred oama (small fishes) in one day."

"You've heard that story so many times already. Oh well, I know you love it. So when I was a young keiki (Child) just about your age, one of my favorite things was to go fishing for oama with my father. The morning was beautiful, and I remember..." Lyn always loved this story because Aunty Haunani's father sounded so wonderful. She was always a bit envious and wondered what it would be like to have a father like Aunty's.

Namio felt as though life was just too long and unbearably painful. He did his very best to lose himself in the numbing embrace of alcohol. He missed his wife dearly, and each night when he'd close his eyes, he found himself reliving that tragic moment when he was asked to make a decision that could have saved his wife's life. The guilt he felt from that night consumed him relentlessly. Every time he looked at his daughter, Kimi, he only saw his wife. She looked so much like her, and every time he looked at his youngest daughter, he couldn't help but think that she was the biggest mistake he had ever made. These thoughts haunted Namio, like trying to escape one's own shadow. Often, Namio would leave in the middle of the night and not return for many days. He'd travel to a small village-town called Laie. There, standing on jagged rocks jetting out into the ocean, he'd curse life itself. Threatening to jump and end the nightmare he lived day in and day out. Alas, when the sun would rise, he'd find just enough courage to return home and survive another day.

On one particular night, Namio was determined to go to Laie and end things once and for all. He waited until he noticed all the lanterns in the home had gone out. Slowly, he took his wife's apron and packed a few things. Being careful not to wake anyone, he made his way outside. Not noticing Nobu sitting on one of the chairs on the porch, he crept down the stairs and was just about to get on his way.

"Eh, so are you going to do it this time?"

Frozen in place to hear a voice from behind, Namio replied, "You're up late."

"Hai (Yes). Just know, either way, you were never here to begin with. The man I once knew died with his wife a long time ago."

"And what about my children?" Namio inquired.

"We will care for them as if they were our own. If you leave tonight, do not come back. They have gone through too much."

"Hai (Yes)," Namio said and bowed in Nobu's direction. Nobu responded with a slight nod.

Namio again found himself looking down from the razor-sharp cliffs of Laie. How inviting the almost black water looked. Yet, once again, doubt filled his mind if he'd ever truly be able to escape the pain that tormented him. Soon came the sunrise, and for the first time, he felt hope, knowing that the option to return home was no longer. Taking hold of this fleeting opportunity, instead of returning to the north side of the island, Namio ventured south.

Now, many years later, Namio found himself working on the boats he once loved so much. As a former potter, he was exceptionally skilled with his hands. Over the past few years, Namio had become a highly talented welder for the military. He loved fixing things and feeling purposeful. He'd often wondered about his daughters and would send money to Nobu and Emi whenever he could. To his dismay, and yet as expected, he never received a reply.

Dear Nobu and Emi,

It has been quite some time now, and I sincerely hope all is well with you. Although I have not yet received any response from you, word has reached me that my youngest child now goes by the name Lyn. I am pleased to hear this, yet not giving her a name is just another regret I will have to carry with me. I've also been informed that Kimi is pursuing her studies to become a nurse. She has always been exceptionally talented with her hands, and much like her mother, she was always eager to help others.

As for me, I continue to work as a welder for the military. I've always held a deep fascination with large ships and their intricate mechanics. Currently, I am stationed on a project involving a boat named the USS Arizona. It is truly massive. I hope the money I am sending is reaching you and that it helps to alleviate some burdens. Although I am uncertain if we will ever see each other again, please know that you all are constantly in my thoughts.

Sincerely,

Namio

Namio lifted his welding mask, relishing in the refreshing scent of the ocean. With the brisk wind in his face, he felt rejuvenated, as though he could endure another day. He found himself wondering what his children were doing at that moment, imagining what they looked like now. He thought to himself that the time had finally come to make amends with his family. Although he was scheduled to work the remainder of the weekend, he was eagerly anticipating some much-needed time off he had accrued, starting on Monday. Yes, he decided, this coming Monday, he'd return to Waialua and begin the long process of righting his wrongs. Feeling both ashamed and nervous, Namio reached into his satchel and pulled out Yukie's apron, pressing his face into the old, now tattered fabric. He took a deep breath and did something he had not done in quite some time: he smiled.

CHAPTER 16

Infamy

Sunday, December 7th, 1941

"Lyn, wake up. It's time to get going," Kimi said as she put on her nurse assistant uniform. "Just think, one day, I'll be a real full-time nurse."

"Sure, one day, but until then, can I just sleep a little longer? The sun isn't even up," Lyn protested as she pulled the covers over her head.

"Listen, why do we have to do this every morning? We're basically orphans, and we've been fortunate enough to live with Aunty Emi and Uncle Nobu all these years. We need to do our part, and now that I am working, it's your job to get breakfast started, pack the lunches, and tidy up a bit."

"Okay, Mom. You've told me this a million times. Go to work already."

"You ungrateful little brat! Don't you ever talk about Mother that way? I would be so thankful if I could become half the woman she was."

The room fell silent. Both sisters knew they had crossed the line. Kimi could hear Lyn sniffling under her covers. She slowed her pace and knelt down near her sister's bedside.

Muffled and under her blankets, Lyn mumbled, "At least you knew her. How will I ever know how to be half the woman she was?"

Kimi pulled the blanket from over Lyn's face. She felt a surge of compassion for her ten-year-old sister, who had tear-streaked, rosy cheeks and large almond eyes looking up at her.

"It won't be hard for you, sis. Each time you look in the mirror, take a deep breath, close your eyes, and smile. When you open your eyes, I promise you'll see Mother looking back at you."

"Kimi, I'm sorry. I know you miss her. I just wish I knew what that felt like. Trust me, I'm sure you are more than half the woman mother was. I love you."

"I love you too," Kimi said, followed by a kiss on her forehead. "Now we need to get going. I think I can hear Aunty and Uncle starting to wake."

Lyn felt invigorated. She jumped up and dashed into the kitchen. Swiftly, she put on an apron, filled a kettle with water, and placed it on the now-lit stove. She then whisked some eggs with a splash of dashi (Soup base). Despite her argument with her sister, this was her morning routine. Uncle Nobu was the first to arise.

"Ohayo (Morning) smells good, Lyn," he would say every morning. Aunty Emi poured herself a cup of coffee and stood outside on the porch. The sun was but a sliver on the horizon, and the sky painted its colors on the ocean like a grove of cherry blossoms in the spring. Aunty Emi would linger on the porch until she finished her coffee. This time was sacred to her, and everyone in the home knew not to disturb her, or else the consequences would be severe.

The last to rise was Ren. He always sauntered into the kitchen shirtless, wearing a pair of boxer shorts and socks. On this particular morning, each sock had a hole, with each of his big toes sticking out. As he meandered through the kitchen, yawning, stretching, with the occasional crotch scratch, he made a pit stop at Lyn on his way to the table and roughed up the top of her head.

"Morning Hey-You, smells good."

Despite Ren's unkempt morning appearance, Lyn's heart always skipped a beat each time she saw him. She detested that he still called her Hey-You. It made her feel like such a child.

Although they were many years apart, Lyn loved Ren far more than just as a brother and hoped desperately that one day he'd see her as more than just Hey-You.

Kimi was finally ready and rushed through the kitchen. For a moment, as she made her way to the door, she paused to watch her little sister. She was amazed at how much Lyn had grown. Closing her eyes and inhaling the delicious scents of food, she knew everything was cooked perfectly. As she opened her eyes, she was drawn to the apron tied around Lyn's waist, and for a moment, she remembered what it was like being ten years old, watching her mother move with such grace and speed, preparing breakfast. She remembered the apron that she wore every day, and now, seeing a similar scene before her eyes, she realized that her little sister was becoming the woman their mother once was.

Peter could not sleep. All night, he wrestled with the nagging idea of abandoning his friends and family to pursue his dream of professional baseball. He could tell that the sun was just beginning to peek over the horizon, and if he didn't talk to someone soon, he knew that this idea would continue to haunt him. Realizing that sleep was a lost cause, he put on his swim shorts, grabbed a towel, and jumped in his car. Jason and his mother, Mae, lived in a cozy house just behind their quaint restaurant. Peter parked the car on the road and crept quietly around to Jason's window. All the lights were off, and he could hear his buddy snoring. It had been quite a night. Peter pressed his face against the screened-in louvers.

"Jason. Wake up. I need to talk to you," he whispered.

"Not now, ladies. I'm trying to figure out why my feet have fingers, and my hands have toes," Jason mumbled in his sleep.

"Oh, brother. This is going to be harder than I thought," Peter said aloud. Scanning the surroundings for anything to wake his friend up, he noticed a water spigot and a hose just below the window. He also spotted a quarter-sized hole in the window screen just above Jason's bed. Peter had that mischievous look in his eyes, the kind that often resulted in a good ear-pulling. It had never stopped him before and would not stop him now. He carefully poked the hose through the hole, lowering it until he heard a thud and a moan.

"Contact," he murmured under his breath. "Well, my friend, you are about to have the wet dream of a lifetime." With that, he turned the hose on.

"Son of a bitch!" Jason yelled.

"Keep your voice down," Peter replied, now turning off the hose.

"Are you serious? What were you thinking!"

"I was wondering the same about you. Why don't you see if you now have toes on your feet instead of fingers?"

"What are you talking about?"

"Never mind. Hurry up and grab your shorts. I need to pull a morning swim before practice," Peter said, returning to his car.

Jason, soaking wet, muttered to himself, "What's the point? By the look of things, I've already done that."

Minutes later, now wide awake, the boys stretched on the sun-warmed beach. Each of them could hear the other breathing in the salty air. As the water gently brushed up against their toes, neither one of them was ready to take the plunge. They knew their bodies would warm up as soon as they started to swim.

Then, out of nowhere, Jason shouted as he sprinted into the water, "First one to turn back is a pineapple pickin' sissy." Peter did not hesitate. Both boys swam until they were gasping for breath. The sun was barely above the horizon as they both tread water, desperately hoping the other would turn back. Soon, their minds began to play tricks on them, and they now felt their exposed legs dangling in the depths more than ever. Neither boy wanted to show fear.

Jason was the first to talk, "So, how deep do you think we're at?"

"Why are you scared? Ready to turn back?"

"Shut up! I could stay out here all day." Peter swore he could see gray shadows moving just below their toes as the light shifted with the rising sun.

"This is stupid. I have practice in a few hours. Maybe we should head in," Peter suggested. Jason knew he had won.

In hopes of not shaming his friend, Jason replied, "Sure, this was dumb. Let's head back." Soon, both boys were back sitting on the shore looking out to sea with their towels draped over their shoulders.

"So what's going on? I know you didn't just drag me out of bed for a morning dip," Jason said, breaking the silence.

Peter had thought all night long about what he should say to Jason, and now that the moment was here, he found himself at a loss for words. Staring down at the sand between his feet, Peter drew circles in the sand, hoping to be saved from such an awkward moment.

"Last night, my dad told me I had a chance to try out for the Japanese Professional Baseball League. Because of the war, they need more players, which could be my chance."

"Wait, you're saying you'd be playing for Japan? Peter, we're Americans. We're at war with Japan."

"Take it easy. We're also Japanese. What's the big deal? I thought you'd be happy for me. Hasn't this been our dream all along?"

"No, that is your dream. Not mine! You know, I didn't grow up with servants. Here in America, I can one day be more than a maid's son. Someone like you wouldn't understand." Jason knew he had crossed the line. However, he wasn't willing to take his words back.

Then, under his breath, Peter mumbled, "Dad was right. It's time I took care of myself."

Jason was about to punch Peter right in the face when, off in the distance, they heard the sound of planes flying in their direction. At first, they thought nothing of it until they saw that it was not just a few planes but hundreds of planes. As the boys looked closer, they could see real bombs attached to these aircraft, and since they were flying low, it didn't take long for them to spot the Japanese flag painted on the wings of the planes.

"You still think we're Japanese. I promise you those guys up there are not our friends."

"I think you're right. Let's get out of here."

Pearl Harbor burns following the Japanese attack, December 7, 1941. Public Domain, U.S. National Archives.

It was just around 7:30 a.m., and Namio was being carefully lowered down the side of the USS Arizona warship. There, he perched on a swing-like bench with his welding equipment. Although he had now worked on many different boats, Namio never ceased to admire their imposing grandeur. Most people did not work on Sundays. However, Namio had plans to reunite with his daughters the following day and needed to complete a few tasks. Pearl Harbor was not your typical military facility. For the most part, this was a pit stop and a place of rejuvenation for those who were on their way home from the war.

Namio enjoyed listening to the happy voices above, blended with music and laughter. He felt a sense of hope that day, knowing that soon he'd be able to mend things, seek forgiveness, and move on with his life. He got to work, aware that the day would quickly become warm and humid. Then, off in the distance, without warning, he heard a sound like a swarm of bees approaching. He thought it might have been airplanes, but it just didn't make sense. To generate such a deafening noise, it would have to be more planes than he could even begin to imagine. Then, the sounds of laughter changed to panic and shouting. Explosions were bursting everywhere. Namio yelled to anyone above.

"Pull me up. Help! Anyone! I'm down here!" Looking up, he could now see the planes flying overhead. The Japanese flag was starkly visible, painted across the sky. The battleships were firing back, but nothing was prepped or ready. The Japanese attacked with ruthless precision, and all could see that every moment had been meticulously planned.

Namio felt the Arizona rock back and forth, being hit by bomb after bomb. He clung to the ropes supporting his bench. Soon, the harbor was ablaze. The oil from the damaged boats seeped and blanketed the water's surface like lava flowing across the land. Namio started to cough heavily and could feel the intense heat radiating from the water below him. Quickly, he wrapped his wife's apron around his face in hopes of not succumbing to the smoke engulfing him. Namio wondered if he'd be able to climb the ropes to safety. Now, as he attempted to stand on the bench, he felt his knees shaking and found his courage waning. Just then, he saw men above trying to leap from the ship he was hanging from to the vessel next to him. All reason had evaporated. Looking at the boat nearest him, he knew that it was well over twenty feet away. Had people gone mad? Every person attempting the jump fell into the fiery water. The screams they emitted and the smell of burning flesh mixed with toxic oil fumes nearly made Namio faint.

"It's now or never," he said aloud. He reached up one of the ropes and wrapped his leg around it. Looking up, he realized that his efforts were now in vain, seeing the rope aflame.

Strands broke fiber after fiber, and Namio knew he would not make it.

"Snap," went the ropes.

Namio felt his body plunge into the water. At that moment, he realized he had passed through the burning oil and was sinking quickly to the ocean floor. Looking down, he saw the heavy welding equipment connected to many hoses entangled around his legs. At first, he tried to free himself. Then, in his last moments of consciousness, he looked up at the burning surface of the water. Either way, he was a dead man. He remembered how quiet and peaceful it was the day his wife died, submerged in the depths of the ocean. He then realized he had a choice to die in peace or to be burned to death. The choice was easy.

Namio closed his eyes and relaxed his body. He could feel the water entering his lungs. At first, instinctively, he fought back, and then he felt himself embracing the darkness. In his final moments, Namio opened his eyes. Once again, his wife, Yukie, looked down at him. How beautiful she looked. She extended her hand, and Namio reached for it. As their hands touched, he was surrounded by light. It was so bright that he shielded his eyes with his arms.

When the light faded, Namio was no longer underwater. The air smelled of honey, and he could feel the soft earth beneath his body. He slowly found his way to his feet. Looking around, he could see that he was standing in a grove of Sakura trees. The wind caressed his face as he stood, hands open, feeling the sun's warmth on his back. Startled to feel something fall into his hand, Namio opened his eyes. It was a single Sakura blossom. At that moment, he knew he had passed on and was no longer part of the living. As he exited the grove, looking ahead, he could see his little home there near his pottery shed. He continued up the hill, and there was Yukie standing in their kitchen window as she always had. She smiled and then spoke.

"Namio, come home," and he did.

The USS Arizona burning after the Japanese
attack on Pearl Harbor, December 7, 1941.
Public Domain, U.S. National Archives.

Interlude

President Franklin D. Roosevelt signs the declaration of war against Japan, December 8, 1941. Public Domain, courtesy of the Library of Congress.

"Yesterday, December 7, 1941—a date which will live in infamy—the United States of America was suddenly and deliberately attacked by naval and air forces of the Empire of Japan... The attack yesterday on the Hawaiian Islands has caused severe damage to American naval and military forces. I regret to tell you that very many American lives have been lost... Hostilities exist. There is no blinking at the fact that our people, our territory, and our interests are in grave danger... With confidence in our armed forces—with the unbounding determination of our people—we will gain the inevitable triumph—so help us God. I ask that the Congress declare that since the unprovoked and dastardly attack by Japan on Sunday, December 7, 1941, a state of war has existed between the United States and the Japanese Empire," declared President Franklin D. Roosevelt, the 32nd President of the United States.

The pungent smell of burning oil pervaded the air, and it didn't matter whether you were looking mauka (toward the mountain) or makai (toward the ocean). A relentless billow of smoke ominously crept over the land like a sinister plague. The death toll from yesterday's attack was still unconfirmed, with thousands of local American Japanese now under suspicion and rigorous investigation. The once vibrant spirit of aloha (love) had all but vanished, only to be replaced with hate and unchecked violence. It was impossible to conceal the color of your skin, the distinctive shape of your eyes, or a heritage deeply rooted in ancient traditions.

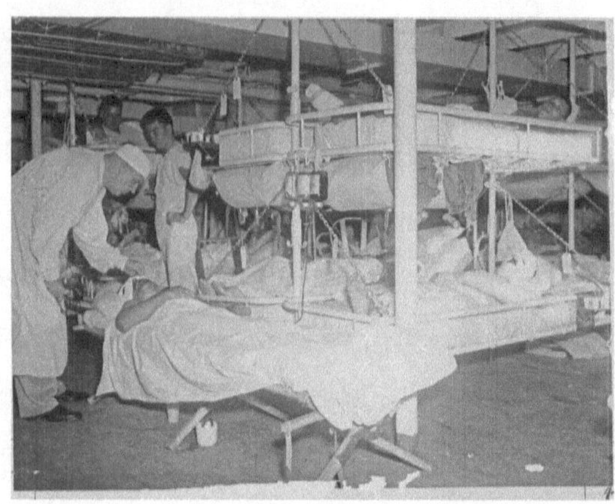

U.S. Navy medical staff care for burn victims aboard the hospital ship Solace following the attack on Pearl Harbor, December 7, 1941. Public Domain, courtesy of the BUMED Library and Archives.

The urgent call for help echoed throughout the land. The demand for resources, vehicles, and medical attention reached unprecedented levels. Extracted from the wreckage were thousands of individuals suffering from severe, agonizing injuries. All nearby available facilities were hastily transformed into makeshift hospitals, including the Pearl Harbor Recreation Center and the Officers' Club. Medical personnel and anyone with training were urgently recruited to assist at various locations. The majority of the patients in these facilities bore the brunt of extreme burns. Many victims, exposed to intense flash burns, screamed in relentless agony as doctors and nurses worked with painstaking precision to remove clothing that had gruesomely fused to the flesh. Day in and day out, no relief could be found as people endured the excruciating pain of their physical healing. Despite this, the emotional healing, the journey of moving forward, was regrettably nowhere in sight.

CHAPTER 17

Mad World

In twenty-four hours, the world had gone mad. Kimi reported to the plantation medical cottage. She noticed that everyone was anxiously gathered around a small radio. She could not believe the words she was hearing. A few moments after the broadcast, the doctor burst into the room.

"Everybody, stop what you're doing. We need to go immediately to the plantation hospitals in Ewa and Aiea."

All were momentarily frozen, shocked to hear such a request. "What are you staring at? We need to get going. Hundreds, if not thousands, are injured."

The medical personnel quickly snapped out of their trance and began to hurriedly gather supplies.

As Kimi made her way into the back of a military truck, she saw Uncle Nobu and Lyn running toward her.

Trying to catch his breath, Nobu said, "Your father..." he stammered off.

Caught off guard, Kimi replied, "My father?"

"Yes, your father has been working at Pearl Harbor as a welder on the warships. Kimi, you need to find him. We must take care of unfinished business."

Lyn couldn't even begin to find the words. She threw her arms around her sister and, with heavy sobs, would not let go.

Kimi crouched down and held Lyn firmly, hands on her shoulders. "Listen, you have to be brave. You are no longer that forgotten child. You need to take care of our family. Uncle Nobu and Aunty Emi need you more than ever. I must go and help. Maybe I will find our father and bring him back."

"With or without him, you must come back," Lyn said.

"I will."

Kimi gave her sister one last hug and loaded herself onto the truck. As the truck drove off down the red dirt road, Lyn thought to herself, "There goes my sister—the bravest person I will ever know."

Kosuke had lost his mind. At that moment, Peter burst into the room. "Father, what is going on?"

"They'll be coming for me. Quick, grab those papers on my desk."

Peter had no idea what his father was talking about. However, the urgency in his father's voice made him realize this was not the time to ask questions. Grabbing the papers and seeing his father with an armful of files, they exited their home to the back near the garden shed. Kosuke then turned over an old, empty steel barrel and threw the documents into it. He then grabbed a canister of gasoline and poured it all over the inside of the barrel.

"Stand back, son." Then, with the stroke of a match, the barrel exploded into flames.

"Father, what is going on?" Peter inquired again.

Without an answer, Kosuke ran back into the house, muttering over and over, "They are coming for me."

It took almost a dozen trips back into the home with armfuls of paper and documents. Peter and his dad threw these items into the fire. Finally, they were done. Now, they were staring at the fire, hypnotized. Kosuke finally spoke.

"It's been hard taking care of our family's fortune. The American economy has not done well, and with this war, I needed to explore other options. To say the least, many of my dealings with Japan have not been in the best interest of this country."

"Wait, what are you saying? Father, are you a..."

"Don't say it. I am doing whatever it takes to ensure that our family's fortune and status will be here for generations to come. Who we are is much bigger than you and me. I am sure one day, when I am no longer here, you will have to make these same types of choices. It isn't a choice between right and wrong. It is a choice to do whatever is needed to uphold our family name."

Peter felt sick to his stomach. His father's words always seemed to make sense, but deep within, he questioned the integrity behind the message.

"Quickly, go into the house and pack a bag. We must leave immediately for Japan to ensure our safety."

"But what about Mother, Aunty Mae, and Jason?"

"There is no time for them. They will be fine."

For the first time, Peter felt rage boiling up inside. He had never spoken back to his father. However, he could not contain it any longer.

"No!" He shouted. "Father, I will not go with you unless I can check on the safety of mother first."

"You are still weak. Still just a scared little boy who needs his mother's teat! Okay, I'll let you suckle one last time, and then you must become a man. I refuse to allow you to be this soft coward of a person. Now, grab your things. We will stop by the restaurant on our way to the docks."

Kosuke and Peter arrived at Aunty Mae's restaurant. As they entered, Chiyoko shouted as she approached Kosuke. "Get out! Get out! Get out! You coward of a man! Did you know? Look me in the eyes and tell me you didn't know about what happened yesterday."

"Pull yourself together. You're a disgrace. You think that I am the only villain in this story. How do you think I put a roof over your head, buy you the fancy clothes you wear, or continue pouring money into your friend's rundown restaurant? Do you think these things just buy themselves? Deep down inside, you all knew that these things don't just magically appear. Every time you took my money, you knew it had to come from somewhere, and none of you ever said anything. So, to hell with you all."

Jason had heard enough. Why did his mother and aunty have nothing to say? They just sat there with their heads down, engulfed in shame. That was it. He couldn't take it anymore. From the back of the restaurant, he rushed Kosuke with a raised fist, ready to strike. Kosuke did not even flinch, and in a flash, Peter stepped in front of his father and blocked the punch, followed by a counterstrike to Jason's chest. His friend was flung to the floor. Stunned by his actions, Peter looked down at Jason and then back to his hands.

"What have I done?" he said to himself aloud.

He then felt his father's hand on his shoulder as he whispered in his ear, "You're becoming a man."

Hearing these words sent chills down Peter's back. Now realizing what he had done, he ran to his friend on the ground.

"Jason, are you okay? I'm so sorry."

Kosuke interrupted as he exited the room, "Ha! That's typical. Peter, I'll give you ten minutes. If you are not in my car, I will assume you have made your decision."

Peter was helping Jason up. Their mothers continued to sit with their heads down, accompanied by the occasional sniffle and sob.

"Come on, let's go eat some lychee," Jason said as they walked outside to the big tree in the backyard.

For a moment, each boy picked and peeled a few fruits, feeling the juices fill their mouths, followed by a vigorous spewing of the seeds.

"I'm sorry," said Jason.

"Me too. He's my dad. I know he's not the best person, but he's still my dad."

"I know. So what are you going to do?"

"I think I'm going to go with him. Am I crazy?"

"You sure are. If you weren't, you wouldn't be my best friend."

Peter could feel tears welling up in his eyes, and before he knew it, Jason punched him in the arm.

"It was getting too emotional," Jason said.

With that, both boys embraced. They firmly patted each other's backs, and despite their macho demeanor, neither one was able to speak through their tears. Time did not stand still, and minutes felt like seconds.

"Remember our pact, American or Japanese, I will always have your back," Jason said as they let go.

"And I yours."

"Don't worry, we will see each other again. Make sure you hit one out of the park for me."

At that moment, Peter felt a reassuring hand on his shoulder. It was his mother, Chiyoko.

"It's time, son. You need to go. He will leave you."

Slowly, they walked down the long, winding driveway. Peter's mind was a whirlwind of thoughts. He knew that his time would be up when he reached his father's car, and he'd have to leave right away, so he deliberately slowed his pace.

"Peter, I want to explain," said Chiyoko.

"No," he replied firmly. "I'm sorry, I have to go. If you ask me to stay, I will. You don't have to feel sorry or obligated to send me with him. If you ask me to stay, I will."

Chiyoko reached down and tenderly held Peter's hand as they walked towards the car. Peter felt like a little boy again. Instead of looking up at his mother's face, he was looking down. He remembered how small his hand once felt in hers, and ironically, he realized how small and fragile her hand now felt in his. How could he leave her unprotected and vulnerable? It was his job to protect her—to protect her from him, his father.

Now, only a few steps away from the car, he could see his father sitting in the front seat, ready to go. Kosuke pressed the horn and urgently waved over to his son.

"Mom, I don't think I can do this."

"I know. When your father announced that we'd be leaving our home in Japan, I also didn't think I could do it, but I did. Have courage, my son. You are not him. I know there are great things you will one day do."

Peter held his mother close. He took one last deep breath with his head nestled on her shoulder. Peter loved the way his mother smelled. To Peter, his mother always smelled of home. With that, he knew that no matter what happened, eventually, he'd find his way back.

"Peter, I'm so very proud of you," Chiyoko said with tears brimming in her eyes.

"And I you. I will come home. I promise."

As Peter and Kosuke drove off, Chiyoko stood watching, her heart heavy with both pride and concern, wondering if her son would really be able to keep such a promise.

CHAPTER 18

Desperation

Emi was in the back room, solemnly burning an offering of incense, while Lyn busily packed the lunches. Ren was putting on his shoes, ready to head out to work. At that moment, two FBI agents abruptly burst through the doors.

"Nobu Takahashi, you are coming with us," one of the agents announced, grabbing Nobu by the shirt.

Ren rushed over to his father, punching the agent directly in the face. Lyn screamed and dropped the lunches she was holding. The other agent immediately drew his gun and pressed it against Nobu's head.

"No one move or I'll blow this man away," he shouted menacingly.

Emi hurried over to Ren and stood between him and the agent.

"Settle yourself, my son," Emi urged.

"Where are you taking my father?" Ren shouted!

"It is none of your concern," the agent coldly replied, leading Nobu outside to a government-marked car.

"Son, it will be okay," Nobu reassured with a brave face as they lowered him into the car's back seat. "Take care of your mother and the rest of the family. I'll be back soon."

With that, the car sped down the dirt road. Ren broke free from his mother's grasp and chased after the vehicle. Emi would never forget the silhouette of her son on his knees, sitting in the middle of the road, enveloped in the dust, in the wake, of the car.

It had been two months since they took Nobu. The family had not heard a single word regarding his whereabouts or condition. Every chance Emi had, she would retreat to the back room of their home, burning incense on behalf of her husband, silently praying for his safe return. Ren, on the other hand, was becoming angrier by the day.

"We have to do something," he said, pacing back and forth in the kitchen. His voice was sharp, carrying a mix of frustration and desperation. "I have to do something. I'm losing my mind. How can this even be happening?" he muttered, more to himself than to anyone else.

"There is something you could do," Lyn interrupted. "Come and sit with me on the porch."

Together, they sat on the porch, a ritual they often shared at the end of each day. The warm hues of the setting sun bathed the yard in a golden glow, casting long shadows across the ground.

"I don't want you to go," Lyn began, her voice soft but steady. "But I know you have to do something. It breaks my heart to see you so hopeless and trapped here in Waialua. Here, take this."

Lyn reached into her apron pocket, pulling out a somewhat crumpled newspaper article from the Honolulu Star-Bulletin, and handed it to Ren.

"Come on, Hey You, you know I'm not the best reader," Ren teased, smirking slightly.

Lyn rolled her eyes, annoyed but choosing to let it slide. She hated when Ren called her "Hey You," but she knew now wasn't the time to argue. Instead, she began reading the article aloud. It described a group of college boys determined to show their patriotism despite being barred from enlisting. Many of them had fathers who, like Nobu, had been taken away under suspicion of treason. These young men called themselves the Varsity Victory Volunteers, also known as the Triple-V. The article explained that their numbers were steadily growing, welcoming anyone willing to join, regardless of education or background.

"This is it," Ren shouted, his excitement cutting through the tension. "Lyn, I could kiss you right now."

For a moment, time seemed to freeze. They stared intently into each other's eyes. Lyn felt her heart racing, her cheeks burning with warmth. It occurred to her that this might be the first time Ren had actually said her name. The moment stretched, feeling infinitely longer than it truly was. Then, Ren cleared his throat dramatically, breaking the spell. He reached over toward Lyn. She leaned in slightly, closing her eyes.

"Was this really happening?" Lyn thought, her mind racing.

At that exact moment, Ren ruffled the hair on Lyn's head and stood up with a grin.

"Thanks, Hey-You. You always have my back. This is exactly what I need to do. I'm sure if I can prove myself to our country, they'll have to let Father go. And, maybe—just maybe—I can finally show Kimi I'm more than just that rascal from our childhood. You're the best little sister a guy could ask for."

Lyn's heart sank, mortified by her own thoughts. What was she thinking? Of course, Ren would never stop loving Kimi, and she would always just be his little sister, Hey-You.

Kimi would go days on end without returning home. Often, she slept on a cot at the plantation hospital in Ewa. When she wasn't working, she tirelessly visited as many medical facilities as possible in search of her father. Occasionally, she would meet someone who knew him. They always spoke of what a hard worker he was and how kind he had been to everyone he encountered. However, no one could tell her exactly where he was on the day of the attack, leaving her with unanswered questions that weighed heavily on her heart.

On this particular day, after carefully replacing bandages on burn victims and soothing their cries of pain, she was called into one of the doctors' offices.

"Kimi, we've been working together for a long time now," the doctor began. "I still remember the day during the influenza pandemic when you would help me mark the doors in the plantation camp. You have real talent, and I believe you could do so much more."

Kimi never complained, always worked diligently, and quickly learned from her experiences. Hearing such words of encouragement felt surreal, almost like a dream.

"I'm sorry," Kimi said, her voice soft with disbelief. "I'm just a bit stunned. I've always dreamed about doing more one day, but never thought it was possible."

"It is very possible," the doctor replied with a warm smile. "Queen's Hospital is starting a training program for up-and-coming nurses. Here is a brochure with all the information. The program requires a recommendation from a licensed doctor, and I would be more than happy to write one for you."

Kimi felt a spark of excitement she hadn't experienced in a long time. She felt like a little kid again, dreaming of impossible things. To her, the idea of being a nurse in a hospital seemed as far-fetched as walking on the moon.

"I don't know," she replied hesitantly. "You are very kind to think that I am ready for such an opportunity. However, I still have too many responsibilities, like caring for my uncle, aunty, and younger sister. I don't think I have the time," Kimi added, her eyes catching on the price printed on the brochure, a silent reminder of her financial struggles.

"Kimi, I am confident that your family will be just fine," the doctor said. "You really need to consider all the good you could do in this world. You've outgrown the plantation, and you've done so much to take care of others. It's time to think about your future."

Not wanting the doctor to know the full extent of her financial situation, Kimi thought it best to end the conversation gracefully. She smiled politely and assured him she would consider it. After thanking the doctor for his kindness, Kimi carefully folded the brochure and tucked it into her pocket.

It was just past six o'clock when Kimi returned home. As she walked into the quiet house, she realized that no one else was there. Kimi was utterly exhausted. She sat down on the old wicker chair in the living area, the worn cushion welcoming her weight, and within minutes, she was fast asleep. She was so tired that she had even forgotten to remove her shoes.

The first to arrive home was her sister, Lyn. Seeing Kimi asleep, Lyn tiptoed to the kitchen to start dinner, careful not to disturb her sister's much-needed rest. Next entered Aunty Emi. She also noticed Kimi fast asleep, her face still and peaceful, but the sight of her shoes still on caught Emi's attention. Carefully, Emi crouched down, gently slipping off Kimi's shoes, hoping not to wake her.

As Emi removed the shoes, her gaze caught a folded piece of paper on the floor near Kimi's hand. It must have fallen from her grip as she drifted off. At first, Emi hesitated, telling herself that it was none of her business. She fought every urge not to interfere, but curiosity tugged at her. She reached for the paper, only to jump at the sudden sound of the door slamming open. Ren had returned from the plantation.

Startled by his loud entrance, Emi let out a small scream. "Baka (Stupid)!"

"What's going on?" Kimi asked groggily, waking up in a daze, her eyes still heavy with sleep.

"Oh, it's just dumb-dumb clomping through the house," Lyn teased from the kitchen.

"What's for dinner? I am starving," Ren said, rubbing his stomach.

"You are always starving. I'm making curry," Lyn replied, rolling her eyes.

Ren paced around the room, his movements restless and deliberate. Then, after a moment, he stopped and spoke. "Everyone, stop what you are doing. I have an announcement."

Ren rarely made big announcements. In fact, his usual routine after coming home was to put on a pair of shorts, take off his shirt, and lose himself in a comic book. Though a hard worker, Ren wasn't known for being particularly serious, so his tone now caught everyone's attention.

"Okay, so I'm not sure exactly how to say this. Well, you know it's been really hard without Dad, and nobody really knows where he is. I've just been trying to find a way to get him back, and..." Ren began, his words tumbling over themselves as he struggled to explain.

Finally, Lyn interrupted, "For goodness' sake, I shared with Ren an article about a group of college boys called the Triple-V who are supporting the war to show their devotion to America. Many of their fathers were also taken under suspicion of treason."

"Yes, that is what I was saying," Ren continued, his voice growing steadier. "Well, today, I quit my job, and I am going to join the Triple-V. Mother, I know we need the money, but I have to do something, or I'm going to lose my mind."

Emi's eyes welled with tears, her emotions visibly overwhelming her.

"Are you upset?" Ren asked cautiously, watching her reaction closely.

"Ie (No), I am just so proud of you," Emi said, pulling her son into a warm embrace. "We will be okay. Don't worry about us. Go get Father and bring him home."

The family talked late into the night, their voices filled with both hope and uncertainty. Kimi, however, couldn't shake the growing knot of anxiety in her chest at the idea of Ren leaving. Since Uncle Nobu had been taken, Ren had stepped into the role of the man of the house, shouldering responsibilities far beyond his years. Feeling overwhelmed, she slipped outside to the porch, letting the cool night breeze wash over her.

After a few minutes, Ren joined her, his presence breaking the silence. He leaned against the railing, gazing into the shadowy yard as if searching for answers in the darkness.

"So, when are you leaving?" Kimi asked softly, her voice barely above a whisper.

"I think I'll begin to pack tonight and try to head out first thing in the morning."

"We are all so proud of what you are doing. I'm sure people will notice, and your father will be back with us soon," Kimi said, her voice steady but filled with emotion.

Ren walked over to where Kimi was standing. His eyes held a seriousness she wasn't used to seeing. "I'm not just doing this for my dad." He placed his hands firmly on her shoulders, his touch both grounding and intense. "I am also doing this for you."

"I don't understand. Why me?"

"My entire life, I have always loved you more than just a sister, but you still see me as that foolish boy playing in the cane fields. I want to show you I've grown up. I am more than what you see."

Kimi's heart began to pound as she stared into Ren's eyes, his words sinking in deeper than she anticipated. She had resisted his advances for so many years, dismissing them as childish infatuations, and yet here they were. She wasn't sure why she did what she did next. Perhaps it was the romance of the night, or maybe it was the lingering fear that she might never see him again. Caught up in the moment, she leaned in without thinking. Before either of them could comprehend what was happening, they were kissing.

Both Kimi and Ren became lost in the intensity of the moment, oblivious to everything else around them. Neither noticed Lyn's eyes, wide with betrayal, peering at them from behind a window overlooking the porch.

"Okay, I've got something to look forward to," Ren said, his tone lightening as he pulled back.

"We'll figure this out when you get back. Please, just stay safe," Kimi whispered.

Ren kissed her gently on the forehead before heading into the house. Kimi remained on the porch, her thoughts a chaotic swirl of emotions. The idea of Ren leaving unsettled her more than she had expected. One thing was clear—if Ren left, she had to stay. Her family needed her. With a heavy sigh, she pulled the nursing school brochure from her pocket, the weight of her own unfulfilled dreams pressing against her chest.

"So, when are you leaving us?" a voice asked from behind her, breaking the quiet.

Kimi turned to see Aunty Emi standing there, her expression calm yet firm.

"Aunty Emi. No, I'm not going anywhere. You can count on me."

"No, I can't."

"Don't be silly. Of course, you can."

"No, we'll be fine. Lyn is old enough to work on the plantation, and we'll manage here. You need to go."

"Go where?"

"Go and do the things that you were meant to do. Become a nurse."

"Wait. How did you know?"

"I found the brochure when I was removing your shoes while you were sleeping."

"Ah, pretty sneaky. It doesn't matter, though. I can't afford it."

At that moment, Aunty Emi pulled out an old cigar box and placed it firmly in Kimi's hands.

"I'm not sure if you will ever find your father," Emi began, her voice trembling slightly. "Uncle Nobu and I were worried that these things might bring you more pain than joy. Every few weeks, your father sent us a letter with some money to care for you and your sister. We haven't spent any of it. We knew there would be a time when you would need it. Please forgive us for keeping these from you."

Kimi opened the box, her hands trembling as she gazed at the neatly stacked money inside. It was more than she had ever seen in one place. Overwhelmed, she turned to Emi and embraced her tightly.

"You never have to ask me for forgiveness. Lyn and I will forever be in your debt. We love you and Uncle Nobu so much."

Emi, unable to hold back her tears, quickly excused herself and ran into the house, her emotions pouring out. Kimi slowly sat down on the porch steps, still holding the box. As she moved the money aside, her eyes caught a letter resting on the top of the pile. With care, she unfolded it and began to read.

Dear Nobu and Emi,

I've decided to come home. I can't live another day without my girls, especially Kimi...

She couldn't read any further. A deep, unshakable feeling settled within her—something inside told her that her father was gone. If he were alive, he would have returned by now. Yet, instead of anger or despair, Kimi felt an unexpected wave of gratitude. Her father's sacrifices and love were evident in every word and every dollar he had sent to ensure their well-being.

Closing her eyes, she let the breeze caress her face as she whispered aloud, "Otosan (Father), arigatogozaimasu (Thank you)."

Graduates of the Queen's Hospital Training School for Nurses, Honolulu, circa 1930s–1940s. Public Domain, courtesy of Hawaii State Archives.

CHAPTER 19

The Triple-V

Ren dreaded emotional moments. The night before had been more than he had imagined, overwhelming in ways he hadn't anticipated. The highlight, without question, was Kimi's kiss. Even now, as he hurriedly packed his duffel bag—crafted from old rice sacks—it felt as though he could still feel the warmth of her lips on his.

The bag, stitched together lovingly by Kimi years ago, carried a bittersweet weight. As he tucked a few belongings inside, his mind lingered on her. For a fleeting second, Ren considered waking her for one last kiss goodbye. The thought of seeing her one more time pulled at him, but he hesitated. Knowing Kimi, he wondered if, by this morning, she might have changed her mind. No, he decided. It was better to leave things as they were, the memory of the previous night left untouched and perfect in its own way.

As he passed by the girls' room, Ren paused in the hallway, his steps slowing as he approached their door. His hand grazed the wooden frame, and he peered inside. The faint moonlight filtering through the window illuminated the serene image of Kimi asleep beside her sister, Lyn. The sight stilled him. For a moment, it felt as if time had stopped, the scene imprinting itself in his mind like a cherished photograph. In a voice so soft it barely escaped his lips, he whispered, "Till we meet again, my love."

Adjusting the strap of his makeshift duffel bag over his shoulder, Ren took a deep breath and turned away. With quiet determination, he stepped out into the cool, dark morning. The faint crunch of his footsteps on the dirt road echoed softly as he walked down the dusty path that led away from the Waialua plantation. The stillness of the early hours seemed to embrace him.

It wasn't long before the sun was high in the sky, casting its relentless heat over the dusty road. Ren trudged forward, knowing that if he stayed on this path, he would eventually reach the small town of Wahiawa. There, at the Army facility called Schofield Barracks, he hoped to find the Triple-V, the group Lyn had told him about during her research.

The road stretched endlessly ahead, with little in the way of company. Few cars passed by, but Ren held out his thumb anyway, hoping for a ride. Deep down, he doubted anyone would stop for a Japanese person. The thought only served to deepen his frustration, his mind circling back to his father. Was he even alive?

Car after car sped past, kicking up clouds of dry dust that stung Ren's eyes. With every passing vehicle, his anger grew. How can I fight for this country when they hate us? he thought bitterly. I've never even been to Japan. I'm just as American as the next guy.

After several more miles, his anger softened into confusion. He wondered what he would find when he reached the Triple-V. Would there be others who felt the same uncertainty he did, or would he be surrounded by unwavering patriots? The more his thoughts churned, the slower his steps became, until he found himself standing still by the side of the road, paralyzed by indecision.

"This is nuts! I can't do this!" Ren shouted aloud to himself. "How can I prove myself to my country if I don't even know if I believe in what we're doing? They've taken my father! They treat us like criminals, and we've done nothing! I've done nothing!"

Ren tilted his face to the sky, his voice rising as if pleading for an answer. Although his family was Buddhist, many of his friends were Christian. Ren wasn't sure what he believed, but in this moment of desperation, he clung to the hope that something or someone was listening.

"Okay," he said, his voice quiet now, almost a whisper. "I'm not sure if you're real. I've never really prayed before, but just in case... If the next car I see picks me up, I'll stay on this journey. But if they pass me by, I'm turning around and—"

"Hey, buddy, who the heck are you talking to?" a voice interrupted.

Startled, Ren spun around, his face flushing with embarrassment. "Seriously?" he muttered under his breath. He turned to see a car pulled over to the side of the road, a young man leaning out of the driver's side window with an amused expression.

Clearing his throat, Ren replied, "I'm not crazy, just a bit confused. Any chance you're heading toward Wahiawa?"

"Well, friend, today's your lucky day. Confused is my middle name, and yes, I'm on my way to Schofield Barracks to join the Triple-V."

"You've got to be kidding me! That's exactly what I was hoping to do, too. Could I ride the rest of the way with you?"

"I don't think so. Just kidding," the young man said with a grin. "I wanted to see that confused look on your face one more time. Of course, you can. Jump on in."

Ren heaved a sigh of relief as he tossed his bag into the back seat of the tan, sun-worn sedan. The dashboard was cracked from years of heat, and the seats were faded, their fabric frayed at the edges. Books were scattered throughout the car, covering the floor and even the passenger seat.

The driver, a young Japanese man, looked neat and proper. His hair was neatly combed with a precise part down the middle, and he wore thick, round, black-rimmed glasses. His pinstriped collared shirt was buttoned all the way up, though he lacked a tie. His freshly pressed beige trousers and polished black-and-white wingtip shoes completed his pristine appearance. Ren couldn't help but wonder if this guy had ever done a hard day's work in his life.

"So, do you only talk with God, or do you talk to people, too?" the driver teased.

"Sorry," Ren stammered. "You just don't look like... um..."

"Don't worry. People have been judging me my entire life. I know I'm not your typical soldier, but this is my country, too, and I want to do something. I'm Arthur. And you are?"

"I'm Ren. My family and I are plantation workers out in Waialua. Thanks again for picking me up. I really appreciate it. It's pretty neat that you have your own car. Your family must be rich."

"Actually, this is my dad's car. We live in Manoa, and he's a businessman in Honolulu. He doesn't even know I have it. By now, I'm sure he's figured it out. I left him a note."

"You stole your dad's car?"

"You bet I did. And I just dropped out of school at the University of Hawaii."

"You dropped out of school?"

"Are you going to do this the entire trip? Repeat everything I say?"

"Sorry. It's just that everything you're saying is so unbelievable."

Arthur laughed. "Let's just say my father has never really approved of me. He's never seen me for who I am, and I want to show him that I can be so much more."

"I get that," Ren said, thinking briefly of Kimi. "Well, Arthur, I won't forget what you've done for me today. I'm sure if we stick together, we can figure this thing out."

"That would be great. Don't worry—I won't tell anyone you're a little bit crazy. Just try to keep your conversations with God a bit quieter in the future."

Both boys laughed, the tension melting away as the car bumped along the road. The dusty outskirts of Wahiawa soon came into view.

U.S. Army soldiers drilling at Schofield Barracks, Oahu, in the years leading up to World War II. Public Domain, courtesy of the U.S. Army / National Archives.

Soon, they arrived at the gates of Schofield Barracks. The sprawling military base loomed before them, bustling with activity. Following directions, Ren and Arthur found their way to a cluster of run-down cottages. Faded signs marked the buildings with the words Varsity Victory Volunteers.

"Well, no turning back," said Ren, his voice steady but carrying a hint of nervousness.

"Were you talking to me?" replied Arthur.

"Knock it off. Grab your stuff," Ren said, rolling his eyes as he adjusted his duffel bag.

Ren hauled his rice sack duffle bag over his shoulder, while Arthur, in sharp contrast, neatly lifted two leather briefcases from the car's trunk. Together, they walked toward a building marked Office and stepped inside, the faint creak of the door echoing in the quiet.

Behind a desk sat a Hawaiian-Japanese man whose weathered skin and broad shoulders spoke of years spent under the sun. He wore a faded shirt with an eagle whose wings formed the shape of a "V." His presence was imposing, his muscular frame making the cramped office feel even smaller. Ren cleared his throat, catching the man's attention.

The man glanced up, his expression casual but assessing. When he spoke, it was in the familiar Pidgin English that Ren had grown up hearing on the plantation.

"So, what you guys like?" he asked, leaning back in his chair.

"We're here to be part of the Triple-V," Ren replied.

"And what? You look like you can. But what about dis guy? What you, one accountant?" the man said, gesturing toward Arthur with a smirk.

"Seriously," Arthur shot back, clearly irritated but trying to remain composed. "Look, I'm here to help, just like you."

"Fo real? I bet dis bruddah can barely lift one hammah," the man said with a laugh.

Ren, fluent in Pidgin and unwilling to let the insult slide, stepped in. "Eh, no ack. He get just as much right to be here as you and me. So what? Where do we need to sign?"

"Wow, no need get huhu (irritated) wit me," the man said, holding up his hands in mock surrender. "Just playing small kine. Look, we only get one more bed, so we can only take one more guy."

"I understand. I'll head back," said Arthur softly, his head lowering in resignation.

"Listen," Ren interjected firmly, "I've slept on the ground almost my entire life. My friend here will take the bed, and I'll find a spot on the floor. You guys can use all the help you can get, so there's no need to send one of us away."

"Whateva's. Shoots den," the man said with a shrug. "I'm Keoni. My maddah is Japanese, and my faddah is Hawaiian. I'm named after my dad, so everyone just calls me Junior."

He extended his hand to Ren, who accepted it with a firm shake. Arthur, however, was not offered the same courtesy. After handing them some bedding and uniforms, Junior led them to a small, weather-beaten cottage with six sets of bunk beds, three on each side of the narrow room.

Junior spoke directly to Ren, barely sparing Arthur a glance. "If you need anything, just let me know. The last bunk on the bottom is open. Catch you, latah."

Ren could tell Arthur felt disheartened as they approached the empty bed. His shoulders slumped slightly.

"I appreciated you sticking up for me back there," Arthur said, his voice low. "I don't mind sleeping on the ground. I've never done that before, but I'm sure I could get used to it."

"Don't worry about it," Ren replied. "I'm serious. Back at my house, I could fall asleep practically anywhere. And as for Junior, he's a punk. There are tons of Juniors where I come from. He's nothing special. As far as I can see, there aren't many Arthurs out there, so be yourself and don't give it another thought."

Their cottage remained quiet for a few hours, and both boys quickly fell asleep, the exhaustion of the day catching up with them. However, the silence was soon interrupted by loud voices and the sound of the door opening and closing.

"Hey, check it out, you guys—new recruits!" someone shouted, his voice filled with excitement.

Ren and Arthur sat up, blinking as a group of Japanese-American boys around their age crowded into the room. Unlike Junior, these boys were friendly and welcoming, their energy infectious. They quickly introduced themselves, eager to learn about the new arrivals.

One boy, who seemed to be the group's leader, stepped forward holding a piece of paper. His demeanor was calm but resolute. "Look," he said, addressing Ren and Arthur. "We're all here to prove to our country that we are not the enemy. This petition has become an oath we've all taken to be here. No one will judge you if you don't want to make this commitment, but know this—if you don't, you do not belong here."

The room grew silent as the boys leaned in to read the petition.

Hawaii is our home; the United States our country. We know but one loyalty and that is to the Stars and Stripes. We wish to do our part as loyal Americans in every way possible and we hereby offer ourselves for whatever service you may see fit to use us.

Although Ren was still unsure where he stood, he was taken aback to hear Arthur reply without hesitation, "I'm in!"

Ren felt a surge of determination and quickly added, "I'm in, too."

"Great," replied the group's leader. "My name is Jason. It's good to meet you both. I'm bunking just above one of you two. I'm from Haleiwa. Where are you both from?"

"I'm from Manoa," Arthur said, adjusting his glasses.

"And I'm from the plantations in Waialua," Ren answered.

"No kidding," Jason said, his expression brightening. "My best friend used to play baseball on the plantation teams down there. You might know him. His name is Peter. Unfortunately, he's not with us. He had an opportunity to play professional baseball...." Jason paused briefly, a hint of regret in his voice, before finishing, "...abroad."

Ren didn't recognize the name Peter, but something about Jason made him feel at ease. His easygoing nature and genuine manner felt familiar, like they were already old friends. Maybe it was their shared roots on the North Shore, tied by the same ocean winds and sun-soaked landscapes of their youth. Whatever the reason, Ren felt sure that their meeting wasn't just by chance.

Courtesy of Ted Tsukiyama Papers, Varsity Victory Volunteers #50, University of Hawaii at Manoa Library. Used with permission for educational and historical purposes.

CHAPTER 20

Back in The Game

All the boys were back for lunch, seeking relief from the relentless heat. The sun blazed high in the sky, and the humidity wrapped around them like a thick, suffocating blanket. The moment anyone stepped outside, their shirts clung to their skin, sticky and damp from the moisture in the air. Some of the guys gathered under the shade of a fragrant plumeria tree just outside the cottage, talking story and sharing cigarettes, their voices mixing with the occasional laughter. A few resumed a poker game they had left unfinished the night before, their focus intent as they played. Others, despite their grimy-covered bodies and the stickiness, lay sprawled on their bunks, stealing what little rest they could before it was time to return to the rock quarry.

The quiet was interrupted by the sound of the door slamming open. Junior burst in with more energy than the moment called for and announced loudly, "I have mail. Jason, you have a letter from Japan. Eh, I neva went open'um. You know they stay checking all da mail from Japan," he said, handing the letter to Jason with a grin.

"Who's writing to you from Japan?" Ren asked, his curiosity piqued.

"Oh, it's... my... um... Aunty's... sister's... brother's neighbor," Jason stammered, the words spilling out unconvincingly. "Eh, don't be so niele (nosey)."

"Sheesh, I didn't really care," Ren replied.

Jason tightened his grip on the letter, feeling a mixture of dread and anticipation. He knew exactly who had written it—his best friend, Peter. It had been ages since he'd heard from him, not since Peter and his father had left for Japan. The letter in his hand felt heavier than it should, carrying the weight of unresolved emotions. Jason hated that he felt ashamed of Peter, a friend who had done nothing more than pursue his dream of playing professional baseball. Yet, deep down, Jason couldn't help but feel like Peter had betrayed them, and he feared the other boys wouldn't understand if they found out.

As the lunch break ended, the boys began to gather their things, their conversations shifting back to the tasks ahead.

Boots shuffled against the wooden floor as they headed out the door.

"Let's go," Ren called, glancing over his shoulder.

"I'll be there shortly," Jason replied.

The cottage grew silent as the others filed out. Now alone, Jason hesitated, staring at the unopened envelope in his hand. He took a deep breath, the air in the room thick and still. Carefully, he unfolded the letter, the paper crackling faintly as he began to read.

Dear Jason,

Well, I am still alive. Dad and I arrived at Aloha Tower later that day. There were lots of people everywhere—military guys with guns. I'm not going to lie... I was super scared. My dad saw his contact, and we moved quickly onto a fishing boat. As soon as we got on the boat, we were led down to this secret compartment with fish everywhere. I can't even begin to tell you how stink it was. We had to stay down there for two days. There were other people with us, and trust me, we were not in the best of company. I must have barfed more times than I could count.

I guess once we were in open water, we were allowed on the deck. We had some pretty close calls where we had to rush down to the fish dungeon—that's what I call it—but for the most part, when we arrived in Yokohama, everything was good.

My dad must be a pretty important guy here in Japan. Most people can tell that I am a foreigner. We probably should have paid more attention when we were at Japanese school. I didn't have much time to relax. The day after we arrived, I tried out for the Japanese Professional Baseball League. I realized quickly that I wasn't as good as I thought I was. However, to my relief, I made it onto one of the teams. I am now a member of the Tokyo Giants. This is no plantation team. The coaches really work our butts off.

I hope you, Aunty, and Mom are okay. I'm sure you're off changing the world and making a difference. I hope one day you'll forgive me for leaving. Maybe when this war is finally over, we can figure this all out. Till then...

A hui hou (Till next time),

Peter

Jason sighed in relief, knowing that his friend was okay. He was happy for Peter, but the anger he felt still simmered beneath the surface. He wasn't sure if he'd ever be able to forgive him for leaving. The betrayal felt heavy, too much to process. Jason hoped the physical labor at the rock quarry would help him work through his emotions as the day wore on.

Varsity Victory Volunteers bridge gang at Schofield Barracks, Oahu, 1942. Courtesy of Ted Tsukiyama Papers, University of Hawaii at Manoa Library.

When Jason arrived at the quarry, he was glad to see his friends hard at work. The sun blazed relentlessly, and the air was thick with heat. Each boy swung his sledgehammer or pickaxe with determination, breaking the jagged rocks into smaller pieces. As the sun climbed higher, shirts came off one by one, leaving the boys in their blue jeans and work boots, their bronzed, sweat-slicked bodies glistening under the harsh sunlight. Their muscles flexed and moved with precision, the rhythm of their work almost hypnotic.

Looking down at his blistered hands and then out at his friends hard at work, Arthur felt his breath hitch. Each of them was mesmerizing in their own way—the way their toned, sun-kissed bodies glistened under the relentless sun, muscles rippling with every deliberate swing of their tools. The fluid grace of their movements, the raw power behind each strike—it was intoxicating to watch. The humid air carried the rich, salty scent of their sweat, mingling with the earthy aroma of dust and stone, creating an atmosphere that made his pulse quicken. Lost in the heat of the moment, his thoughts spiraled until a sudden sharp voice jolted him back to reality, leaving him flustered and breathless.

His focus was shattered by a loud voice. "Eh, booksmart! What the hell are you looking at?" Junior shouted, his tone sharp and accusing.

Startled, Arthur stammered, "Sorry, I was just lost in thought."

"Oh yeah? You like what you see?" Junior sneered, his eyes narrowing.

"No. I mean, yes. I mean, I'm happy to see the progress we're making," Arthur replied awkwardly, his words tumbling over each other.

"No talk smart with me. Like me break your face like I break these rocks!" Junior snarled, tossing his hammer to the ground and storming toward Arthur with quick, deliberate steps.

Arthur's heart pounded in his chest. He had never been in a fight before, and the fear gripped him. He wanted to walk away, but standing now might seem like an invitation to escalate the confrontation. As Junior closed the distance, Arthur sat frozen, unsure of what to do.

Just as Junior was a few steps away, Ren and Jason stepped in, placing themselves between Junior and Arthur.

"What you like, Junior?" Ren asked calmly, his tone firm but steady.

"Eh, dis is between me and dis stupid piece of shit!" Junior barked, pointing at Arthur.

"His name is Arthur," Jason interjected. "And he's here doing his best, just like the rest of us."

"But I swear, dis guy was looking at me like one wahine (girl)!" Junior snapped.

Jason smirked and said, "Seriously, Junior, you need to spend a bit more time down on Hotel Street." His comment sent the group into loud, spontaneous laughter, easing the tension in the air.

Jason clapped Junior on the shoulder and added, "Look, the sun's hot today, making us all think crazy. Let's call it quits early and hit the town tonight. I'll buy you a drink."

"Okay, maybe you're right," Junior said, shrugging. "I'll let you buy me a drink, but I don't want one from that guy," he added, jabbing a finger in Arthur's direction before walking off.

As Jason and Junior headed toward the other boys, Ren turned back to Arthur. "You okay?" he asked.

Arthur nodded, still shaken but grateful.

"Like I told you that day when you picked me up on the side of the road, I've got your back," Ren said. "Let's get cleaned up. Sounds like we're all hitting the town tonight."

Arthur managed a small smile. "Go ahead. I'll be there in a minute. I just need to catch my breath," he said.

Ren nodded and walked off, leaving Arthur alone on the boulder. This was the first time he had almost gotten into a fight. Although he was terrified, it was also exciting. Arthur had never felt so alive in his life. He was very grateful for his friends—grateful to have friends. Despite the hard work and being physically out of shape, Arthur realized that day that he could do this because he had such good friends like Ren and Jason. Standing up from his boulder, now all alone, Arthur looked down to see a pee-drenched stone, which shrouded him in a wave of embarrassment.

That night, piled into the back of a military truck, the Triple-V boys made their way to Smith's Union Bar on Hotel Street. They had been overdue for a break, and the promise of a night to unwind brought a sense of relief to the group. Each boy entered the bar with laughter on his lips, most with a girl on his arm—some even with a girl in each. Drinks quickly began stacking on tables as money flowed freely from pockets.

The air was thick with the smell of sweat, spilled beer, and cheap perfume, but it was alive with energy and celebration.

Arthur, however, sat alone at the bar. Despite the attention of several women who approached him, he waved them off with polite but firm refusals. He nursed his drink quietly, his thoughts miles away.

"Hey, drinking alone doesn't seem like much fun," Ren said, sliding onto the stool next to him.

"Oh, me? No, I'm fine," Arthur replied.

"Look, is Junior still messing with your head?"

"Something like that."

"Seriously, you have to let it go. Just stay close to Jason and me. We've got your back—we won't let anyone mess with you," Ren said firmly. He leaned closer, adding with a teasing grin, "Now, my friend, let's find you a lady. I'm sure we'll find someone just your type."

Arthur rolled his eyes. "I'm not so sure about that," he muttered under his breath.

Before Ren could respond, the atmosphere of the bar shifted. A group of young men in military uniforms strode in, their loud chatter and infectious energy commanding the room. The group was unmistakably Japanese, and their uniforms marked them as part of the Hawaii Army National Guard. Their arrival was electric, and the room buzzed with curiosity and excitement.

"A round of drinks for the house, on me!" one soldier shouted, throwing his arms wide with a grin. The room erupted in cheers, the noise rising like a wave.

One of the soldiers raised his voice above the din. "They took away our weapons. They called us traitors. And now, gents, we are back in the game! Tomorrow, we ship off to the mainland—Honolulu to Oakland, Oakland to Camp McCoy, Wisconsin—where we'll get the training we deserve to kick some Nazi ass!"

Another wave of cheers swept through the bar, louder and more celebratory than before. Jason, catching wind of the soldier's words, moved through the crowd toward him, his curiosity piqued.

"Excuse me," Jason said. "This is great news. Do you know if they'll open enlistment for the rest of us who want to do more?"

The soldier turned to him, "I don't know," he admitted. "But when we get there, we'll make sure we train harder than anyone else. If asked to wake up, we'll wake up earlier. If asked to run, we'll run faster. If they ask us to fight, we'll fight harder. Trust me, there will be no question why we're here."

"Mahalo (Thank you)," Jason said, nodding in respect before stepping back into the crowd.

Ignoring the beckoning calls of his friends and the women vying for his attention, Jason found his way to a quiet table in the far corner of the bar. He reached into his pocket, pulling out Peter's letter. His fingers brushed the edges of the worn paper as he unfolded it, and he stared at the words for a long moment. Speaking softly, as though Peter could hear him, Jason murmured, "I'm sorry, my friend, but you chose wrong. We are moments away from the fight, and we are ready. We are ready."

CHAPTER 21

Letters

Dear Ren (From Lyn),

I had hoped you would have come home to visit by now, and I wouldn't have to write this letter. I often see articles about the Triple-V in the newspaper. It sounds like you are truly working hard. Things have been rather quiet here at home. Kimi isn't around much. She shared with me the letters from our father. We are pretty confident that he died in the bombing of Pearl Harbor. I wish I could feel more sadness about this, but honestly, I really didn't know him well. Your parents are the closest thing I have to a mother and father. It's easier to express this in writing than face-to-face, but I want you to understand that just because the same people raised us, that doesn't necessarily make us brother and sister. I'm not a little kid anymore. I am more than that nickname "Hey-You." Just as you long for Kimi to recognize you as so much more, I hope that one day, you'll see me as Lyn, a person who has always strived to take good care of you. This might be a hopeless thought, but please know that I will always be here for you, no matter what.

I'm sure you are wondering about how Kimi is doing. For the most part, she stays in the nurse's quarters at Queens Hospital. When she is home, she sleeps most of the day. The training she is undergoing is very intense, and she often works through the night. Kimi is such a diligent worker, and we are all so proud of her. We both hope that you will come home soon. Your mom burns incense every day for you and Uncle Nobu. I'm still uncertain about which religion to believe in, but I know this, for what it's worth, you are in my thoughts and prayers daily. Hang in there.

Much aloha,

Lyn

My dearest Peter (From Chiyoko),

I just received your letter and I am relieved to hear that you arrived safely in Japan. I often reminisce about our home in

Yokohama and feel as though that era was a lifetime away. When I look in the mirror, I can barely recognize myself, yet when I gaze at your picture, I still see the goodness in this world. I understand that when we parted, things were difficult to grasp. I often judge your father too harshly, but I acknowledge that he has done his best to provide well for us all. With the ongoing war, I harbored fears that I might never see you again. I am so proud to hear that you are now playing professional baseball. Your talent truly shines through.

Aunty Mae is doing well, and the restaurant is busy with soldiers. In fact, I have taken up cooking as a way to pass the time. I never envisioned myself learning to perform the tasks our servants usually handle for us. However, I have discovered great satisfaction in learning these new skills. Jason frequently comes by to help repair and maintain things for us. He is a good boy, though we are concerned about him. He has changed. He has become consumed with the war, and we fear that if permitted, he will enlist in the military. His friends are always eager to assist, especially in moving the heavy boxes for Aunty and me. One boy, in particular, whose name is Ren. He mentioned that he grew up on the Wailua plantation. Do you know him from your baseball days there? I'm sure you are quite busy. Please take good care of yourself. Make sure you eat well, and when the time is right, please come home to me, with or without your father.

Douzo genki de (Take care of yourself),

Mom (Chiyoko),

My love, Emi (From Nobu),

I have no way of knowing if this letter will ever reach you. I was in a camp in Hawaii for some time, but recently, they transferred us to a very cold place on the mainland. From what I've overheard, I am now in a state called Wisconsin, at a place they refer to as Camp McCoy. Many of us are unsure of the reason for why we are here. There are a few Japanese military survivors from the bombing who are held as prisoners alongside us. We receive the bare minimum to survive, and the living conditions are extremely harsh, with mud everywhere. I am doing all I can to keep my feet warm and dry. However, many men have lost toes, and some have lost their entire feet. I know my words will cause you concern, and I share these details only so that you can let someone know that we need help. There is no way to escape. I have witnessed others who have tried, only to be killed in their attempts. With that, I understand that my best chance of reuniting with you all is to remain patient and cooperative, continuing to nurture the hope that I will one day return home.

I am a very hard worker and feel I am well-liked among the soldiers here. I have made a few friends who have agreed to send this letter to you on my behalf. It is risky to send a letter because any intercepted attempts are seen as acts of treason. The government suspects that we may be embedding secret messages in our letters to Japan. Despite the risks, I felt it was important to reach out to you. I'm sure you and the family are very worried. Rest assured, I will be okay. This war is difficult and unpredictable. I know Ren can be somewhat of a hothead. There is talk here of Japanese American soldiers training nearby from Hawaii. People say that they fight like lions.

There is also speculation that they might be deployed to France to demonstrate their loyalty to America. Please, I beg you to make sure Ren does not get involved. Tell him to be patient, and I will return home as soon as I can. I trust our girls are managing well. Did Namio ever connect with them, as he mentioned in his last letter? I'm sure it was a heartfelt reunion. I miss my old friend dearly and hope that we can all gather together soon. I'd better sign off now to avoid drawing attention. I love you deeply and miss the gentle touch of your hand.

Till we meet again,

Nobu

Japanese American families arrive at an internment camp on the mainland USA, 1942. Harsh conditions mirrored the fear and prejudice faced by Japanese Americans across the country during World War II. Public domain, Dorothea Lange, U.S. War Relocation Authority.

Office of War Information (OWI)

Office of the Director

October 2, 1942

The President

The White House

Dear Mr. President:

For both Mr. Eisenhower and myself, I want to recommend that you take two actions designed to improve the morale of the

American-citizen Japanese who were evacuated from the Pacific Coast:

(1) Two bills in Congress – one aimed at depriving the Nisei (Second generation of American Japanese AKA AJ) of citizenship and the other proposing to "intern" them for the duration of the war – have heightened the feeling that this may after all be a racial war and that, therefore the evacuees should be looked upon as enemies. A brief public statement from you, in behalf of the loyal American citizens, would be helpful. I think WRA and the Justice Department would concur in this recommendation.

(2) Loyal American citizens of Japanese descent should be permitted, after individual test, to enlist in the Army and Navy. It would hardly be fair to evacuate people and then impose normal draft procedures, but voluntary enlistment would help a lot.

This matter is of great interest to OWI. Japanese propaganda to the Philippines, Burma, and elsewhere insists that this is a racial war. We can combat this effectively with counterpropaganda only if our deeds permit us to tell the truth. Moreover, as citizens ourselves who believe deeply in the things for which we fight, we cannot help but be disturbed by the insistent public misunderstanding of the Nisei; competent (sic) authorities, including Naval Intelligence people, say that fully 85 percent of the Nisei are Loyal to this country and that it is possible to distinguish the sheep from the goats.

Respectfully yours,

Elmer Davis
Director

Letter to the Secretary of War from President Roosevelt
February 1, 1943

My dear Mr. Secretary:

The proposal of the War Department to organize a combat team consisting of loyal American citizens of Japanese descent has my full approval. The new combat team will add to the nearly five thousand loyal Americans of Japanese ancestry who are already serving in the armed forces of our country.

This is a natural and logical step toward the reinstatement of the Selective Service procedures, which were temporarily disrupted by the evacuation from the West Coast.

No loyal citizen of the United States should be denied the democratic right to exercise the responsibilities of his citizenship, regardless of his ancestry. The principle on which this country was founded and by which it has always been governed is that Americanism is a matter of the mind and heart; Americanism is not, and never was, a matter of race or ancestry. A good

American is one who is loyal to this country and to our creed of liberty and democracy. Every loyal American citizen should be given the opportunity to serve this country wherever his skills will make the greatest contribution -- whether it be in the ranks of our armed forces, war production, agriculture, government service, or other work essential to the war effort.

I am glad to observe that the War Department, the Navy Department, the War Manpower Commission, the Department of Justice, and the War Relocation Authority are collaborating in a program which will assure the opportunity for all loyal Americans, including Americans of Japanese ancestry, to serve their country at a time when the fullest and wisest use of our manpower is all-important to the war effort.

Very sincerely yours,
(Sgd) FRANKLIN D. ROOSEVELT

Thus began The AJ, Nisei, Hawaii 442nd Regimental Combat Team.

Color guard of the Japanese American 442nd Regimental Combat Team standing at attention as their citations for bravery are read near Bruyères, France, November 12, 1944. Public domain, U.S. Army Center for Military History.

CHAPTER 22

At The Steps of The Palace

"Hold still, Mr. Johnson," Kimi said gently as she examined the patient's swollen glands. "Well, it seems as though you are having an allergic reaction. Try to breathe slowly, and the doctor will be here shortly."

"Hello, Kimi. I'll take it from here."

"Doctor Tom? I thought Doctor Ishikawa would be handling things on this floor today?"

"You and me both. However, just as I was about to leave for the day, a messenger brought an urgent message to Doctor Ishikawa, and just like that, he said he had to go. Who knows?

These young interns often have better things to do, I guess. So, Mr. Johnson, what was the last thing you recall eating?"

This news piqued Kimi's curiosity. Young Doctor Ishikawa was not known to shirk his duties. She couldn't remember the last time he had called in sick. At that moment, she heard shouting and the sound of doors opening and closing. It wasn't an angry ruckus. The air was charged with excitement. Peering out the window, she was astounded to see young men either jumping into their cars or sprinting toward downtown Honolulu. Initially, her heart started to race, fearing another attack, but as she looked closer, noticing that all these young men were of Asian descent, she wondered if it had something to do with their fathers being taken under suspicion of treason. At that moment, hope surged in Kimi's heart, thinking perhaps Uncle Nobu had been released.

With that thought, she said, "Excuse me, Doctor Tom, but I must go too. I am terribly sorry."

"Sure. Why not? It's not like I had plans this evening," the doctor muttered under his breath.

Not paying any attention to what the doctor had said, Kimi replied, "Great, thank you for understanding." She quickly gathered her things and joined the throng of people running towards hope.

Soon, Kimi found herself in the vibrant heart of downtown. As she looked around, she saw thousands of young Japanese men, all about her age. Everyone was talking excitedly, making it difficult for her to grasp what was happening.

"Is it true," someone shouted near her.

"It is! It was only a matter of time."

"What is?" Kimi chimed in.

"The war, they are going to let us enlist."

"How many?" another voice shouted.

"Hundreds. Maybe thousands." With that revelation, the crowd erupted in cheers and shouts of adulation.

Kimi slowed her pace to a stop as the crowd surged forward, pushing and shoving past her. Uncle Nobu was still not coming home. Despair sank deep into her heart, swiftly followed by panic. "Ren!" she said out loud to herself. At that moment, she realized she had to get home. What actions could she take? What words would she say? Had Ren already enlisted?

"You don't have to do this!" shouted Emi. "Please, son, didn't you read the letter from your father? You need to be patient. Why? Why do you want to fight for this country when they have taken your father? Look at how he is living. Please, just be obedient. I can't lose you both." Emi pleaded, now on her knees, tears cascading down her face.

"Mother, since I've been gone, I've learned that I am not just fighting for Father or myself. It is so much more than us. I am fighting to show that freedom belongs to everyone, regardless of race." Ren was now on his knees too, holding his mother's hands. At that moment, Kimi walked through the door. "Mama, I am fighting for..." he stammered, then looking up at Kimi, "I am fighting for my children and their children. My entire life, I have sought purpose, and now I have found it." Still holding his mother's hands, still looking at Kimi, "I will come home. I promise."

Kimi could feel tears streaming down her face. Her heart sank at the thought of losing her mother, then her father, then Uncle Nobu, and now possibly saying goodbye to Ren for the last time—it was simply too much. With that, she turned and ran. Kimi sprinted down that long dirt road and did not stop until she reached the water. It was the same beach she had run to as a child, where she saw her father enter with total desperation. She remembered that day vividly, as if it were yesterday, and for a brief moment, now as an adult, she began to truly understand the depth of her father's hopelessness.

Slowly, she waded into the water, now up to her knees. Did she possess the courage to keep walking, to take the only action she felt she had control over? How serene it would be to let all of this just fade away? Closing her eyes and taking a deep breath, the roar of the ocean, though loud, somehow managed to drown out all the noise in her head. At that moment, she felt a hand grasp hers, fingers interlacing.

"I love him too."

Slowly opening her eyes, she looked down at their entwined hands, then at a face awash with tears ready to spill over. Lyn. For a long moment, time seemed to stand still, their hands clasped, gazing out at the horizon.

Kimi was the first to break the silence, "This is my very special place. Miracles happen here." Kimi had never shared with her sister what had transpired with their father at that beach. "That's what we need—a miracle. Lyn, do you believe in miracles?"

Lyn paused to consider, then replied softly, "I do, and I know Ren will come back to us—both of us. But until then, we have each other, and that will never change. Promise?"

"I do."

Sunday, March 28, 1943

The sun shone brightly, yet it was slightly overcast. Drops of water glistened on the plants like jewels adorning the mountains after a light morning shower. The cool tradewinds blew gently offshore, sweeping across the land. Jason could hardly believe this day had come.

"Arthur, wake up. It's time," Jason said.

"Just five more minutes," groaned Arthur.

"Seriously. Wake up. We need to meet Ren down on King Street."

Jason came into view, rubbing the sleep from his eyes. He stood in all his glory, dressed in his newly pressed military uniform, his hat neatly tucked under his arm. Arthur thought to himself how striking Jason looked. He considered Jason the complete package—strong, handsome, and with that deep voice, he could melt the hearts of the best of them.

"Um, Arthur, you're doing it again," Jason said uncomfortably.

"Doing what?"

"You know, staring. Hurry up and get dressed. We need to go meet Ren."

Quickly, Arthur snapped out of it and got dressed. Both boys had enlisted in the 442nd Regimental Combat Team along with their friends in the Triple-V. Soon, a military truck honked its horn outside their cabin.

"Eh, hurry up! Sheesh, you guys, you move slower than mud drying in a pothole on a rainy day," shouted Junior from the driver's seat.

"Cool your jets, Junior. We're coming already," replied Jason as they jumped in the back of the truck with other members of the Triple-V.

"So what, Arthur, had to do your hair or something la-dat!"

"Enough already, Junior. If I hear one more comment like that about Arthur, I won't hesitate. We are now all on the same team. If we don't watch out for each other, it could mean one of us doesn't come home. You understand," said Jason sternly.

As his words set in, Junior didn't respond and just nodded, and with that, they were off.

Ren was there to meet them as they unloaded from the truck on King Street.

"Eh, what took you guys so long?" Ren inquired with a raised eyebrow.

"Well, if it wasn't for..." Junior stammered, catching Jason's stern gaze. "Neva mind. Had traffic and stuff la-dat."

For a moment, they were all speechless, taking in the crowds of people who had gathered to honor them as the new soldiers. A farewell ceremony was set to be held at the entrance of Iolani Palace. That day, two thousand six hundred and eighty-six American Japanese enlisted volunteers would march through Honolulu to commence their military service. Hundreds of people thronged the streets to pay their respects. Soon, the leaders of their unit began to call the soldiers to order.

"Jason. Jason," a voice echoed through the crowd.

He recognized the voice instantly. "Mother, I am here."

Battling her way through the crowd were his mother and Aunty Chiyoko. Without hesitation, she enveloped her son in a warm embrace, her tears staining his starched, pressed collar.

"How can you be leaving me? I thought this day would never come. Is there nothing I can say to make you stay?" she asked, her hands tenderly cradling his face as she searched his eyes desperately.

"There is nothing you can say. I love you, but I need to go."

"I know you do. I will be here when you come back. Please come back," she implored, embracing her son one last time with an urgency that conveyed the depth of her fear of possibly losing him forever. As she released Jason, she turned and threw herself into Chiyoko's arms, her body racked with deep, sorrowful sobs.

At this moment, Chiyoko placed a lei around Jason's neck and whispered, "You are family, more than you know. Please be careful and come home. I know Peter will worry, and with him, we all eagerly await your return." After one final, heartfelt hug, Mae and Chiyoko reluctantly retreated back into the crowd.

Nearby, another voice called out, beckoning Arthur. Confused, Arthur looked around. Standing off to the side was a very well-dressed businessman with salt-and-pepper hair, black-rimmed glasses, and the thinnest pencil-like mustache imaginable.

"Father?"

"Yes, I am here, son."

"But I don't understand, all this time and not a word. Why are you here?"

"Well, we don't have much time, and yes, I was pretty upset when you stole the car. Look, I know we see this world very differently, and I don't understand you, but you are my son, and I love you very much."

Arthur had never heard his father speak to him in such a heartfelt manner. His heart raced, and though touched, he felt a surge of anger welling up inside him.

"Now you say this! Now you tell me you love me, only moments away from me leaving, maybe even leaving for good. This is when you choose to say these things."

With his head bowed, trying to conceal the tears brimming in his eyes, his father replied, "Yes, this is where I choose to share these things. Please forgive me."

Realizing his father's sincerity, Arthur felt his anger dissolve, replaced by a longing for reconciliation. "Father, this is all I ever wanted. It was for you to be proud of me. To be proud of the man I've become."

Looking up, his voice filled with tenderness, his father replied, "I am." This was the first time Arthur recalled his father embracing him. He then presented him with a lei. "Please take care of yourself. We can talk more when you return."

Still in disbelief, Arthur rejoined the ranks. Slowly, the march began, with the crowd shouting, "Go For Broke!" It was a momentous scene. As they approached the stretch to the palace, another desperate call cut through the noise.

"Ren! Please, Ren!"

"Kimi? Where are you?" he replied. Navigating his way out of rank and scanning the crowd, he felt a pang of disappointment but was soon relieved to see Lyn waving him down.

"It was too much for Kimi and your mother to be here. I had to see you one last time."

"I'm so glad you came. You've always been there for me. I love you!"

"I love you too." The gravity of the moment overwhelmed Lyn, leaving her little time to process his words.

"I have to go," said Ren.

"I know. Be safe, and we'll see you soon," Lyn replied, draping a lei around his neck and kissing his cheek. As his figure dwindled in the distance, she was left wondering if this farewell might be their last.

Gathered on the steps of the palace, everyone shared a united hope of seeing each other again someday.

On March 28, 1943, more than 2,600 Nisei volunteers from Hawaii gathered at 'Iolani Palace for a farewell ceremony before departing to join the 442nd Regimental Combat Team. Thousands of family members and supporters filled the capitol grounds, proud of the young men who volunteered to fight for a nation that had once questioned their loyalty after Pearl Harbor. The Honolulu Star-Bulletin called it "one of the most striking and significant scenes of the war." From this moment, the 442nd would become the most decorated unit of its size and length of service in U.S. military history. Photo courtesy of Nisei Veterans Legacy, public domain.

CHAPTER 23

Mud and Rain

France, October 14, 1944

The 442nd Regimental Combat Team pushed through the misty Vosges Mountains. Each step dragged them deeper into exhaustion. The forest was a haunting labyrinth of towering pines cloaked in fog and icy rain, which soaked through their olive-drab uniforms, boots, and socks. The mud clung to their feet like lead weights, and the bitter cold was relentless. Fatigue seeped into every muscle. Combat had become their routine, with enemy artillery and tree bursts sending deadly shrapnel ripping through the ranks. The unforgiving conditions reflected the grit it took to liberate Bruyères and Biffontaine from entrenched German forces.

Huddled in waterlogged foxholes, the men sought small distractions from their misery. Junior, always the first to break the silence, nudged Ren with a grin, his rifle resting across his lap. "Eh, da mud no badah me just like anadah day in da lo'i (Hawaiian Wet Taro Patch)," he said, raising one eyebrow.

Ren smirked, shifting uncomfortably in the mud. "Wat you know about one lo'i thought you was from Ewa Beach. Dat place is dryer den toast." The joke earned a few low chuckles, and a rare moment of relief was felt amongst the group.

Arthur adjusted his weathered helmet and sniffed the air. "This forest smells like home. When I was a kid, my dad and I would walk through Manoa Valley just after a light rain," he reflected as distant artillery broke the stillness.

"Eyes open, boys," Jason interjected, his tone calm but commanding as his sharp eyes scanned the misty tree line. "We've got a job to do."

The men shifted, fatigue etched into their faces as they prepared to move. The mud squelched underfoot, and the dense underbrush made every step an ordeal. Ren adjusted the strap on his helmet, sliding up to Jason. "Hey, Jas," he muttered, keeping his voice low, "you ever think about the smell of home? Kalua pig, maybe some malasadas?"

A faint grin flickered across Jason's face despite the weight of his M1 Garand. He chuckled softly, his breath fogging in the frigid air. "Ren, if we survive this war, I'm taking you out for the biggest plate of laulau you've ever seen. But for now, keep your head in the game."

Up front, Junior raised a hand, bringing the squad to a halt. His sharp eye cut through the haze as he muttered, "Stay tight, boys. Bruyères is close, and the Germans aren't going to make this easy." When Junior spoke without any pidgin, everyone paid attention.

Just then, the squad was pinned down by enemy fire. They quickly found refuge in a shallow trench, rain pooling around their boots. "If one more branch falls and hits my helmet," grumbled Junior, "I'm paddling my ass back to Hawaii."

Nearby, Ren peered through fogged binoculars from a makeshift observation post, muttering to Arthur, who always seemed to be beside him, "Another day in paradise, huh? At least the Germans are as cold as we are." Now, making his way down from his post, Ren just sat in the mud, staring at a damp photograph of Kimie, which he had pulled from his inside jacket pocket. "I wonder if she got my last letter," he said quietly, looking at the night sky. "Maybe we are both gazing at the same stars."

The battle for Bruyères was a clash of armies and a test of will. The Germans fiercely dug in and fortified their positions with machine gun nests, mines, and tanks. The forest, soaked and shrouded in fog, became a deadly game of resilience. Shells burst in the treetops, sending lethal fragments raining down—a constant, inescapable danger. However, the men of the 442nd pressed on, their resolve unbroken. They weren't just fighting for victory. They were fighting to prove that loyalty and courage were stronger than prejudice. Their motto, "Go For Broke," echoed in every step forward.

Soldiers of the 442nd Regimental Combat Team advance through the mist-shrouded Vosges Mountains in eastern France, 1944. Public domain, U.S. Army Signal Corps.

The next day, the assault on Bruyères began as usual, under a shroud of rain and desperation. The hills, heavily defended by German forces, were a maze of machine-gun nests and hidden bunkers. Rain turned the slopes into slick, grease-like slides, forcing the men of the 442nd to claw their way uphill through mud and relentless enemy fire. The eerie wail of "screaming meemie" rockets ripped through the air, shaking the ground and the soldiers' nerves alike.

Pinned down under fire during an ambush, Jason led his men to save another nearby squad trapped by German guns. Jason threw a grenade, silencing one machine-gun nest. At that moment, a sniper's bullet grazed his arm, sending him to the ground. As he fell, Jason's voice rose above the chaos, "Go for broke!"

Nearby, Ren crouched behind a tree, clutching his rifle tightly. Jason's words echoed in his mind, filling his entire body with renewed determination. The squad pushed forward with Jason's cry driving them as they fought to claim the blood-soaked ground.

*Members of the 442nd Regimental Combat
Team march through the mud toward Bruyères,
France, in October 1944. Public domain, U.S.
Army Signal Corps.*

For three days, the 442nd pushed forward toward Bruyères, encountering fierce resistance outside the town. German forces unleashed a storm of machine-gun fire and mortars, halting their advance. Tree bursts from enemy shells rained shrapnel down, splintering branches into deadly projectiles. Using fallen logs, the soldiers hastily reinforced their foxholes.

In the midst of the chaos, Jason's squad prepared to flank an enemy machine-gun position. Jason whispered, crawling through the wet underbrush, "Stay low, stay quiet. And if you get shot, try not to scream."

Ren stifled a nervous laugh. "Classic Jason—always the ready."

A German patrol suddenly emerged from the trees, triggering a burst of rifle fire. Grenades arced through the air, and the forest erupted in chaos. When the smoke cleared, the squad had taken prisoners and neutralized the machine-gun nest. Jason clapped Junior on the back, his face grim but proud. "Good work. But don't get cocky—we still got miles to go."

As they regrouped, the crack of rifle fire shattered the uneasy quiet. "Ambush!" Arthur yelled as the men dove for cover, bullets snapping through the trees.

Jason's voice rang out, sharp and decisive. "Suppressive fire on that ridge! Ren, Junior, and Arthur flank left!"

Adrenaline surged as Ren and Junior sprinted through the trees with Arthur close behind, ducking low as dirt and bark exploded around them. With hearts pounding, the boys fired into the enemy's position, their aim steady despite the chaos that surrounded them. The German gunfire faltered, and the soldiers just behind pressed forward with reinforcements, driving their foes back.

That night, the forest fell eerily quiet, save for the crackling of a small fire around which the men sat. They shared rations, their faces drawn from exhaustion and loss. Ren stared at the familiar photograph of Kimie in his hands, the creased edges worn from countless moments like this.

Arthur settled beside him, breaking the silence. "You miss her, don't you?"

"Every day," Ren replied softly. "I'm here for her. For all of us. What future will we have if we don't prove we belong?"

Arthur nodded, his expression unreadable in the flickering firelight. "You think everyone back home gets it? What we're doing here?"

Overhearing the conversation, Jason said in his low, unwavering voice, "They'll get it when we win."

The men fell silent, some scribbling letters to loved ones, others simply staring into the flames. In the distance, thunder rumbled. Whether it was from a brewing storm or artillery, none of them could tell.

The next morning, word came that over 200 Texan soldiers of the 141st Infantry Regiment were trapped, encircled by German forces deep within the dense Vosges Mountains. Supplies were dwindling, and reinforcements had been deemed impossible. Then the call came in. The 442nd Regimental Combat Team would be sent to do the impossible.

"They're calling us to do the job no one like do," muttered Junior, his voice laced with fatigue as he packed his gear.

"Go for broke," said Jason with a grin, the familiar motto rolling easily off his tongue.

"Damn right," Ren replied, a faint smile breaking through the weariness.

As the men readied themselves, the weight of the mission was heavy in the air. They carried more than rifles and grenades. They carried the hopes of their families, the pride of their communities, and the honor of proving their loyalty to a country that had not always believed in them. Their uniforms, soaked and caked with mud, bore testament to days of unrelenting combat. The red "Go for Broke" patch on their sleeves stood as a silent vow. They would not falter.

The trail toward the 141st was a nightmare. The rain was relentless, making the ground cling to every step. Mud gripped their boots and seeped into their waterlogged socks, the chill biting deep into their bones. Helmets glinted dully under the gray morning light as rain dripped from their brims.

Jason's voice cut through the steady drum of rain. "Hurry it up! If we stop, we freeze!"

Arthur trudged along, muttering to himself, "This isn't like Hawaii. I'd give anything for even a bowl of cold saimin right now."

Ren smirked, overhearing his complaints. "Trust me, if we get out of this alive, when we get back home, I'll make you enough noodles to sink a boat."

The exchange earned a few tired chuckles, a brief moment of relief in the grim march. But the laughter died as artillery fire erupted ahead, the distant booms shaking the forest. Shrapnel tore through the air, splintering tree trunks and sending the men diving for cover.

Crouched behind a crate with a map spread out before him, Jason barked orders. "We're flanking to the right! Watch for tripwires—they've booby-trapped the trails." His calm, measured tone steadied the nerves of those around him, though his eyes betrayed the tension of the mission.

Japanese American soldiers of the 442nd Regimental Combat Team climb a steep hill near Bruyères, France, October 24, 1944. Public domain, U.S. Army Signal Corps / Courtesy of the Seattle Nisei Veterans Committee.

As night fell, the advance became a brutal crawl. The Germans were dug in, their machine guns spitting death from concealed positions in the thick forest. Shadows danced under the faint light of a rising moon, each one a potential ambush. Bullets cracked through the air, snapping branches and boring into the mud.

"They're dug in deep," yelled Ren.

The 442nd pressed on, inching closer to the trapped battalion. Each step was a victory over exhaustion, fear, and the brutal elements. Every now and then, the crackle of the radio pierced the much-coveted silence.

"We're holding, but barely..." came the faint transmission from the 141st, the desperation in their voices cutting through the static.

Jason turned to his squad, his face set with determination. "We'll reach them," he said firmly, his voice a steady anchor amid the chaos. "We're the 442nd. No one's out of reach on our watch."

Exhausted but unbroken, the men steadied themselves. Tomorrow would bring one of the toughest battles of their lives, but they marched on with the unwavering resolve that had come to define the 442nd. They weren't just fighting for the men trapped ahead—they were fighting for the honor of proving that no obstacle, no prejudice, and no enemy could break them.

CHAPTER 24

Secrets Told

Sotaro Suzuki, an unidentified All-Nippon player, Lou Gehrig, Hisanori Karita, and Babe Ruth during the 1934 Japan–U.S. baseball tour that helped introduce professional baseball to Japan. Public domain, Yoko Suzuki Collection.

The crack of a bat echoed through the stadium, but Peter wasn't paying attention. His grip on the bat loosened as his mind drifted. The crowd's murmur, the slap of leather gloves, and even the rhythmic shouts of his teammates blended into a distant hum. He was far from the dusty diamond of Meiji Jingu Stadium, lost in the familiar smells of home—the salty tang of the ocean, the faint aroma of plumeria, and the smoky sweetness of char siu grilling at Aunty Mae's restaurant.

"Peter-san! Focus! Where's your head?" Coach Yamamoto's sharp voice jolted him back to reality.

Startled, Peter blinked and turned toward the dugout. "Hai! I'm here, Coach!" he called back, though his voice lacked conviction.

The next pitch came, but his reaction was slow. The ball smacked into the catcher's glove, and Peter just stood there at the ready.

"That's strike three!" the umpire bellowed, shaking his head.

Peter sighed, dropping his bat as he walked back to the bench. His teammates avoided his gaze, muttering amongst themselves.

"Another out because of him," one said under his breath.

"We can't afford this, even in practice," another grumbled.

Peter sat down on the wooden bench, gripping his cap tightly in his hands, staring at the ground. His mind was spinning, guilt gnawing at him. He thought of Jason—his best friend, his brother in everything but blood. Jason was thousands of miles away, fighting for America.

"Jason's risking his life," Peter whispered to himself, his voice trembling. "And I'm... here."

A teammate, Kent, plopped down beside him, frowning. "You okay, Peter? You've been off for weeks now."

Peter hesitated, then shook his head. "I'm fine."

"Doesn't look like it." Kent leaned closer, lowering his voice. "You're always in your head. Whatever it is, you gotta shake it off. The team's starting to notice."

Peter rubbed his face with his hands. "It's just... everything feels wrong. Being here, playing baseball, while... while others are out there fighting."

Kent frowned, considering Peter's words. "The war's hard on everyone. But you can't carry the world on your shoulders."

Peter looked up, his jaw tightening. "How can hitting a ball and running bases matter when people we care about, who are fighting for us, might not make it back alive?"

Not knowing how to answer, Kent patted Peter on the shoulder and said, "I'm sure you'll figure it out. Now let's play ball."

After practice, Coach Yamamoto called Peter into his small office under the stands. The walls were lined with faded photos of past players, some of whom had gone on to make history in the league.

"Sit," Yamamoto said, gesturing to a wooden chair across from his desk.

Peter obeyed, sitting stiffly, his hands folded in his lap.

Yamamoto studied him for a moment, his expression unreadable. "Peter-san, you're a good player. You have talent. But talent means nothing if your mind is elsewhere."

"I know, Coach," Peter said, his voice low. "I've just been… distracted."

"Distracted?" Yamamoto's voice hardened. "You think you're the only one with troubles? Look around you. Half of this team has family fighting in the war—or worse, gone. Yet they still play with heart because they know they must."

Peter felt a surge of defensiveness. "It's not that simple. I didn't want to come here, Coach. My father brought me. And now I feel… stuck. My best friend is out there, risking his life, and I'm just playing baseball."

Yamamoto leaned back in his chair, crossing his arms. "So you think you don't belong here? That this game is beneath you?"

Peter hesitated but then shook his head. "No. It's not that. It's just… I don't know who I'm doing this for anymore."

The coach sighed, his tone softening. "Peter, I took you on because I saw something special in you. Baseball isn't just about skill. It's about discipline, focus, and pride. If you can't find a reason to play for yourself, then find a reason to play for others. Play for your friend. Play for your family. But most of all, play to prove that you belong—wherever you are."

Peter nodded slowly, though the weight in his chest remained. "I'll try, Coach."

Yamamoto leaned forward, his voice quiet but firm. "Peter-san, trying isn't enough—not here, not in this league, and not in these times. I can't let you continue to drag the team down."

Peter's heart sank, and his throat tightened. "Coach, please—"

"I've made my decision," Yamamoto interrupted. "You're dismissed from the team, effective immediately. Pack your things."

Peter stared at the coach, disbelief and shame washing over him. He stood silently, nodded once, and left the office, the sound of the door closing behind him echoing louder than any roar of a stadium crowd.

That evening, Peter sat on a low stool in the cramped apartment he shared with his father. The sparse but meticulously organized room reflected Kosuke's obsessive need for control. Every item had its place, and the silence hung heavy in the air, suffocating.

"Fired?!" Kosuke's voice roared, shattering the stillness like a thunderclap. He slammed his hand on the table, rattling the teacup that sat on it. The sound reverberated through the small space. "How could you be so incompetent? You disgrace this family!"

Peter flinched but kept his gaze steady. "Otousan (Father), I—"

"Don't speak!" Kosuke barked, cutting him off. He stood abruptly, his face twisted in fury. "You ran away from Hawaii like a sniveling coward, and now you can't even hold onto a baseball bat! What's next? Will you crawl back to your mother just like the sniveling baby you are?"

Peter's face burned hot, his hands trembling as they clenched into fists at his sides. He stood abruptly, his voice shaking but rising in volume. "I didn't run away! You dragged me here! And I'm not the coward—you are!"

Kosuke's eyes widened, his rage barely contained. "Watch your tongue, boy, before I—"

"No! You watch yours!" Peter interrupted, his voice breaking as he stepped closer to his father. "You think you're better than me? You hide in the shadows, dealing in dark places, profiting off people's suffering. That doesn't make you strong—it makes you weak. It makes you pathetic. And I'll tell you this: I will never be like you."

"You ungrateful little shit," Kosuke hissed, his hand curling into a fist. "Everything you have, everything you are, comes from me!"

"Everything I am?" Peter shouted, his voice cracking with emotion. "The only thing you've given me is shame! Do you think this is a life? I hate you! I wish you were dead!"

Kosuke's face twisted in an ugly snarl, his entire body shaking with fury, but Peter didn't give him the chance to respond.

Peter stormed toward the door, ripping it open. "And you know what?" he said, returning for one final blow. "I should've listened to Jason. I should've stayed in Hawaii and done my duty, fought for something real instead of letting you drag me into your disgusting world."

The words hung in the air like smoke. Kosuke stepped forward, his fists clenched as though he might strike, but Peter didn't flinch. He slammed the door behind him, the force of it rattling the walls, and left without looking back.

The ship returned to Hawaii, docked at Honolulu Harbor early in the morning. Peter stepped off the gangway, the salty air hitting him like a long-lost friend. He closed his eyes, breathing deeply as the warm sun bathed his skin. It felt like home—a sensation he hadn't realized he'd been starving for.

At Mae's restaurant, Peter paused just outside the door. He peered through the window and saw his mother, Chiyoko, laughing softly as she did her best to help. For a moment, he stood frozen, his throat tightening.

Finally, he pushed the door open. A small bell chimed, and Chiyoko turned. Her words froze mid-sentence as her gaze locked on him. Her eyes widened, and a gasp escaped her lips.

"Peter?" she whispered.

"Hi, Mom," he said, his voice trembling.

She stopped what she was doing and rushed to him, her arms wrapping tightly around his neck. "Peter! You're home!" Her voice broke, and she buried her face in his shoulder.

"I'm here, Mom," Peter whispered, holding her tightly. "I'm not leaving again. Never."

"You're thin," she said, pulling back to inspect him, her hands on his cheeks. "Are you eating enough? How did you get here? Why didn't you tell me you were coming?" The questions spilled out of her in a rush, but her joy was unmistakable.

"Mom, I'm fine," Peter assured her, his voice thick with emotion. "I just... I had to come home. I couldn't stay in Japan any longer."

From the doorway to the kitchen, Aunty Mae appeared, wiping her hands on a towel. "Well, if it isn't the baseball star," she teased, but her grin faltered when she saw his face. "Oh, boy, you've been through it, haven't you?"

"Hi, Aunty Mae." Peter managed a weak smile. "I've missed you."

"Missed me? You're the one who vanished." Mae crossed her arms but then softened, shaking her head. "Come sit. You look like you could use a good meal."

They sat together at one of the small tables in the dining area. Chiyoko brought Peter a bowl of saimin and a plate of manapua, her eyes rarely leaving him as he ate. Mae sat across from him, her sharp eyes watching closely.

"So," Mae began, "what happened over there?"

Peter hesitated, setting his hashi (chopsticks) down. "I got fired," he admitted. "I wasn't playing well. My head wasn't in it."

Mae raised an eyebrow. "And your father?"

Peter's jaw tightened. "We had a fight. A big one. I said some things I can't take back, but I'm not sorry."

Chiyoko reached for his hand. "What kind of fight, Peter?"

"The kind where you realize your father is the person I tried to pretend he wasn't," Peter said bitterly. "He's involved in things, Mom. Dark things. And I saw..." He shook his head. "It doesn't matter. I just couldn't stay."

Mae exchanged a glance with Chiyoko, but neither said anything. Peter noticed the silence and frowned. "What? What is it?"

"Nothing, son," Chiyoko said quickly, standing. "We're just glad you're back."

One afternoon, Peter was helping Mae move boxes in the back storage room. He lifted a particularly heavy one and nearly stumbled into a side door left slightly ajar. His brow furrowed as he heard muffled voices from inside.

He set the box down and pushed the door open just a crack. Inside, three men sat around a table, stacks of cash and several guns spread out before them. One man lit a cigarette, his tattooed hands briefly illuminated by the flickering flame. Another counted bills with a practiced rhythm, muttering to himself. The third tapped a pistol against the table absent-mindedly.

Peter's stomach dropped. He quickly backed away, his heart pounding in his chest. He waited until the men's voices faded before retreating to find his mother.

"Mom," Peter said sharply as he walked into the kitchen, his voice low but urgent. "What's going on here?"

Chiyoko turned, startled. "What do you mean?"

"I saw them," Peter said, his voice rising slightly. "In the back room. Men. Guns. Money. What the hell is happening? What are you and Aunty Mae involved in?"

Chiyoko's face darkened, and her voice turned sharp. "It's none of your business, Peter."

"None of my business?!" Peter exploded. "Mom, this is dangerous! Those men—what are they doing here?"

"It's your father's business," Chiyoko said, her tone clipped.

Peter stared at her in disbelief. "Father's business? Are you serious right now? You're letting all of this happen here?"

"The only thing you need to worry about," Chiyoko said firmly, "is that this keeps us alive. That's all."

Peter's voice rose again, shaking with anger. "Keeps us alive? Mom, this isn't survival—it's a death sentence! You're letting his poison seep into everything."

Chiyoko's face softened slightly, but her tone remained steady. "You don't understand, Peter. This is how it has to be."

Peter ran a hand through his hair, frustration and disbelief clouding his thoughts. "I can't believe this. You and Aunty Mae... you're better than this. How can you let him control everything, even from Japan?"

Chiyoko didn't respond. Her silence was deafening, and Peter could see the weight of unspoken truths behind her eyes. Stunned, he turned and left, unable to stomach the situation any longer.

The next day, Chiyoko had arranged to meet Peter at Mae's restaurant for lunch. She fidgeted nervously as she folded and unfolded a letter she had spent the night writing. Her hands trembled with the weight of the truth it held—decades of a secret she was finally ready to reveal.

Chiyoko left for the restaurant earlier than planned, unable to wait at home. Her thoughts swirled as she rehearsed how she might break the news. She clutched the letter tightly as though the paper might give her courage.

As she turned the corner onto the street leading to the restaurant, a sleek black town car slowed beside her. The door opened, and two sharply dressed men stepped out. Their suits were immaculate, but the tattoos peeking from under their sleeves betrayed their ties to the Yakuza. Chiyoko froze in her tracks.

"Mrs. Tanaka," one of them said in a cold, dark tone.

Chiyoko stepped back instinctively. "Please," she said quickly, her voice shaking. "We need more time—we'll get the money."

Her plea was cut short as one of the men grabbed her from behind by the arms, yanking her back. The other stepped closer, drawing a gleaming knife and pressing it to her throat.

"You're the first," he hissed, his tone venomous. "If we don't get our money, your son will be next."

"Don't... please..." Chiyoko's voice was barely audible as tears filled her eyes. She thought of Peter, waiting for her at the restaurant, and the letter she held in her hand. She tried to twist away, but the man held her firmly.

Without another word, the knife moved. A sharp, sickening slice cut through the air, and Chiyoko collapsed to the ground, clutching at her neck as blood poured from the wound.

Peter was running late, guilt already nagging at him as he jogged toward Mae's restaurant. As he neared the dirt driveway beside the building, he noticed a figure lying motionless. His steps faltered, his stomach knotting with dread.

"Mom?" he called hesitantly, quickening his pace. When he saw her, everything around him blurred.

"Mom!" Peter dropped to his knees beside her, his hands shaking as he gently lifted her head. Her face was pale, and her breath came in shallow gasps.

"No, no, no," he murmured, his voice breaking. "Mom, stay with me. I'm here. I'm here."

Chiyoko's eyes fluttered open. She struggled to focus on his face, her lips moving soundlessly. Her trembling hand reached out, clutching something—her letter. She pressed it weakly into Peter's hand before her arm fell limp.

"Mom, no—stay with me! Please!" Peter cried, his tears falling onto her blood-stained dress. He cradled her in his arms, rocking back and forth, but her breathing slowed until it stopped entirely. Chiyoko's body went still.

"Mom!" Peter shouted, his voice raw and desperate. "No! You can't... You can't leave me!"

He clutched the letter, now marked with her blood, as sobs racked his body. Shaking, he unfolded it, his eyes scanning the words through blurred vision. As he read, his tears turned to shock, then confusion.

"Jason... Jason's my brother?" Peter whispered, his voice hoarse. "How... how is that even possible?"

His grief and the revelation collided violently in his mind. Jason, his best friend, was family—but the truth only deepened the pain. His mother was gone, and Peter was left to piece together a lifetime of secrets and loss.

CHAPTER 25

Promises in The Fog

The forests of the Vosges Mountains were a living nightmare. The trees loomed like silent sentinels, their twisted branches clawing through the thick fog that clung to everything. The air was damp and heavy with the metallic scent of rain and blood.

Jason adjusted his helmet, his fingers trembling slightly despite the calm determination etched on his face. The weight of his rifle, now as much a part of him as his limbs, rested heavily on his shoulder. He glanced to his right, where Ren crouched against the trunk of a tree. The rhythmic scrape of Ren's knife against a whetstone echoed faintly in the oppressive quiet, a metronome counting down the minutes to battle.

Jason broke the silence, his voice low but tinged with dry humor. "Ren, are you sharpening that knife for the Germans or just your nerves?"

Ren smirked without looking up. "Both," he replied simply, his tone casual, though the tightness in his jaw betrayed the tension simmering beneath the surface.

Junior trudged over, his boots squelching noisily in the muck. He carried himself with an air of authority, but there was an edge to his movements—a stiffness that suggested exhaustion or maybe fear. He stopped a few feet away, wiping sweat from his brow with a filthy sleeve.

"Captain says we move in five," Junior announced. "This ridge won't take itself."

Ren let out a low whistle, his knife pausing mid-stroke. "Hell of a ridge to die on," he muttered, more to himself than anyone else.

Jason shot him a pointed look, his expression hardening. "Better us than the boys up there," he said firmly. "They're out of food, out of ammo. If we don't break through, they're done."

Nearby, Arthur was hunched over his gear, checking and rechecking the straps on his pack. Though his hands moved with the precision of habit, his face betrayed him—his eyes darted nervously. He knew he was the weakest of the group, and though the war had made him stronger, there was still a flicker of sensitivity in everything he did.

Jason caught his eye and gave him a reassuring nod. "You good, Arthur?"

Arthur swallowed hard. "Yeah," he said, though the word came out shaky. "Just... ready to get this over with."

Jason chuckled softly, a sound that didn't quite match the gravity of their situation. "Aren't we all."

Jason reached into his jacket then, his fingers brushing against the worn edges of a folded piece of paper tucked safely into his inner pocket. Ren, ever observant, noticed the movement and cocked an eyebrow.

"What's that?"

Jason hesitated momentarily, his fingers lingering on the paper as though it carried a weight beyond its physical form. Finally, he shrugged and pulled it out, holding it up briefly before tucking it back into his pocket. "A letter," he said simply. "For Peter. My best friend back home. Just in case."

Ren studied him, his smirk fading into something more serious. "You don't plan on needing it, do you?"

"Nobody plans for this kind of thing, Ren. Just... better safe than sorry."

Ren nodded slowly, his gaze dropping to the knife in his hand. He resumed sharpening it, the metal scrape filling the silence. "Fair enough," he murmured, leaving the subject to rest.

The unspoken understanding between them lingered in the air, heavy as the fog surrounding them. Jason glanced at the others—Ren, Junior, Arthur—and felt the strange mix of fear and resolve that always came before a fight. They were tired, battered, and scared. But they were here, together, and that would have to be enough.

"Two minutes!" came the call from Junior. The men exchanged brief, grim looks before rising to their feet. Jason adjusted his rifle, squared his shoulders, and took a deep breath.

"Let's go save those boys," he said, his voice steady.

The others nodded, and one by one, they stepped forward into the gray abyss, leaving behind their last moments of peace.

The climb was a waking nightmare. The hill loomed above them, steep and unforgiving, its surface churned into a treacherous bog by relentless artillery. Every step was a gamble. The smell of gunpowder and charred earth filled their lungs, mixing with the tang of sweat and fear. Visibility was reduced to a few miserable yards. The thick fog wrapped around them like a suffocating veil, hiding the deadly precision of the German defenses.

Mortars shrieked through the air like banshees before slamming into the earth, sending shards of shrapnel and chunks of mud flying in every direction. Machine guns raked the hillside, their shots bursting, tearing through the battle. Men screamed, their voices high and desperate, lost in the chaos. Some cries stopped abruptly—cut off by death. Others lingered, agonizing reminders of those who hadn't been lucky enough to die quickly.

"Keep moving!" Jason's voice rang out, sharp and commanding. But even he sounded frayed, his words edged with desperation.

Jason and Ren were at the front, hunched low as they pushed forward, their rifles clutched tightly in their hands. The world around them was chaos—a storm of noise and violence that threatened to drown them at any moment. Then, without warning, a burst of machine-gun fire erupted ahead.

"Down!" Jason roared, shoving Ren to the ground as the bullets chewed through the trees and earth around them. Splinters of wood rained down as the machine gun tore into the forest, slicing apart anything in its path.

Behind them, a sharp cry rang out. Jason whipped around to see Junior stumble, his foot catching on a hidden root. He went down hard, tumbling awkwardly down the slope. The crack of his leg snapping was sickeningly loud, even over the chaos of the battle.

"Junior!" Jason shouted, panic lacing his voice. He made to move toward him, but a fresh volley of gunfire erupted, forcing him to dive for cover. The deafening rat-a-tat of the machine gun drowned out all other sounds.

"Damn it," Ren swore, slamming his fist into the ground. "We're pinned!"

Jason's eyes darted between Junior, writhing in agony a dozen yards down the slope, and the ridge ahead. He could see the faint silhouette of the machine gunner through the fog, the barrel flashing as it spat death into their ranks.

"He's not gonna make it if we don't do something!" Jason shouted over the gunfire.

Ren gritted his teeth, his jaw tight. "If you go, you're dead, Jason! That thing's locked in on us!"

Jason didn't respond. His mind raced as he scanned the chaos, his hands gripping his rifle so tightly that his knuckles turned white. Another scream cut through the fog—a soldier somewhere to their left, torn apart by a mortar blast.

"Cover me!" Jason barked, not waiting for a reply. He broke into a low sprint, weaving through the trees as the machine gun adjusted its aim. Bullets whizzed past him, one so close he felt the heat of it graze his cheek.

"Jason, you crazy son of a bitch!" Ren yelled, rising just enough to fire off a few shots toward the enemy position. His rounds pinged uselessly against the metal shield of the machine gun, but it was enough to force the gunner to duck for a moment.

Junior clawed at the mud, his nails digging into the wet earth as he tried to drag himself forward. The pain in his leg was unbearable, a fiery, searing agony that shot up his body with every movement. His breath came in shallow gasps, each more desperate than the last. He looked down at his leg and felt his stomach in his throat—it was twisted grotesquely, the bone jutting unnaturally beneath the skin.

The sound of footsteps crunching through the muck froze him in place. He turned his head slowly, the hairs on the back of his neck standing on end. A German soldier emerged from the fog, his uniform dark and smeared with mud. The man's rifle was already raised, and the barrel pointed directly at Junior's head. The soldier's expression was cold and emotionless, his eyes narrowing as his finger moved to the trigger.

Time seemed to stretch, every second dragging out into an eternity. Junior's heart thundered in his chest, his mind racing as he stared down the barrel of the rifle. This was it. He was going to die here, alone and helpless. His hands trembled as he tried to reach for his weapon, but it was useless—his rifle was out of reach, and even if he had it, he wouldn't be fast enough.

The crack of a rifle shot shattered the stillness, deafening in the foggy quiet. Junior flinched, his body tensing as he waited for the pain to hit, but it didn't come. Instead, the German soldier staggered, his eyes wide with shock. A red bloom spread across his chest, soaking through his uniform as he fell onto his back with a thud.

Junior blinked, still holding his breath. He looked up to see Arthur stepping out of the fog, his rifle still raised, a thin wisp of smoke curling from the barrel.

"You okay?" Arthur asked, his voice calm but tinged with urgency as he scanned the area for more threats.

Junior's chest heaved as he tried to catch his breath. "I... I think my leg's broken," he gasped. "I can't stand."

Arthur moved quickly as he knelt beside Junior. His movements were efficiently practiced, but his expression was tight with worry. He glanced down at Junior's leg, his mouth pressing into a grim line.

"Yeah, that's broken," Arthur said bluntly. "You're not walking out of here."

Junior shook his head, panic rising in his voice. "I'll just stay here. Someone will come back for me."

Arthur's eyes narrowed, and his voice turned sharp. "Not an option, Junior. You stay here, and you're dead."

Junior's face twisted, his discomfort shifting into something deeper—shame or maybe fear. "I'm fine," he muttered, his tone defensive. "I'll wait."

Arthur exhaled sharply, his patience wearing thin. "Listen to me, you stubborn ass. It's not contagious." He leaned closer, his eyes locking onto Junior's. "You don't have to like me. Hell, you don't even have to respect me. But I'm not leaving you here to die, so shut up and let me save your life."

Junior hesitated, his face a mix of anger, fear, and something else—maybe regret. The sound of German shouts in the distance snapped him out of it, and he gave a reluctant nod.

"Fine," he muttered. "But just... hurry."

Arthur wasted no time. He grabbed Junior under the arms and hoisted him onto his back, grunting slightly as he adjusted the weight.

Resting for a moment, Junior spoke, his voice tight with emotion. "Why'd you come back for me? You could've just... kept going."

Arthur grunted, his tone matter-of-fact. "Because that's what we do. We don't leave anyone behind. We're on the same team."

Junior fell silent, his head hung low. The shame that had burned in him earlier was still there, but it was dulled now, replaced by something he couldn't quite name. Maybe gratitude. Maybe a sense of respect.

As the sounds of battle raged around them, Arthur continued his rescue, one step at a time.

Meanwhile, Jason and Ren pressed forward. The final ridge loomed ahead, a brutal stretch of terrain where the German defenses dug in deep. Mortars shrieked overhead, slamming into the earth and leaving craters filled with bodies and shattered limbs.

"Stay close!" Jason barked, his voice hoarse from shouting over the havoc. His rifle roared, cutting down a German soldier who had popped up from a foxhole.

Ren was a shadow beside him, his movements sharp and practiced. His rifle barked with precision, each shot punching through the chaos with deadly intent. "We're not gonna make it if we don't clear that ridge soon!" Ren shouted.

Jason didn't answer immediately. Machine gun fire shot around them, forcing them to dive into a shallow ditch.

"We don't have a choice!" Jason growled, shoving a fresh clip into his rifle. "If we stop now, those bastards up there die hungry and alone. Move!"

They scrambled up the slope, their boots slipping in the blood-slick mud. The screams of their fallen brothers echoed behind them, guttural cries that would haunt their dreams. Jason's focus narrowed to the trench ahead, a jagged line in the earth where the last of the German defense held strong.

They reached it together, breathless and battered, their weapons snapping up instinctively. Jason fired first, his rifle's deafening bark cutting down a German soldier who had raised his own weapon too late. Ren followed, his blade flashing as he drove it into another soldier.

The trench was chaos. Bodies piled against the walls, some still twitching, their lifeblood pooling in the filth. Jason moved with relentless purpose, his rifle an extension of himself. Every shot was precise, and every movement was calculated.

At the far end of the trench, Jason turned to Ren, a flicker of triumph lighting his eyes. "We did it!" he shouted. "Ren, we—"

The sharp crack of a sniper's rifle cut him off mid-sentence. Jason's body jolted violently as the bullet tore through his chest, the force of the impact sending him staggering. His eyes widened in shock as he crumpled to his knees, his rifle slipping from his fingers and landing in the muck.

"Jason!" Ren roared, dropping to his side. He pressed his hands against the wound.

Jason's lips moved, his voice barely audible over the chaos. Ren leaned closer as he struggled to hear. "Ren... my pocket," Jason rasped, his eyes locking onto his friend's. "The letter... for Peter."

Ren's hands trembled as he fumbled for the letter, pulling it free from Jason's jacket. It was crumpled and damp with blood, the ink smeared but still legible. "You're gonna deliver it yourself, Jason. You just have to hold on, okay? You hear me? Hold on!"

Jason coughed. Blood at the corner of his mouth. "No... you have to," he said, his voice weaker now, each word a struggle. "Tell him... I forgive him. We're still brothers... always."

Tears blurred Ren's vision as he clutched the letter, his head shaking in denial. "I promise," he whispered, his voice cracking under the weight of his grief. "I swear, I'll tell him."

Jason's lips curled into a faint, bittersweet smile. His chest hitched once, twice, and then, in his last breath, he whispered, "Go for broke." His hand, which had been clutching Ren's arm, fell limp.

Ren sat frozen, the battlefield noise receding into a distant hum. For a moment, the world around him ceased to exist, his focus entirely on Jason's lifeless form. Gently, almost reverently, Ren laid his friend down, smoothing the fabric of his uniform.

He rose slowly, the letter clenched tightly in his hand. His expression was a mask of fury and grief, his body trembling with the weight of his loss. The roar of the battle crashed back into focus, and Ren turned, Jason's rifle now slung over his shoulder.

"For you, Jason," Ren muttered, his voice low and deadly.

With that, he moved forward into the chaos, his steps steady and purposeful, the promise to his fallen friend driving him forward into battle.

Arthur and Junior were among the first to stumble into the clearing where the Lost Battalion huddled, their breaths ragged and shallow. The men they found were little more than shadows of soldiers—gaunt and hollow-eyed, their uniforms hanging loosely from their bodies. Some were slumped against trees, rifles resting limply in their laps, while others stood guard with a desperate determination that betrayed their exhaustion.

"What the hell?" Arthur muttered, his voice barely above a whisper as he took in the scene. He tightened his grip on Junior, who was still slung over his back, his broken leg wrapped in a crude splint. "They look half-dead."

Junior, pale and sweating from the pain, managed a weak nod. "Yeah... but they're alive. That's what matters."

One of the trapped men, a lieutenant whose face was streaked with grime, staggered forward. His eyes, bloodshot and sunken, lit up at the sight of Arthur and Junior. "Reinforcements?" he rasped, his voice cracked and dry.

Arthur nodded, his expression grim. "What's left of us. We're here to get you out."

The lieutenant's face crumpled with relief, and he reached out to clasp Arthur's shoulder. "Thank God. We thought... we thought they'd given up on us."

Ren arrived moments later, emerging from the trees. His face was set, his eyes dark and unreadable, his rifle still gripped tightly. He didn't speak as he took in the battered soldiers, his gaze flicking briefly to Junior before settling on Arthur.

"Let's move," Ren said, his voice low but commanding. He didn't wait for a response; instead, he stepped forward to help one of the weaker men to his feet.

Arthur glanced at him, catching the tension in his face, the hollowness in his eyes. "Jason?" he began, but Ren cut him off with a sharp shake of his head.

"Not now," Ren said. "We need to get these men out of here before the Germans regroup."

Together, they began the slow, agonizing march back down the hill. The terrain that had been treacherous on the way up was now covered in debris. The survivors leaned heavily on their rescuers, their movements sluggish and mechanical, their minds numb from days of fear and hunger.

Arthur gritted his teeth as he adjusted Junior's weight on his back. "You okay back there?" he asked, his voice strained.

Junior let out a dry chuckle that turned into a wince. "I've been better. But hey, at least I'm not doing the walking."

Arthur smirked despite himself. "Yeah, lucky me."

The forest around them was now quiet, the echoes of gunfire replaced by the groans of wounded men. Ren walked at the rear, his steps steady but heavy, his mind consumed by the weight in his pocket. The letter felt impossibly heavy, as though it carried all the grief and guilt he hadn't allowed himself to feel. Jason's voice echoed in his mind, a haunting reminder of the promise he had made.

Ren's gaze drifted to the gray skies above, the clouds thick and unmoving. His fingers brushed against the pocket where the letter rested. The words Jason had spoken before he died replayed over and over, each one cutting deeper than any wound.

"I'll get it to him, I swear," Ren whispered, his voice barely audible over the sound of trudging boots. His grip on his rifle tightened as he forced himself to keep moving.

Arthur caught the whisper, glancing over his shoulder. For a moment, their eyes met, and something unspoken passed between them. Arthur nodded, understanding without needing to ask.

The march continued in silence, each man bearing the weight of all that had transpired. The forest, though battered and broken, stood as a solemn witness to their struggle, its branches reaching skyward as if in mourning for those who would never leave its depths.

By the time they reached safety, the survivors of the Lost Battalion were barely conscious, their relief overshadowed by sheer exhaustion. Ren, Arthur, and Junior stood among the chaos of medics, their faces etched with weariness. As the last of the rescued men were taken away, Ren reached into his pocket, his fingers brushing the letter one more time.

"We got them out," Arthur said quietly, his voice tinged with both pride and sorrow.

Ren nodded but said nothing, his thoughts elsewhere. He stared into the distance, the letter a constant reminder of the promise he still had to fulfill.

Members of the 442nd Regimental Combat Team escort survivors of the Lost Battalion to safety after their rescue in the Vosges Mountains, France, October 1944. Public domain, U.S. Army Signal Corps.

CHAPTER 26

Echoes of The Past

The late afternoon sun poured its golden hues into Aunty Mae's living room, transforming the space into a warm bath of light and shadows. Peter, sitting in the overstuffed armchair that had once been his mother's cherished favorite, cradled a steaming cup of tea. Between him and Mae, on the low wooden table, a delicate sakura teapot gleamed under the light, its single cherry blossom imprint sparkling as if clutching the day's last moment.

Peter's face, usually vibrant and full of life, was now pale, visibly drained by sleepless nights and the depths of his grief. "I still can't believe she's gone," he murmured, his voice so soft it was almost swallowed by the quiet of the room. "I keep thinking she'll walk through that door with her smile... her warm, comforting smile that always seemed to light up the room."

Mae, her own face a mask of calm composure, poured herself a cup of tea. Her movements were slow, deliberate, almost meditative. "Your mother was a remarkable woman," she began, her voice steady but her eyes distant, lost in memories. "She possessed a strength that most of us can only dream of." Mae paused, taking a deep breath as if the next words required a feat of courage. "There's something you need to know, Peter. Something she wanted you to understand before she passed. It's about Jason."

Peter's eyes, red and raw from his tears, widened slightly. He placed a worn letter on the table—a letter his mother had handed him, filled with revelations never spoken. "I know... Jason is my brother. But how? How is that possible?"

"It is possible," Mae confirmed, her voice a blend of sorrow and resolve. "Your father, Kosuke... he... he forced himself on me years ago, on the boat that brought us here from Japan. That's how Jason came to be." Her eyes shimmered with the threat of tears, a testament to the pain of the past. "I've carried this secret for so long, but your mother knew. She helped me raise Jason and loved him in her own way. She was stronger than I could ever be."

Peter's hands clenched into fists. His entire body tensed as if to brace against a physical blow. "No," he whispered, shaking his head violently. "No, you're wrong. Jason... Jason's just a friend, not my brother. My father..." His voice trailed off, choked by anger as the truth set in. "My father is a monster."

Mae reached out, her hand trembling as she placed it gently over his. "Hate won't bring you peace, Peter. I've learned that the hard way. I hated your father for what he did to me, hated him so much I nearly lost myself to it. But your mother... she saved me. She showed me that there can be salvation even in the worst times. And from the darkest moments, sometimes, the greatest blessings emerge."

Peter jerked his hand away, his eyes stormy, his jaw set hard. "How can you expect me to forgive him? He's the reason she's dead. And now Jason... he doesn't even know the truth. He's off fighting in France. I can't even tell him."

Mae's expression softened her voice, a whisper of hope amidst the turmoil. "When Jason returns, we will tell him together. We'll face this, finally, as a family."

As Peter's anger faded, replaced by an overwhelming sorrow, his shoulders slumped. Mae handed him a napkin, her touch light. They sat in silence. The room filled only with the gentle ticking of the clock and the soft clinking of the tea set as the sun dipped below the horizon, taking its light and leaving shadows to fill the spaces between them.

In the fading light of the day, Mae gently lifted the sakura teapot, its porcelain surface catching the last rays of the sun. "Do you recognize this, Peter?" she asked, holding the artifact with a reverence that filled the air with an unspoken history.

Peter peered at the teapot, his thoughts tangled with grief and confusion. "It seems familiar, but I can't place it."

Mae's lips curled into a wistful smile as she cradled the teapot closer. "Your mother bought this from a young potter in Yokohama. She was no older than you are now. She gave him a gold coin for it—more money than I'd ever seen. She was moved by his love for his wife, a love so profound that it touched her deeply. She envied them." Mae's voice grew softer, more reflective. "She envied their freedom to love, something she knew her status would never allow. Bound by tradition and the expectations of arranged marriages, your mother longed for a love that was truly her own—a choice denied to her and possibly a future you might face someday."

"Why are you telling me this now?" Peter's brow furrowed, his voice tinged with a mix of curiosity and sadness.

Mae extended the teapot towards him. "Because it's yours now," she declared, her tone solemn. "Your mother wanted you to have it, to remember that real love, the kind she yearned for but could never fully embrace, is worth fighting for. She believed in the power of chosen love over those made by others."

Taking the teapot, Peter traced his fingers over the smooth outline of the cherry blossom.

A week later, he stood by his mother's grave near the Byodo-in Buddhist temple in Kahalu'u. This place, though reflective of a faith not her own, had always brought her peace, perhaps reminding her of a home that once was, now out of reach across the ocean.

The funeral had been a somber affair, attended by many who respected and loved Chiyoko. Yet, as the crowd began to disperse, a sleek black town car pulled up, shattering the reflective atmosphere. Kosuke, his father, emerged flanked by two bodyguards, his presence like a dark cloud over the day's mourning.

Fury ignited within Peter, raw and uncontainable. He charged, his voice erupting in a violent outburst. "You bastard! How could you show your face here? I'll kill you!" His grief had morphed into a fierce rage.

The bodyguards intercepted him swiftly. One grabbed around his arms while the other pressed a cold, threatening knife to his throat. "Go on then, do it! Kill me!" Peter screamed, spit flying. "I've got nothing left to live for. You might as well finish it!"

Kosuke watched with icy detachment. "Your rage will serve you well," he remarked coldly. "Harness it because you'll need it to lead. I'm preparing you to take over, whether you like it or not."

Despite his struggles, Peter was thrown to the ground, his body slamming against the dirt. Kosuke's chilling gaze lingered for a moment before he retreated to the safety of his car. As it drove away, Peter lay face down, his body battered, his spirit crushed, yet a vow formed in his mind— one day, I will be the man who takes your life.

Months had dragged by, each weighed down by the unresolved tension between Peter and his father. After being diagnosed with a rare and aggressive neurological disorder, Kosuke's health rapidly deteriorated. Initially manifesting as mere headaches and brief moments of confusion, the symptoms quickly escalated to severe cognitive decline, culminating in a devastating stroke that left him comatose, tethered to the life-sustaining hum of hospital machines.

The repeated calls from the hospital finally pierced Peter's wall of reluctance. Each ring was a stark reminder of Mae's wise counsel. "Go," Mae had urged, her voice blending concern with wisdom. "Find a way to forgive him, or that hate will destroy you."

Now, standing in the sterile quiet of the hospital room, Peter gazed down at the withered figure of Kosuke. The man who had once loomed over his nightmares was now just a frail shell, his existence maintained by the relentless beeping of machines that monitored his fading vital signs.

Overwhelmed, Peter slumped into the chair beside the bed, burying his face in his hands as he wrestled with his emotions. His thoughts were interrupted by a gentle tap on his shoulder, prompting him to look up. Before him stood a young woman whose presence was strikingly breathtaking; her beauty was undeniable—not merely in her physical appearance, with her soft, almond-shaped eyes and the graceful way her sleek black hair cascaded in gentle waves—but in her composed and deliberate movements, which radiated a soothing grace.

"I'm sorry to disturb you," she said, her voice soft yet assured, drawing Peter further from his somewhat embarrassing jaw-dropping moment. "Are you Peter?"

He nodded, finding himself at a loss for words, captivated by her calm and caring demeanor. "Y-yes. Who are you?"

"I'm your father's nurse," she responded. "If you need anything, please don't hesitate to ask. I'm here to help."

Her professional demeanor suggested that she was comfortable navigating complex emotional situations, asserting a quiet yet firm presence that demanded both sensitivity and strength. This combination of traits struck Peter as profoundly attractive.

Peter cleared his throat, striving to find composure. "Thank you. I... I'm just trying to figure out what to do next."

The nurse nodded understandingly. "It's a difficult decision that no one is ever truly prepared for. If you'd like, I can sit with you for a while or give you some time alone to think."

Her offer, delivered with sincere warmth, made Peter feel less isolated within the cold, clinical room. "Could you... Could you stay for a bit?" he asked quietly.

"Of course," she answered, pulling up a chair beside him. As she settled in, she spoke about the medical aspects of Kosuke's condition in a gentle tone, her explanations clear and thoughtful, her movements fluid and graceful, each gesture reinforcing her words.

After a brief pause, she added softly as she stood to leave, "Please don't hesitate to contact me if you need anything. If you can't find me, I won't be far. My name is Kimi."

CHAPTER 27

Bound by Choice

In the sterile quiet of the hospital, Peter often found himself at his father's bedside, the relentless beeping of life support machines punctuating the heavy silence. These sounds underscored the unresolved tensions, much like the oppressive, stale air that hung over the ward. His father, Kosuke, remained immobile, his existence tethered to the life-sustaining machinery. Against this cold, clinical backdrop, it was Kimi's kindness and empathy that brought Peter solace during his frequent visits.

One evening, tucked away in a secluded alcove far from the hospital's constant activity, Peter's voice carried a sense of vulnerability. "Kimi," he began, hesitating, his gaze not quite meeting hers, "I'm faced with a decision about... about my father." The weight of his confession filled the space between them.

Kimi, sensing the deep turmoil stirring within him, placed a reassuring hand on his arm. "What about him?"

He sighed heavily, a sound laden with dread. "The doctors... they've said there's no chance for recovery. They suggested that it might be time to... to let him go." His voice broke with the gravity of the decision.

Kimi's expression softened, her voice gentle and full of compassion. "That must be incredibly difficult for you, Peter."

"It's more than just a decision. My father was responsible for my mother's death. It was his actions that led to her being murdered." The bitterness in his tone was heavy as he spoke the harsh truth.

Kimi's eyes widened. "Peter, that's terrible. I can't even begin to imagine how you must feel."

Turning away, his gaze lost in painful memories, Peter continued, "I've despised him for so long. Now, to pull the plug—it feels too merciful, too gentle for someone as horrible as him. It feels like I'm letting him off too easily."

Listening intently, Kimi moved closer, her presence offering warmth in the stark reality of the hospital. "Carrying this burden won't bring you peace. Maybe letting go is less about what he deserves and more about freeing yourself."

Peter's eyes met hers. "How do you always know what to say?" he asked.

Kimi offered a sad smile. "I don't always, but I've seen enough to know that holding onto pain can poison your soul. Letting him go might be how you find your own peace."

He nodded slowly, her words beginning to soothe the turmoil within. "It's just so hard, knowing it's all in my hands. I wish things were different. I wish he had been different."

Kimi squeezed his hand, her voice a soft echo of strength. "I know. But this is your chance to end the cycle of pain. It's your path to healing."

Peter exhaled deeply, feeling a slight easing of his burden under Kimi's empathy. "Thank you, Kimi. For listening, for being here."

As they walked back to the nurses' station, their steps slow and measured, Peter felt a flicker of resolve stir within him. Kimi's words had provided a refreshing perspective, hinting at forgiveness, or at least acceptance, and a path forward from the shadows of his past.

Each visit to the hospital deepened his connection to Kimi. The hospital corridors, with their relentless beeps and muffled announcements, seemed to recede into the background when they were together, replaced by a sanctuary of shared understanding and feelings. As they sat side by side in a nearby courtyard, watching the sunset, their conversation turned to memories steeped in nostalgia.

Kimi's voice brightened with excitement, her eyes reflecting the vibrant hues of the sky. "Peter, did you know I grew up on the North Shore, too? On the Wailua Sugar Plantation. There's a beach access at the end of the service road that runs through the plantation. Do you know it?"

A spark of recognition lit Peter's face, and he turned towards her. "Yes, I played baseball near there as a kid with the plantation teams. I can't believe our paths might have crossed back then."

"I have an idea. Meet me there, at that beach, tomorrow?" Kimi suggested, her voice vibrant with excitement, casting aside all concerns for social norms.

Peter nodded, his smile slow but sincere. "I'd like that," he said. "It'll be like discovering a piece of our history together." The idea of intertwining their past with the promise of a shared future seemed to warm the day.

Kimi reached out, her hand lightly touching his. "Maybe we'll find an old baseball that made its way to the sand."

Under a sky with the tender blush of dusk, Kimi and Peter sat on the sand, reminiscing about their childhood memories.

"Peter, this place..." Kimi's voice was a soft murmur, her eyes scanning the horizon where the ocean seemed to kiss the sky.

"It's where miracles happen. And now, with you here, it feels like I'm experiencing another one."

As the sun began to set, bathing the ocean in a stunning display of gold and crimson, they sat side by side on the soft, sandy shore. Their toes playfully touched, mingling beneath the gentle caress of the waves that lapped softly at their feet.

"Do you remember the day we first met in the hospital?" Kimi asked.

Peter smiled, the warmth of the memory spreading through him. "How could I forget? Everything was so cold and dark, and there you were—a light full of warmth and hope."

"You seemed so strong, even in such a difficult time, but I could see you needed someone."

"That day," Peter said, his voice thick with emotion, "you brought peace to my world. Being with you just felt like... home."

Kimi reached out, her hand finding his beneath the shallow surf. Peter turned to face her more directly, his hand tenderly brushing a lock of hair from her face. The last rays of the sun danced in her eyes, adding a celestial glow to the moment.

Peter leaned in, his breath tinged with a mix of strength and nervous anticipation. Kimi, feeling the gravity of the moment, closed her eyes, surrendering to the sensation. She felt his hand move to cradle the back of her head gently. As their lips met, she tasted the salt on his, the sea's essence blending with their own.

Slowly, Kimi leaned back, pulling Peter into the soft, wet sand with her. The weight of his body on hers was a comforting pressure, a protective embrace she had longed for. In that moment, their kiss deepened further, fueled by the pent-up passion and the exhilarating danger of their forbidden love.

Their kiss deepened, igniting every sense. Wrapped in each other's arms, with the ocean water washing over their entwined legs, they lost themselves in a passionate embrace that spoke of deep longing for each other. The cool breeze mingled with their heated breaths, crafting an intensely romantic atmosphere that seemed lifted from the pages of a romance novel.

In that perfect, stolen moment, their passion was a beacon, shining brighter than the last light of day, speaking a language of love so profound that words could not do it justice.

There, in the embrace of the incoming tide and under the emerging stars, they held each other, the ocean's gentle rhythm promising new beginnings and unspoken promises.

The romantic moment was abruptly disrupted by the sound of someone clearing his throat just up the beach. Startled, they turned to find Ren standing a few feet away, his figure outlined against the dimming light. He was dressed in his crisply pressed military uniform, the medals gleaming faintly in the light of dusk, his expression a complex tapestry of hurt and betrayal.

"The war is over," Ren's voice broke the heavy silence, each word heavier than the last, laden with the weight of battle-worn exhaustion and unexpected heartache.

Kimi and Peter jolted from their intimate embrace and quickly scrambled to their feet. Kimi's heart skipped a beat at the sight of Ren. For a fleeting moment, she forgot about Peter and started to run toward Ren. But Ren quickly raised his hand and shouted, "No. This was not the homecoming I expected. How could you?"

Tears began to form in Kimi's eyes as her emotions threatened to spill over. Every day before she had met Peter, Ren was always on her mind and worries. Now he was home, and he wanted nothing to do with her. Confusion and sorrow swirled within her. "Ren, I'm sorry..." she managed to say, her voice trembling.

Peter, hearing her apology, felt a pang of worry. Why was she sorry, he thought.

Ren continued, his voice a mix of anger and disbelief, "I stopped by our house first. When you weren't there, I knew I'd find you here. I knew this was your special place. But to come here and see this... I'm doing all I can to prove my loyalty to our country, and to speak of loyalty, and find this. How could you?"

Peter, ever the peacemaker, stepped forward, his voice steady but filled with a nervous desire to ease the tension. Extending a hand, he introduced himself, "I'm Peter."

Ren's reaction was startled as he heard the name. "What did you say your name was?"

"I'm Peter."

"Sure you are, and I bet your best friend's name is Jason."

The air thickened with confusion—Peter stunned, Kimi confused, and Ren, standing there, lost for words.

Peter clarified, trying to bridge the gap between them, "Actually, Jason is more than my best friend. He's my brother."

Ren's demeanor shifted slightly, though his anger lingered. He remembered the heavy promise he carried. "Kimi, I'm still angry, but the message I must deliver is much more important."

"What message? Is Jason okay? Is he home?" Peter asked, a sudden dread filling his voice.

Ren's heart sank as he reached into his pocket. His fingers found the letter. Though it was worn and weathered, still smeared with Jason's blood, he handed it solemnly to Peter.

As Peter read the letter, his knees buckled, grief washing over him in an unforgiving wave. Ren crouched down beside him. "Jason was a good man and friend, and he wanted me to tell you that he forgives you and that you will always be his brother." Overwhelmed by the magnitude of the news, Peter buried his face in his hands and began to sob.

Ren turned to walk away, but Kimi ran after him. Turning back to her, Ren faced Kimi's pleading eyes. "What do I do?" she asked desperately.

"You need to choose," Ren replied.

Looking back at Peter, holding the blood-stained letter from Jason, kneeling in the sand, and then at Ren, who stood tall and proud in his uniform, transformed from a boy to a man by war and loss, Kimi made her decision. "I will always love you, but as my brother and nothing more. I'm sorry." With those final words, she turned and ran back to comfort Peter.

Understanding her choice, Ren accepted it with a heavy heart. He knew that if Peter was Jason's best friend, he must be a good man. With a deep sigh, he reached into the same pocket that had carried the letter and pulled out the picture of Kimi that had brought him comfort during his darkest times. After one last look, he dropped it in the sand and walked away, never looking back.

Later that evening, Peter lay on his bed, fingers interlaced behind his head, staring blankly at the ceiling. The day's weight pressed heavily on him, his thoughts consumed by Jason's letter. The realization that Jason had died without ever knowing they were brothers gnawed at him, an ache that seemed to cut deeper with every passing moment. Yet, amid the grief, a fragile sense of hope stirred within him. Kimi had chosen him over Ren—a person she had known her entire life. Somehow, her choice felt like a light breaking through the shadows of his loss. It was a quiet miracle, an act that began to fill the void he had carried for so long, a void he thought might never be healed.

A gentle knock at the door broke his concentration. He sat up, his stomach lurching as unease rippled through him. Who could it be? For a fleeting moment, he feared it might be Aunty Mae, and the thought of delivering the news of Jason's death to his mother was more than he could bear in his fragile state.

"One minute, please. I'm coming," he called out. Rising slowly, Peter crossed the room, his mind racing with possibilities as he reached for the door. Taking a deep, steady breath, he opened it.

Standing there, bathed in the soft glow of the hallway light, was Kimi, dressed in an exquisite traditional kimono. Peter froze, utterly stunned. The sight of her was mesmerizing. The delicate bamboo comb nestled in her hair, the flawless precision of her makeup, and the perfect folds of her silk kimono—all of it was elegance and reverence for a tradition older than them. She looked like a vision, an embodiment of timeless grace and beauty.

Kimi tilted her head, an amused smile playing on her lips. "Are you going to just stare, or will you let me in?" she said.

Peter swallowed hard, nodded, and stepped aside, barely able to string together a coherent response.

As she entered, Kimi covered her mouth to stifle a light giggle. The soft rustling of her kimono fabric echoed in the quiet space, each sound heightening the tension in the room. Her eyes moved with quiet purpose as she surveyed the apartment until they landed on a low table and two floor pads that Peter's mother had once insisted he keep to honor tradition. Though Peter had never used them, they seemed destined for something profound tonight.

Kimi gestured for him to kneel at the table, her movements speaking volumes without needing words. There was an unspoken intimacy in her gestures, a quiet but unmistakable command. Peter followed her lead, feeling strangely vulnerable yet profoundly drawn to her presence.

She began gathering the utensils she had brought, arranging them meticulously. Her every movement carried a delicate precision, a reverence that made the air in the room feel charged. As she worked, her gaze fell upon a teapot on the counter. Its intricate design, with a subtle sakura blossom etched into its surface, held her attention. She lifted it, turning to Peter, silently asking for permission. He nodded in agreement.

With the teapot in hand, Kimi began the tea ceremony. Though she had never performed one herself, she often watched Aunty Emi perform the ritual for her husband, Nobu. It was a gesture of deep love and respect, a way of expressing emotions too profound for words. That night, Kimi poured that same devotion into her every movement.

She turned off the lights and lit candles instead. Their soft, flickering glow cast a golden hue over the room, transforming the ordinary space into something sacred and intimate. The crimson silk cloth she unfolded shimmered faintly in the candlelight as she methodically cleaned each tool. Her hands moved in a steady rhythm, each gesture deliberate, each motion steeped in meaning.

Peter knelt silently, his eyes fixed on her. The elegance of her movements and the calm she brought into the room were unlike anything he had ever experienced. The tension in the air thickened, not with unease but with a magnetic pull that seemed to bind them closer. The faint scent of matcha began to fill the room as steam curled upward from the teapot. The earthy aroma mingled with the faint perfume she wore, a subtle, intoxicating blend that made his heart beat faster.

Kimi whisked the vibrant green powder into a frothy surface, the soft sound of the bamboo whisk against the bowl filling the silence with its soothing rhythm. When the tea was ready, she turned to Peter, holding the bowl with both hands. Her eyes met his, and time seemed to stop at that moment.

The weight of the day, the loss, the grief—it all fell away as he became very aware of her, just her.

She extended the bowl with quiet reverence, inviting him to share in this ritual. Peter accepted it carefully, his fingers brushing against hers briefly, sending an electric current through him. He turned the bowl twice before drinking, as tradition dictated. The warmth of the tea and its earthy richness grounded him.

Kimi's hands trembled ever so slightly as he handed the bowl back, a fleeting crack in her composure. Her vulnerability was evident, and it mirrored the tenderness he felt for her. She resumed cleaning the utensils with the same care and precision, yet her movements had a sense of finality. The ritual was ending, but the atmosphere lingered—heavy with emotion, unspoken yet profoundly felt.

The room was silent except for the faint hum of the city outside, but something unbreakable had formed between them in that silence. Kimi's act was more than a ceremony. It was a declaration, a quiet offering of her heart. And in Peter's chest, where grief and emptiness had dwelled, a new sense of belonging began to take root.

The couple knelt across from each other, locked eyes, each gaze heavy with unspoken emotion. The room seemed to dissolve around them, leaving only the weight of their connection. Peter felt tears trail silently down his cheeks. Finally, breaking the silence with a trembling voice, he whispered softly, "Domo arigatou gozaimasu" (Thank you so much).

Kimi didn't speak, only nodding in quiet acknowledgment. Her eyes shifted back to the teapot, her fingers tracing the delicate imprint of the sakura blossom etched into its surface. There was something deeply familiar about it that stirred a distant memory. She picked it up carefully, her hands reverent as they inspected its flawless craftsmanship. Her fingertips lingered over the engraving, and she murmured, almost to herself, "This is the most beautiful thing I have ever seen. How did you come to possess such a wonderful piece of art?"

Peter's voice softened further as he explained that it had belonged to his mother. He recounted how she had acquired the teapot long before his birth on the bustling docks of Yokohama. His words painted vivid scenes, a chance encounter, and the precious exchange that led the teapot into their family's care. Kimi's eyes widened as he spoke, her heart racing as recognition began to take hold.

Carefully, she turned the teapot in her hands, her breath catching as she slowly examined its base. The name inscribed there stopped her immediately—"Ikeda." Her fingers trembled, and a gasp escaped her lips as tears began to stream down her face.

Peter, alarmed by her reaction, leaned forward. "Kimi, what's the matter? Are you okay?"

She nodded shakily, fighting to steady herself, though her voice wavered as she spoke. "Peter, the name written on this pot... it's my last name. I am Kimiko Ikeda. My father was Namio, a humble potter who sold his work on the docks of Yokohama. He often spoke of a woman of great nobility who purchased his finest creation—a teapot he called his masterpiece—for one gold coin. It was through her generosity that my family was able to come to Hawaii. But soon after we arrived, my mother passed away from disease, and my father was killed during the bombing of Pearl Harbor. I have so little left of them... and now, here in my hands, I hold his last creation."

Peter reached out, his voice steady and warm. "I want you to have it," he said, gesturing to the teapot.

Kimi shook her head, overwhelmed. "No, I couldn't. This is too much of a gift."

"It isn't," Peter insisted. "It was never meant for me. Kimi, I love you. Please take it."

Her breath hitched, the words washing over her with a force she hadn't expected. Tears glistened in her eyes as she clutched the teapot closer. "I love you too," she whispered.

For Kimi, who had spent so much of her life caring for others, this moment felt like nothing she had ever known. The barriers she had built around her heart melted away in Peter's presence. Setting the teapot aside with trembling hands, she began to disrobe slowly, her movements tentative yet deliberate. Her kimono slid from her shoulders, revealing her bare vulnerability. Her heart raced as she knelt before him, exposed and unsure but certain of her love.

Peter's lips curved into a gentle, loving smile as he took her in, his eyes soft with admiration and understanding. Kimi rose to her feet, her steps quiet yet purposeful as she moved behind him. She knelt again, her fingers brushing his shoulders as they reached around to unbutton his shirt. Each movement was unhurried, every touch intentional. She could feel his heart pounding beneath her fingertips, the warmth of his skin rising to meet her cool hands.

The room's ambiance deepened into an intimate cocoon as Kimi delicately traced the lines of Peter's chest. As the fabric parted, revealing the warmth of his skin, she explored the contours of his body with a soft touch. Peter's breath caught in his throat, his body embracing her every caress. Her touch was light yet full of intent, each movement crafted to stoke the fire of anticipation between them.

Kimi leaned in, her lips finding the sensitive skin of his neck. She kissed him softly there, feeling his pulse race under her lips.

Turning to face her, Peter caught Kimi's gaze. She reached for him, their lips meeting in a kiss that started tender and hesitant but quickly ignited into passion.

The air around them was charged with electricity, every touch and kiss deepening their connection. Peter lifted Kimi off the ground, her legs wrapped around his waist, drawing him closer, her movements bold and inviting. Peter cradled her in his arms as he carried her to his bed.

Their bodies moved in perfect rhythm, breath meeting breath, the tension between them building until everything inside them broke free in a single, trembling release. The world seemed to narrow to the sound of their inaudible words—ragged, desperate, alive. Kimi clung to Peter as though the moment itself might vanish if she let go. Her body quivered with aftershocks that blurred pleasure and disbelief. For a long while, neither spoke. They simply held each other, allowing the rhythm of their hearts to slow and the silence between them to grow soft and real.

Their breathing came in short, uneven bursts at first. Peter's chest rose against hers, then fell in sync as the pace of life gradually returned. Kimi lay still, listening to the quiet settle around them like a warm blanket. Their exhales were the only proof that the world still turned. Across the room, the Sakura teapot glimmered in the thin spill of moonlight, her father's creation now a silent witness to her existence. She traced the line of Peter's arm, trembling with both tenderness and fear. She was the daughter of a poor potter, and he was the son of nobility. In the hush that followed their passion, she felt the truth settle upon her. They had crossed a threshold that could never be undone.

The warmth of his skin lingered against hers, but already the chill of the coming dawn crept in. That night, they had become one, daring to love across every divide that bound them. Yet, as the first light began to touch the horizon, Kimi knew that love, no matter how pure, could not change the world that awaited them beyond this room.

CHAPTER 28

The Unyielding Path

Ren walked the service road back from the beach, each step echoing a memory of youthful days spent with Kimi and his family on the plantation. The road felt longer, his heart heavier, knowing that Kimi had taken another path. His love for her had spurred him to feats of bravery, but now, what did it all mean if they couldn't be together?

As the familiar silhouette of his old plantation home came into view, his mind was flooded with fond memories. Ren remembered the night before he left, standing on that weathered porch, fueled by his desire to prove himself by joining the Triple-V and Kimi's kiss that sealed his choice. Yet, even in that moment, her eyes never seemed fully committed.

Climbing the steps to the home that still held his deepest roots, Ren paused, his hand on the doorknob. The house was silent; the family was still out tending to the plantation, and the echo of emptiness greeted him. Yet, this was home—its familiarity a bittersweet comfort amidst the shards of his broken dreams with Kimi.

He opened the door, the scent of aged wood enveloping him. There, the old wicker chair sat as if waiting like an old friend. Sinking into it, the weave of the wicker cradled his weariness. His eyelids fell shut, and sleep, deep and restorative, claimed him.

Emi's steps on the porch paused as her eyes caught the gleam of polished military shoes. A surge of hope fluttered through her mind, her hands trembling as she pushed the door open slowly. Her eyes found Ren, asleep in the chair, a sight she had imagined in countless dreams. Tears blurred her vision as she approached tenderly, her hand resting lightly on his chest, feeling the rise and fall of his breath—a confirmation of his realness. She wept silently, overwhelmed.

Ren stirred, his eyes opening. "Mom, is that you?" he whispered.

"Hai (Yes), my son, I am here," Emi's voice choked with emotion.

Leaping from the chair, Ren wrapped his arms around her, his embrace desperate. "You've come home," she said repeatedly.

The sound of crying had reached Lyn before she entered the house. Dropping her groceries, she rushed in, her heart pounding with dread, only to stop at the sight of Ren, alive and whole. There he was, now a soldier marked by the scars of war, looking up, momentarily confused by her transformed appearance.

"Who is this beautiful woman standing in front of me?" Ren thought to himself.

Lyn's face warmed with a shy blush. "Say something, you big dummy."

Ren smiled, his heart swelling. "I just can't believe it's you. You've grown up. I guess I can't call you 'Hey You' anymore."

Lyn rushed into his arms, her laughter mixing with tears. "I've missed you. I prayed every day that you'd come home to us."

"I know you did. And now I am home," Ren echoed, a smile tugging at his lips.

"I didn't know you were religious," he teased gently.

"I'm not, but seeing you here, I might start believing."

As they settled into a familiar cadence, Lyn's voice took on a hesitant note. "Have you seen Kimi yet? I think she's home for the weekend."

Ren's expression shadowed momentarily, a flicker of pain crossing his features. "Yes, we've seen each other," he admitted, quickly shifting the focus. "So what's for dinner?"

Lyn laughed, a sound of pure relief. "Classic Ren. I knew you were still in there," she said, turning to retrieve the scattered groceries, her heart freer than it had been in a very long time.

The next day, the morning sun cast its first light over the hospital as Kimi and Peter walked together, hands entwined. Her grip on Peter's hand tightened and loosened intermittently, a silent testament to the turmoil swirling within her.

As they approached the looming glass doors, Kimi pulled her hand away from Peter's. She cast her eyes downward, suddenly conscious of her humble origins.

Peter, sensing the shift, glanced at her with a furrowed brow. "Hey, is everything alright?" His voice was soft.

Kimi forced a small smile, avoiding his gaze. "It's just... being here with you, like this—it feels like crossing a line I shouldn't."

Peter wanted to reach out to bridge the gap with reassurance, but the doors before them opened, and the reality of their surroundings pressed in. They stepped into the stark, sterile environment, the hospital's corridors unfolding before them.

Entering Kosuke's room brought another layer of tension. Standing at the bedside was a figure that seemed to draw the air from the room—a tall Japanese man in a sharp black suit, his presence as imposing as his attire.

Kimi moved mechanically to her nursing duties, her professional mask sliding into place. Peter, however, approached the stranger with a mix of curiosity and apprehension. "I don't mean to be rude, but who are you?" His tone was polite yet firm.

The man adjusted his glasses, his gaze assessing Peter before responding in a very heavy accent. "I am Mr. Tadashi, your father's lawyer. The time has come for you to assume your responsibilities regarding the family business. Your father's passing is overdue, and we cannot delay the necessary decisions any longer."

Peter's jaw clenched, his initial politeness fading. "With all due respect, Mr. Tadashi, I believe I'm quite capable of managing my family affairs without your help."

Mr. Tadashi nodded politely, though his eyes were cold. "Very well. You have until three o'clock today. After that, I will take the necessary actions per your father's request." With a curt bow, he departed, leaving a heavy silence in his wake.

Kimi rushed to Peter's side once they were alone. Her voice was a whisper of concern, "I'm so sorry. Are you okay?"

Peter exhaled sharply, his hands balling into fists at his sides. "He's right, you know. It's time. But I'm not sure I'm ready for this."

"You never really are," Kimi responded softly.

Peter nodded, a determined look settling over his features. "Okay, let's do it."

A hospital clerical worker entered. After Peter signed the necessary forms, Kimi began to disconnect the life-support machines. Yet, as the moment finally approached, Peter stopped her with a gentle hand. "I want to be the one to do this."

Kimi stepped back, giving him space, and nodded in understanding. Peter leaned over his father, whispering words too soft for Kimi to hear, "I told you that I'd be the man to take your life. I will spend every moment from here on out trying to forget you and maybe one day forgive you, not because I love you but so that you will never have power over me again. I want you to know I have found love, chosen love, and that is something you can never take away from me." He then reached out and disconnected the life support.

After a few minutes, Kosuke took his last breath. Kimi moved in to check for a pulse, her professional calm masking the emotional weight of the moment. "He's gone," she declared quietly.

Peter staggered back, the reality of his actions catching up with him, and found a chair to sit in. Kimi sat beside him, drawing him close. She held his gaze, her eyes reflecting a mix of sorrow and support. They leaned into each other and engaged in a tender kiss.

As Peter and Kimi's lips parted, the unexpected voice of Mr. Tadashi sliced through the moment, chilling the air around them. "Interesting, very interesting," he observed dryly, his eyes flicking from one to the other. "This does complicate things." He approached Peter with deliberate steps, extending an envelope. "Upon your father's death, I deliver his last will and testament to you, his only living heir."

With a sense of dread, Peter took the envelope, his fingers trembling slightly as he broke the seal. Inside, the will unfolded.

The Last Will and Testament of Kosuke Tanaka

To Peter,

As you read this, know that my passing marks not just an end but the beginning of your true test. You are now the bearer of our family's legacy, a responsibility that demands not only stewardship of our fortune but strict adherence to the path I have laid out for you.

You are to uphold the Tanaka name through calculated guidance of our business interests and through the fulfillment of the marital alliance arranged in your childhood with a woman of significant family influence in Japan. This union is not up for debate—it is a strategic imperative designed to fortify our dynasty.

Be warned: any deviation from these directives will result in severe repercussions. You will lose everything, including Mae's restaurant, an asset of our family in Hawaii. Mr. Tadashi has been tasked to oversee your compliance with these terms. He will not hesitate to intervene should you falter.

Consider this your final mandate. Fail to comply, and you will find yourself stripped of all titles and holdings. Succeed, and you preserve the might of our lineage.

Act wisely. Your every decision now bears the weight of our ancestral honor.

Kosuke Tanaka

Mr. Tadashi waited patiently, his expression unreadable as Peter absorbed the contents of the document. "Your father was quite explicit," Mr. Tadashi explained further. "The wedding arrangements are set a week following your father's funeral. Your attendance is mandatory. Should you fail in your duties, the consequences will extend beyond personal losses to include Mae's restaurant, which, unbeknownst to you until now, is part of your father's estate."

Peter's reaction was immediate, his body tensing as he faced the dead man lying on the bed. "You would take this from me," he yelled, his voice hoarse with fury. "Still, from the grave, you find ways to control me!"

Kimi's eyes welled with tears as she approached him cautiously. Turning to face her, Peter's voice broke. "I'm not leaving. I don't care. I love you. I won't do it. I won't leave you."

But Kimi, her own voice thick with emotion, shook her head. "I'm sorry, Peter, but it is your duty, your destiny. Perhaps I was only here to bring you peace during this difficult time. I am and will always be the daughter of a poor potter, and you will always be the gold coin."

Peter started to protest, to deny the path laid out for him, but Kimi was resolute. With a deep, respectful bow, she turned and walked away. "No, no, please," Peter pleaded, his voice echoing down the sterile hospital corridors.

Kimi ran. Her steps, firm yet heavy with sorrow, as she disappeared, leaving Peter alone with his future delivered.

Kimi didn't pause as she fled the hospital, her feet finding familiar paths that led her back to the comfort of home. As she approached the porch, cherished memories of laughter and warmth welcomed her even before she reached the door. Inside, the sounds of joy—the unmistakable timbre of Aunty Emi's laughter, Ren's deeper chuckles, and Lyn's animated storytelling—filtered through the walls. The aroma of a home-cooked meal mingled with these echoes of familiarity, tugging at her heart.

With a deep breath to steady her nerves, Kimi pushed the door open. Lyn was the first to see her, her face lighting up. "Kimi! Our Ren has come home to us!" she exclaimed, rushing to embrace her.

Kimi's eyes darted around, landing on Ren. Their last conversation hung in the air like a boulder ready to crush them, and her heart clenched with the fear that perhaps too much had changed, that things were broken beyond repair. But then Ren smiled gently and mouthed, "It's okay." The relief that washed over Kimi was more than she could handle. She couldn't hold back her tears as she ran into his arms. His embrace was strong and comforting, a haven from her swirling thoughts.

After some time, they separated, and the evening unfolded with laughter and talk-story over a hearty meal. Ren shouted out from his favorite chair, "Lyn, you outdid yourself. I can't remember the last time I ate that good." As Emi and Lyn gathered dishes, Kimi slipped out to the porch, seeking solace in the night air.

Ren followed shortly, joining her in silence. The last time they stood here, things had been so different—a kiss that had meant so much at the time, now a bittersweet memory. Breaking the quiet, Ren's voice was hesitant. "So when's the wedding?"

Kimi jerked slightly, surprised. "How did you know?"

"Do you think Peter is the one?" Ren asked.

Kimi turned to him, her eyes glistening in the porch light. "I thought he was, but I can't be with him. It's all too much." She shared the events at the hospital, her words tumbling over each other as she explained the impossible choices laid out before her.

They settled on the porch steps, Ren's arm coming around to comfort her. "I'm sorry, I want you to know that I really am."

Then, with a teasing smirk, he added, "So, now, do I have a chance?"

Kimi chuckled despite her tears, nudging him playfully. "Knock it off."

Their light moment was suddenly interrupted by the sound of a military car pulling up. Ren's heart skipped a beat. It was a car just like the one that took his father away. Together, they watched as the car door opened slowly.

"Could it be?" Kimi whispered.

As they squinted into the twilight, footsteps hurried behind them. Emi burst through, pushing past to reach the figure emerging from the vehicle. "Nobu!" she cried out, throwing her arms around a man much thinner and older than when they had last seen him.

He winced slightly at her tight embrace. Ren, Kimi, and Lyn gathered around, their hearts swelling with the overwhelming joy of their reunion. They were once again a family.

CHAPTER 29

Veils of The Unsaid

Peter searched the hospital corridors, his footsteps echoing with a mixture of urgency and despair. At the nurse's station, he approached a weary-looking nurse, his voice tinged with a hint of hope. "I'm looking for Kimi Ikeda. Can you tell me where I can find her?"

The nurse searched for her schedule and timecard, her eyebrows knitting in confusion. "Kimi? She clocked out a few hours ago. Took some time off, which is unlike her. She never takes days off."

Peter's heart sank. "Do you have any idea where she might have gone? Any information would be helpful."

"I really can't say, sir. Maybe try her home?"

Grasping at straws, Peter headed to the plantation where he thought she lived. Arriving at the cane fields, he remembered Kimi lived with her Uncle Nobu, but his surname wasn't Ikeda. This made his search more complicated.

For two days, Peter knocked on countless doors, hoping to see Kimi's familiar face. At one particular house, he felt a strong hunch. He knocked, waited, and listened. There were faint sounds inside, like whispers of a presence. But no one answered.

Defeated, Peter walked to the beach at the end of the service road where he and Kimi had shared their first kiss. The sun was setting, casting a warm glow over the sea. He sat down on the sand, feeling the weight of despair.

As he stared into the horizon, lost in thought, the sound of footsteps in the sand startled him. He turned quickly, half-expecting, half-hoping it was Kimi. Instead, it was Ren.

Ren sat beside him, his gaze fixed on the slowly setting sun. After a moment of silence, he spoke softly, "It hurts, doesn't it? Watching someone you love choose a different path."

Peter looked away, unable to meet Ren's eyes. "It's over. She left me, and here I am, chasing her shadow."

Ren shook his head slightly, his voice filled with sincerity. "Peter, it's not about her leaving. You don't see it—Kimi and I... we're not meant to be. She's always trying to do what's right, and sadly, I'm not what's right for her. You are."

Peter frowned, puzzled. "What are you talking about, Ren?"

Ren sighed, turning to face Peter fully. "Kimi visited with me. She believes in you. Believes that you can make a difference with your resources and your status. During the war, I learned about sacrifice and the importance of putting others before yourself. I learned that best from Jason, and now Kimi sees that potential in you."

Peter's eyes were drawn to the circles he drew in the sand, his mind racing. Ren's words hung in the air as Peter processed them. He finally spoke, his voice barely above a whisper. "Ren, I'm supposed to leave on Monday. Please tell her we must talk and to meet me at my apartment as soon as she can."

Ren nodded, understanding the pain that Peter was going through. He patted Peter on the shoulder and stood up, preparing to leave. "I'll tell her. You know, sometimes Kimi can be wrong."

As Ren walked away, Peter remained on the beach, the waves crashing in the background, matching the turmoil inside.

It had been five days since Peter last ventured outside his apartment. The world had continued its relentless pace, but for Peter, time seemed to halt, punctuated only by the daily deliveries that kept him fed. He lay on his bed, clutching at the sheets that still held Kimi's faint scent.

The sharp knock at the door jolted Peter from his thoughts that morning. He leaped up, his heart pounding with hope and dread. Could it be Kimi? He raced to the door, flung it open, and his heart sank. There stood Mr. Tadashi, his face impassive, his stance imposing.

Mr. Tadashi surveyed Peter with a barely concealed disdain. "Well, I've seen better," he remarked dryly.

Peter replied defiantly, "I'm not going."

Mr. Tadashi stepped inside, closing the door with a soft but firm click. His voice was calm, but there was a chilling undertone to his words. "Peter, this is not a negotiation. I'm not your friend. I've done some wonderful, terribly wonderful things. Your father, Kosuke, broke many men stronger than you, and I was his instrument."

A cold smile flickered across Mr. Tadashi's face as he continued, "Although your father is no longer with us, my loyalty to his wishes remains unwavering. So, let me outline what will happen if you continue this stubbornness. I will send a car to Mae's restaurant. She will be evicted immediately and thrown onto the street, left to mingle with those she belongs with—the beggars."

Peter felt a surge of anger and fear as Mr. Tadashi paused, his eyes cold and calculating. "And if that's not motivation enough, perhaps a visit to the hospital will be in order. Kimiko Ikeda—wasn't that her name?"

The mention of Kimi's name broke Peter's resolve. His voice cracked as he shouted, "Stop! Please, I'll do whatever you ask."

Mr. Tadashi's smile broadened in satisfaction. "Of course you will," he said smoothly.

Peter noted, "I just need to pack a few things."

Mr. Tadashi shook his head, his expression unyielding. "There's no need for that. We've already sold this apartment. Everything you need will be provided for you along the way."

Before Peter could protest, two henchmen appeared at the door, their presence a silent threat. They stepped forward, expressions void of empathy, and escorted Peter out. The door shut with a definitive thud.

Ren had delivered the message from Peter to Kimi, who sat quietly for a moment, absorbing the weight of the words. "I did the right thing," she finally said, though her voice carried a hint of uncertainty.

Ren sighed deeply before replying, "You know how hard it is for me to discuss this with you. I'm not one for ever disagreeing with you or any of the women in our home, but I'm not so sure this time."

Kimi looked up, her brow furrowed in confusion. "What do you mean?" she asked, her voice tinged with worry.

Ren glanced away, struggling with his words. "It's just that... true love is something that should go beyond tradition. It isn't something that just goes away. It's like a dream that stays with you, even in the darkest times," he explained.

Kimi felt a pang of guilt twist in her gut, realizing Ren was speaking from his unspoken feelings for her. She reached out, placing a comforting hand on his shoulder. "Ren, I know you will find what you are looking for someday," she said softly.

At that moment, Lyn approached the house. Ren's demeanor shifted as he noticed her, a subtle lightness overtaking his features. Kimi observed the transformation, a smile playing on her lips. "Maybe that person is closer than you think," she hinted.

Ren turned to see Lyn walking toward them, her presence like a balm to his unsettled heart. Memories flooded back—the day he left for war, and only Lyn had been there to bid him farewell. Lyn had been a constant throughout every hardship and decision, her support unwavering. How had he been so blind?

As Lyn reached them, she greeted Ren with a look of love and pure admiration. Now fully aware of his feelings, Ren returned her gaze with newfound affection. "How's it going?" Lyn asked.

"Better now," Ren replied, his heart lighter than it had been in a long time.

Meanwhile, Kimi, struck by a sudden realization of her mistake, rushed back to Peter's apartment. When she arrived, the door stood ajar, revealing a scene of disruption. Large, strong men were busily packing Peter's belongings into a truck. Desperate, she approached one of the workers. "Do you know where Peter has gone?" she asked urgently.

The worker paused, then replied without much interest, "We're just here to clear out the apartment, ma'am. Everything's going into storage."

Kimi's heart sank as she slumped into one of the unpacked chairs. All around her, pieces of her Peter were being boxed away. Then, her eyes caught a glimpse of the sakura teapot on an end table—a precious relic from her past. She quietly slipped it into her bag and left, feeling defeated.

As the airplane descended into Japan, Peter looked out the window at the foreign and yet familiar landscape. The advancements in aviation had shortened the distances between continents, but the distance between his heart and the events awaiting him in Japan felt immeasurably vast. The silence between him and Mr. Tadashi during the flight was filled with unspoken tensions. Each man was lost in his thoughts.

Upon landing, Mr. Tadashi turned to Peter with a stern and instructive look. "I will leave you with the driver," he began, his voice devoid of warmth. "You will be fitted for a tuxedo to be married in, then he will drop you off at your family's home in Yokohama."

Peter nodded silently, his mind a swirl of apprehension. "All of your necessary provisions will be there, and the household help will be at your service. Please take the time to freshen up. Tonight, you will meet your future in-laws. Since you have no parents, I will accompany you, and you will represent them. You will meet your future bride the following day at the Yokohama Union Church," Mr. Tadashi continued, each directive slicing through Peter's numbed spirit like a knife.

"Let's just get this over with," Peter murmured as he followed the driver to the waiting car. He felt like a pawn in a game, his personal desires and the remnants of his love for Kimi being swept aside by strategic alignments.

Upon arrival at the stately two-story building that was to be his temporary residence, servants greeted him at the entryway. They escorted Peter to a beautiful room, which one servant indicated with a touch of nostalgia. "This was your mother's room," she said.

The room was elegantly furnished, with a spacious adjoining bathroom featuring a free-standing bathtub. Despite never having known his mother in Japan, Peter felt a deep connection, as if her presence lingered in the air he breathed.

Lost in thought, he looked out the tall windows, watching the bustling street below. He closed his eyes, recalling how Kimi's father had sold the Sakura teapot to his mother for a single gold coin. The memory brought tears to his eyes, blurring the view of the street vendors.

His thoughts were interrupted by a knock at the door. An older gentleman entered, bearing a finely pressed suit for the evening's engagements. "Would this suit be appropriate for tonight, sir?" he inquired with a respectful bow.

Peter nodded, and the man began to leave, but then paused, turning back with a more personal tone. "I'm sorry, sir, to hear about your mother's passing. We all loved her dearly, especially my sister Mae."

Startled, Peter responded, "You're Mae's brother?"

The servant bowed again. "I am. I receive letters from her occasionally. I know all about you, and I was heartbroken to hear about the passing of my nephew Jason."

Encouraged by this connection, Peter invited the man to sit, and they conversed for over an hour. Peter shared his fears, his pressures, and the unbearable weight of decisions, not his own. The servant listened with empathy, his kind eyes soothing Peter's spirit. "Many horrible things can happen in this world, but I know, and Mae knows, that these are just things. However, there are some things that not even death can take from us. Please don't worry about Mae. She will be fine," he reassured Peter, placing a comforting hand on his.

That evening was draped in the formalities of tradition and expectation, a somber setting for Peter's introduction to his future in-laws. The grandeur of the room, underscored by the quiet clinking of fine china and the soft murmurs of the staff preparing the dining area, did little to ease his spirits. Mr. Tadashi led the way into the room, his presence commanding and somewhat overbearing as he introduced Peter to the family.

"May I present Peter Tanaka, the esteemed son of Kosuke and Chiyoko Tanaka," Mr. Tadashi began, his voice carrying across the room to where the in-laws were gathered. They stood, a couple of rigid postures and scrutinizing gazes, their polite smiles barely masking their appraisal of him.

"Welcome, Peter. We have heard much about you," said his future father-in-law, his handshake firm, his eyes searching. "Your father spoke often of his ambitions for you. It is our honor to welcome you into our family."

"Arigato (Thank you)," Peter managed to say, his voice nearly a whisper against the weight of expectations.

The man's wife then stepped forward, her demeanor kind but distant. "We hope you will find happiness in this union and bring honor to our families," she said, gesturing toward the table. "Please, let us dine and discuss the future."

As they settled at the dining table, conversation flowed around Peter, mainly directed at Mr. Tadashi. Topics ranged from business arrangements to family alliances, none of which involved Peter's personal feelings or choices.

"Peter, you must understand the importance of this merger—not just for our families but for the broader strategic alliances it represents," Mr. Tadashi explained, his voice firm as if instructing a child. "Your marriage will symbolize a new beginning, a union of strength and prosperity."

Peter listened, his heart sinking further with every word that painted a picture of his life as a series of transactions.

The ceremonial aspect took over as the meal concluded and documents were presented for signing. Peter found himself mechanically performing bows, his movements mirrored by those of his in-laws. Each bow seemed to solidify his role in this orchestrated future.

"Everything is in order," Mr. Tadashi announced as he checked the documents Peter had signed.

The in-laws nodded, their expressions satisfied, their thoughts already moving beyond the dinner to the implications of the alliance. As they rose from the table, farewells were exchanged with the same formal politeness as their greetings.

Peter was left alone as the room emptied. The echo of the departing footsteps reminded him of his isolation. He stared out a nearby window, watching the night deepen over the city.

"I never wanted this," Peter whispered to the empty room, his voice filled with a mix of resignation and defiance.

Tuesday, April 9, 1946

The morning sun had barely risen, casting a soft light through the windows as Mae's brother helped Peter into his tuxedo. The room was quiet, except for the soft rustling of fabric.

"Well, what do you think?" Peter asked, turning to face the mirror, his expression uncertain.

"You look very nice," the servant replied.

Peter met the servant's eyes in the mirror. "No, seriously, what do you think?" he pressed, seeking a more genuine response.

The servant chuckled softly, easing the tension in the room. "I think if I wore all those layers, I might be very hot," he remarked.

The laughter that followed was a relief to Peter. It was a sound so rare in recent times that its presence was both surprising and profoundly needed.

As they drove toward the church, the city bore scars of the war, with buildings still in ruins and the streets cluttered with rubble. The government's efforts to rebuild were evident in the busy crews and the construction sound filling the air.

Arriving at the church, Peter's heart sank. The structure was severely damaged, with its doors barely hanging on their hinges, and the surroundings served as a stark reminder of the hardships of war. Despite this, the church held historical significance for Peter's family. It was where his parents had married, and now, he was supposed to follow in their footsteps under pretty much the same circumstances.

Off to the side of the church stood a sakura tree, scarred by the war, with most of the wood charred and blackened. Yet, at the tip of its branches, a few green leaves sprouted—signs of life amidst destruction. Peter's gaze lifted in search of blossoms, but only the bare branches initially met his eyes. As he was about to turn away, disheartened, a gentle breeze stirred, and a single sakura blossom drifted down, landing softly on his shoulder.

The delicate touch of the blossom was a stark contrast to the harsh reality surrounding him. It felt like a sign, a moment of pure beauty, and a reminder of renewed possibilities. This small token of nature's resilience fortified him, and he took a deep breath, readying himself to step forward.

The church doors creaked open just then, revealing the interior where his bride-to-be knelt at the altar. She was dressed in a flowing white gown with a long train that cascaded down the steps. Her face was veiled, adding to the surreal nature of the moment.

As he stood there, Mr. Tadashi joined him, his presence a reminder of the arrangements and expectations that had been laid upon him. The gathered audience stood, their movements rustling like leaves as they turned their attention to him.

"It's time, Peter," Mr. Tadashi urged in a voice that seemed to strip all warmth from the moment.

Peter looked down at the sakura blossom now in his hand, its presence grounding him. He closed his hand around it, feeling its fragile texture. At that moment, clarity washed over him, and he turned to Mr. Tadashi, his decision made.

"Mr. Tadashi, there are some things you can't take from us. I've decided to choose love," Peter declared, his voice firm with newfound resolve.

Peter carefully placed the blossom into his pocket without waiting for a response. Then, with a deep breath and a heart full of determination, he turned and ran. He ran from the church, from the life that had been meticulously planned for him, toward a future he would choose for himself.

Peter didn't look back as he made his way to the airport. With the bit of money he had, he boarded a plane, leaving behind the expectations, the obligations, and the life that was never his. He flew towards a new beginning, guided by the simple yet profound belief in chosen love.

Kimi sat alone on her special beach, her gaze lost in the vast expanse of the horizon. The soft murmur of the waves seemed to echo her thoughts as she whispered to herself, "I will never love again." Her voice was a mere breath, carried away by the gentle sea breeze.

As she settled deeper into her thoughts, footsteps on the sand startled her. She turned slowly, her heart skipping a beat. To her surprise, it was Ren, his expression a mix of concern and gentleness.

He sat beside her without a word, mirroring her position and looking out at the sea. After a moment of shared silence, he finally spoke, his voice soft and gentle. "You okay?"

Kimi nodded, her eyes still fixed on the sand where she aimlessly drew circles with her finger. Ren watched her momentarily, then took a deep breath before sharing his news.

"You were right. My soulmate was always here, right in front of me. Tonight, I'm going to ask Lyn to marry me," he announced.

The sadness in Kimi's eyes gave way to a spark of joy, and she threw her arms around Ren's neck, pulling him into a tight embrace. "I'm so happy for you both. Now you really will be my brother," she said.

As they embraced, someone cleared their throat from up the beach, which made them both turn. They jumped to their feet, startled by the interruption. Standing there, somewhat awkwardly, was Peter. His eyes locked on Kimi's, filled with an emotion she couldn't quite read.

"I'm sorry, but am I interrupting something?" Peter asked.

Kimi couldn't contain the surge of feelings that overtook her. Tears welled in her eyes as she ran toward him, throwing herself into his arms. Peter caught her effortlessly, wrapping his arms around her as she sobbed into his shoulder.

Between kisses and tears, Kimi said, "I told you this was a place where miracles happen." The words were muffled against his chest, but Peter heard them all the same.

Ren, sensing the deeply personal moment unfolding, chose to step away, giving them space. He walked past the couple, pausing briefly to place a reassuring hand on Peter's shoulder. Ren whispered to Peter in a low voice, "I guess she was wrong."

Peter nodded slightly, focusing on Kimi, who was still clinging to him. Ren smiled softly and continued walking back to his home.

Mae sat in the quiet of her restaurant, surrounded by the comforting yet bittersweet familiarity of its walls, the scent of delicious food that had once been served, and the soft hum of the refrigerator in the background. Each sound seemed to echo with memories of busier, happier times. Today, however, marked the end of an era. She was here for the very last time. As she reflected on the journey that had brought her to this point, her brother's words from years ago when they lived on the streets echoed in her mind: "Even when you lose everything, there are some things they can't take from you." A gentle smile tugged at the corners of her lips despite the sadness. She had faced loss before and rebuilt her life from nothing. She could do it again.

The sound of the door opening and the familiar jingle of the small bell pulled her from her thoughts. She looked up to see a young man enter hand in hand with a beautiful girl.

"Aunty Mae, I'm not sure if you remember me, but my name is Ren. Your son Jason was a dear friend of mine during the war," he said, his voice filled with warmth and familiarity.

Mae's expression softened as memories of Jason and his friends filled her thoughts. "Oh, Ren, of course I remember you. But I'm sorry to rush you off. We are closed now. Permanently. I'm just waiting for the new owners to arrive."

Mae's words hung in the air, tinged with a hint of sadness and embarrassment. She glanced away, unable to hide the emotion welling up inside her.

It was then that the young woman accompanying Ren stepped forward. She moved gracefully and knelt beside Mae, still perched on an old wooden stool near the counter. Gently, the young woman took Mae's weathered hands in hers.

"Aunty Mae, my name is Lyn, and my fiancé, Ren, and I are the new owners. We don't want to see you leave. We want you to stay and help us as long as you are willing," Lyn said, her voice earnest and full of hope.

Mae looked up, meeting Lyn's eyes, which radiated sincerity and compassion. Before she could respond, Ren added his plea.

"Jason always took care of others, most of all me. He would have wanted this. Please let us return the favor by caring for you," Ren implored.

Mae felt a wave of emotion crash over her. She had braced for a farewell to the place she had poured her heart into, but here was an unexpected chance to remain part of its future. Her eyes glistened with tears as she nodded slowly, overwhelmed by their kindness.

"Yes, I... I would love that. Thank you, both of you," Mae managed to say, her voice choked with emotion. "This place, it's more than just walls and recipes—it's a part of me, and I couldn't bear the thought of leaving it behind completely."

Ren and Lyn smiled. They helped Mae to her feet and began discussing their future together.

CHAPTER 30

The Path to Forgiveness

Wednesday, January 1, 1997

In the lush embrace of Makiki Valley, an old wooden house stood proudly, its grass meticulously cut by hand, and a long driveway was greeted by the welcoming branches of an old mango tree. At the end of this driveway, a carport sheltered a 1986 light brown Toyota Camry, which, despite its years, still gleamed as if brand new.

Beside the carport, a row of repurposed coffee cans served as makeshift planters. Young papaya trees reached skyward, surrounded by a variety of herbs and seedling vegetables, all thriving in their rusted coffee cans. Beyond the carport, a flourishing garden featured a shelf adorned with old screen frames, now rebuilt to shelter stunning orchids, their vibrant colors striking against the white, chipped, weather-painted back wall of the carport. Nearby, a lychee tree stood proudly in the backyard along the fence, much to the delight of visiting grandchildren who feasted on the fruit until they were covered in hives.

The house radiated an air of timeless charm and rarely welcomed guests through its formal front door. Instead, friends and family entered through the kitchen at the back, drawn by the promise of something delicious simmering on the stove. The air carried a unique blend of scents—mosquito punk smoke mingling with the nostalgic aroma of an old library. Inside, aged wood released its deep, comforting fragrance, blending with the subtle mustiness of curtains.

The home had rich, dark wooden floors, their surface polished smooth by the tread of countless bare feet. It also featured built-in cabinets and an old tiled shower, its deep base cleverly serving as an ofuro (a traditional Japanese soaking tub). Tucked away at the back, a sewing room hosted a well-used fitting mannequin, witness to the creation of everything from homemade aloha shirts to intricate wedding gowns.

It had been an exciting New Year's Eve, filled with fireworks, delicious food, lively music, and energetic "talk story." But today was reserved for honoring tradition, a time for reflection on the past and thoughtful contemplation of the future.

Kimi, though weary from the festivities of the night before, was already bustling around her home, diligently sweeping floors and chopping vegetables. As she prepared for the family gathering, her movements were methodical and efficient, a testament to her enduring vigor at the age of eighty-seven.

As she neatly arranged the countertop, she heard the familiar creak of the back door, and a cheerful voice called out, "Auntie Kimi, do you need a hand?" It was her niece, Jenna, the middle daughter of her sister Lyn, who had followed in Kimi's footsteps to become a nurse.

"Your mom should be here soon," Kimi replied. "You know she'll want to take over the kitchen as soon as she steps in."

Jenna laughed, tying on an apron. "Mom's the master chef, after all. But I swear she couldn't do it without you." The two women shared a warm smile and got to work side by side.

Just then, Lyn bustled in with her husband not far behind. "Kimi, I hope you've left something for me to do!" Lyn exclaimed, her eyes scanning the kitchen.

Ren chuckled, leaning casually against the doorway. "I brought reinforcements," he announced as three of their grandchildren followed him inside, their voices filling the house with youthful energy.

Lyn's oldest daughter, who had become an accountant, was the next to arrive. "Auntie, your house always feels like home," she said warmly.

Her son, now successfully running Mae's Cafe, soon entered with a broad grin. "And smells like heaven, too. Guess it runs in the family," he said.

Jenna gently motivated her siblings towards the living room. "Let's give these two some space to work their magic. We'll set up things in here."

As the family scattered, filling the home with the lively sounds of preparation, Kimi leaned closer to Lyn. "You know, I couldn't do this without you. This, all of this—was always the thing you did best."

Lyn nodded, her eyes misty with emotion. "It's more than food, isn't it? It's about keeping the heart of the family beating strong."

Kimi, now a widow, often sat in her quiet living room, surrounded by the memories of Peter, her late husband, who had passed away a few years ago. He had died peacefully in his sleep, still holding Kimi's hand as they lay in bed—just as they had every night of their long, shared marriage.

As soft light filtered through the window on a misty morning, Kimi reflected on those final, tender moments. "He was such a good man, always grateful for every day we had together," she whispered.

Kimi then smiled, her thoughts turning to her son, whom they named Jason. Remembering the difficult pregnancy, she recalled how worried Peter had been. Due to complications, Jason remained their only child.

Her thoughts lingered on Jason, her face glowing with pride as she reflected on the man her son had become. Now a successful surgeon at Queen's Hospital and a father, she thought, with way too many children.

Kimi chuckled softly, her heart swelling with gratitude for her enduring legacy. She was also deeply thankful for Jason's wife, a wonderful woman from Kailua. Though not Japanese, her devotion to culture and tradition was such that she might as well have been. Kimi mused, "I couldn't have asked for a better daughter-in-law."

As Kimi straightened the last cushions in her living room, a firm knock echoed at the door. She hurried over, expecting to see the rest of the family and friends. Instead, she was surprised to find Peter and Ren's old war buddies, Arthur and Junior, standing on her doorstep.

"You guys are early!" Kimi exclaimed with a warm smile, stepping aside to let them in.

Junior, who walked with a noticeable limp from an old war injury, hobbled into the house. Arthur followed close behind, playfully teasing him, "Hurry up, Junior! You can't use that leg as an excuse forever."

Junior bellowed back, "Oh, lay off, Arthur! That's easier said than done."

They were like part of the furniture in Kimi's home, always settling into the same two worn chairs facing the TV. As they made their way to their usual spots, Arthur picked up the newspaper from the coffee table and began to look through it.

Meanwhile, Junior started his ritual grumble as he patted the cushions, searching for the TV remote. "Where did that damn thing go again?" he muttered, his fingers digging between the cushions.

Lyn transformed the kitchen into a whirlwind of culinary activity in no time at all. Pots started boiling, and the sizzle of frying could be heard from the stovetop. The sweet aroma of char siu began to fill the air from the oven. From his favorite chair in the living room, Ren called out, "Smells good hun, I'm starving!"

Kimi set up a card table in the corner of the living room and pulled out a deck of Hanafuda cards. "Arthur, Junior, come on over," she called to the men, gesturing to the newly set-up card table.

They ambled over, Arthur with a newspaper still in hand and Junior finally victorious in his battle with the TV remote. Kimi poured each of them a small glass of sake, setting the tone for a relaxed afternoon. As they settled in, Junior nodded appreciatively at the drink. "Ah, Kimi, you always know how to hurt a guy," he chuckled. Arthur dealt the cards.

The afternoon was filled with the vibrant buzz of family. Each grandchild made their way to greet Grandma Kimi first, who enveloped them in warm, loving hugs. They then scurried to Aunty Lyn for samples of her cooking. Before they could dart off to play, each child paused in front of a cherished picture of Grandpa Peter on the back bookshelf. The portrait was adorned with a tangerine, some mochi, and a small teapot featuring a delicate sakura imprint. The children respectfully bowed their heads briefly, then immediately scampered over to see Uncle Junior.

Despite having heard the tales countless times, the kids gathered around, their eyes wide with childlike wonder. Arthur and Ren shared a smile at the sight of the eager young faces. However, it was Uncle Junior, known for his colorful language and lack of filter, who captivated the children's fascination the most.

One of the oldest grandchildren piped up, his voice bubbling with excitement. "Please, Uncle Junior, tell us again how you saved Uncle Arthur when he fell down the mountain during the war!" A chorus of pleas followed, the other children chiming in eagerly. Arthur rolled his eyes with a playful grin while Ren let out a mocking, exasperated breath, shaking his head.

Junior leaned back in his chair, a twinkle in his eye as he prepared to launch into his well-rehearsed story. "Well, you see, the hill was covered in fog, and I rushed the Germans singlehanded—"

Arthur interrupted, "Singlehanded?"

Junior waved him off. "Details, Arthur, details. It adds to the drama."

As Junior spun his exaggerated tale, the room gasped at his supposed heroic antics. Despite the yearly embellishments, Arthur never corrected him publicly. They were more than friends. They were brothers in every sense but blood. Arthur lived with these stories, renting a room to Junior in his modest home in Manoa. Despite Junior's post-traumatic war life, marked by failed relationships and fleeting jobs, Arthur had never ceased looking out for him. Listening to Junior recount the tale in some strange, roundabout way, when Junior told the story, Arthur felt a sense of appreciation. It was Junior's unique way of saying' thank you.

As Junior continued with his war stories, his narrative took a colorful turn that earned him a light smack on the back of his head from Lyn. "Watch your mouth, Junior, before I tell them what really happened," she scolded playfully yet firmly.

Laughing, Lyn then called everyone into the living room. "Come on, gather around," she announced with enthusiasm.

Kimi took her customary place at the top of the circle as the matriarch. She waited patiently for everyone to join hands for a prayer, a tradition that had deepened with their strong Presbyterian faith. Over the years, Kimi and Lyn became known for their homemade guava jelly, which was sold at the monthly church bazaars, and Jason, her son, served as an altar boy during his youth.

Once the circle was complete, with Jason at Kimi's right side, she nodded to him, indicating that he should address the gathering. "Welcome, everyone. As we stand here to usher in the New Year, let us remember all we are thankful for," he began, his voice steady and clear.

After his introduction, Jason turned to his mother, inviting her to share a few words. Kimi looked around at the faces of her family, her heart swelling with pride and love. "Looking at all of you, I'm overwhelmed by the legacy we've created together," she began, her voice thick with emotion. "My husband, your grandfather, was a man of great sacrifice and bravery. Because of his choices, we have grown into such a wonderful family."

She paused, her gaze sweeping tenderly over her loved ones. "The most important thing we can do in this life, and to honor him, is to choose to be kind to one another. Let's hold that in our hearts as we start this new year."

Turning back to Jason, she gave him a nod. "Jason, would you lead us in prayer? Bless our meal and our family."

Jason took a deep breath, feeling the weight and warmth of the moment. "Let us bow our heads," he said. As the family bowed, Jason began, "Dear Lord, we thank you for this food, for the hands that prepared it, and for the love that surrounds us. Bless this gathering, and help us to live with kindness and courage, just as we were taught by those who came before us. In Jesus' name, amen."

Before they began the meal, Jason made one more announcement. He shared that the family had gotten together to get Grandma Kimi an early birthday present. Kimi was going to be turning eighty-eight years old this coming March. In the Japanese culture, they would be celebrating her Beiju Birthday. This milestone is considered especially lucky due to the resemblance of the kanji for eighty-eight to the character for rice, which symbolizes prosperity and good fortune. In light of this historic birthday, everyone had chipped in to buy her a trip to Japan. Kimi, having grown up quite poor, had never been to Japan before; she longed to visit the village where her parents had grown up. Tears filled her eyes, and she bowed deeply to her family and, in a soft voice, said, "Arigatou."

People found cozy spots to eat all around the house, as traditional Japanese New Year's food was served, complemented by a few sides from other local cultures, a result of past plantation life. Kimi was preparing to serve her son Jason his favorite dish: Ozoni, a traditional Japanese New Year's soup. "Jason, you've always said this was your favorite," Kimi remarked, handing him his bowl filled with savory broth and soft mochi.

"It's not New Year's without it, Mom. I look forward to this all year," he replied.

As he savored the first sips, Kimi watched him, her thoughts drifting to her late husband, Peter. "Watching you eat that reminds me of your father," she remarked softly, the corners of her eyes crinkling with tender emotion.

Jason paused, his expression softening. "I like to think he's still with us, especially at times like this."

Kimi nodded, her heart swelling with emotion. "He is, in so many ways," she agreed, then hesitated, her voice taking on a more serious tone. "Jason, I need to share something with you—something I've never spoken of before."

Jason set his bowl down, giving his mother his full attention. "Of course, Mom. What is it?"

Kimi took a deep breath, her voice low and solemn. "Your father was very brave, not just because he provided for us and always strove to do what was right, but because he made a significant sacrifice before you were born." Jason listened intently, sensing the gravity of her words. "Your father was arranged to be married in Japan to a woman of noble status. But I was just a lowly daughter of a poor potter who grew up on the plantations. Despite his noble lineage in Japan, he renounced his fortune and obligations to be with me."

Jason's eyes widened, the revelation adding a new depth to the father he remembered. Kimi continued, "I am forever grateful for his choice, but a part of me lives with the shame of that decision. The woman he was supposed to marry was left waiting at the altar. As we plan our trip to Japan, I need to do something. I want to find a way to make amends, even after all these years."

Jason reached across the table, taking his mother's hand in his. "Of course, Mom. We'll do whatever it takes to make things right."

Kimi squeezed his hand, relief and gratitude mixing in her expression. "Thank you, my son. It means the world to me to finally fix this wrong."

Tuesday, March 25, 1997

A few days after celebrating her eighty-eighth birthday, Kimi and her son Jason found themselves on a plane bound for Japan. Kimi, though she had never visited Japan, spoke fluent Japanese, a skill her son hadn't inherited. Instead, Jason was more familiar with Hawaiian songs than with any Japanese phrases. Despite this, he enjoyed watching Japanese historical sagas on the local Japanese TV channel.

As they arrived in Yanaka village, they were greeted by streets that artfully balanced contemporary life with echoes of the past. Yanaka was renowned for its vibrant food scene and thriving arts community.

Their journey led them to a cemetery adorned with countless acres of sakura trees, a sight of breathtaking beauty. Although her parents' home no longer stood, the air was filled with a sense of closeness that seemed to bridge the gap between the past and present. The cherry blossoms were in full bloom, creating a canopy of soft pink that transformed the sky into a watercolor painting.

Kimi was overwhelmed by the beauty and the surge of emotions as they walked under the blossoming trees. Turning to Jason, her voice filled with awe and a touch of wonder, she said, "This is exactly like I imagined. Hearing my father, Namio, talk about this place was as though it never really existed. Thank you, Jason, for bringing me here."

As they made their way into town, the air was brisk and invigorating, and Kimi and her son wandered through the quaint, historic streets of Yanaka Village, where the echoes of the past lingered around every corner. They decided to pause their exploration for a warm meal, entering a traditional ryotei that seemed to whisper of old Japan.

As they settled into the low seating, a bowl of steaming soup was placed before each of them, accompanied by plates of hibachi-grilled meat, its salty-sweet aroma tantalizing their senses. Kimi took a sip of the broth, its warmth spreading through her, evoking deep memories.

"This is incredible," Jason remarked, tasting the hibachi meat.

Kimi nodded, her eyes misting slightly with nostalgia. "Yes, it reminds me of the food my mother made when I was very little. You know, my grandparents owned a place just like this one."

Her gaze drifted around the restaurant. "I wish we could have found our family's graves. However, being here and walking these streets... I feel so close to them. They must have walked these paths many times, maybe even stopped in places like this."

The conversation deepened as they continued their meal, each bite serving as a bridge to the past.

After spending several meaningful days in Yanaka, Kimi felt a growing urge to visit Yokohama, driven by a need to right the wrong. As she stood before the Union Church, memories and stories shared by Peter filled her mind. The weight of long-held guilt tightened around her heart, the echoes of a past decision haunting her.

Kimi stepped into the church, her eyes tracing the long aisle leading to the altar at the far end. The quiet hush of the sacred space enveloped her as she imagined the young woman who had been left waiting there, the victim of a broken promise. "How humiliating it must have been for her. How deeply sad," Kimi murmured to herself, her empathy stirring deeply within her.

The pastor, noticing Kimi and Jason, approached them. "May I help you?" he asked.

Kimi reached into her pocket and pulled out a small, weathered piece of paper. She unfolded it carefully, revealing the name Aiko Matsuda. "I am looking for someone," she began, her voice steady but filled with emotion. "She would be about my age now. She was supposed to be married here many years ago."

The pastor's expression turned thoughtful. "I was recently transferred here," he explained, "and while the Matsuda family has been a significant supporter of this church for many years, I'm afraid I don't recognize the name Aiko. However, the Matsuda family does have a considerable section in the church cemetery."

Kimi nodded, a mix of relief and apprehension crossing her features. "Could you show me?"

"Of course," the pastor replied, his voice reassuring. He led Kimi through the back doors of the church and out into the cemetery, where the Matsuda family graves were carefully tended, each headstone a silent testament to the family's long-standing connection to the church.

The pastor guided Kimi and her son through the aged gates of the cemetery. As they walked among the ancient gravestones, Kimi felt the weight of centuries under her feet. Some stones were eroded by time and were nearly unreadable. The more she read the names, the more vividly she recalled the stark differences between her own humble origins and the noble lineage of Aiko Matsuda. Her husband, Peter, had forsaken so much for a life with her.

Suddenly, Jason's voice cut through the air. "Mom, come and look!" he called out excitedly.

Kimi hastened to where her son stood. There, etched in stone, was the name they had been searching for. Kimi had harbored guilt for years, wondering if her love story with Peter had inadvertently wrecked another's life. The grave before her was well-tended, the area around it freshly groomed, with incense still smoldering from a recent visitor.

Kimi knelt at the base of the gravestone, her fingers tracing the barely legible inscriptions. From her bag, she retrieved the small Sakura teapot and handed it to Jason. "Son, please fill this with water," she asked softly.

Once the teapot was filled, Kimi used a small rag dampened with the pot's water and gently cleaned the stone. As she worked, she spoke quietly, as if Aiko herself could hear. "I'm sorry for any pain we caused you. I hope your life was full of happiness despite everything."

She bowed deeply, her forehead touching the ground, a gesture of deep respect and profound apology.

When she straightened and looked again, the cleaned stone clearly bore the following message: Here lies Aiko Matsuda, loving wife, mother, and most of all, cherished friend. Tears welled up in Kimi's eyes, relief setting in. It seemed Aiko had found her own path to love and fulfillment.

Sensing his mother's emotional release, Jason gently helped her to her feet. "Are you okay, Mom?" he asked, his voice laden with concern.

"Yes, Jason, I am now," Kimi replied. "She found happiness. That's all I needed to know."

Turning away from the grave, they left the cemetery slowly, leaving behind the girl who was left at the altar and the perfect Sakura teapot.

The End

If you enjoyed *Sakura: The Last Blossom*,
please take a moment to leave a quick review.

Your feedback helps other readers discover the story
and supports future books by **M. K. Hirokawa**.

(Scan the QR code below to share your review.)

Nonfiction Historical Index

1603

- Establishment of Yanaka Hills, Yanaka Village ("Old Tokyo"), and Sendagi as part of the historical area known as Yansen.

1859

- Yokohama established as a major port.

- The Queen's Hospital is founded in Hawaii by Queen Emma and King Kamehameha IV.

1864

- Land in Laie, Oahu, Hawaii is acquired by Mormon missionaries.

1865

- Eugene Van Reed is appointed as Hawaii's consul general in Japan to recruit plantation workers.

- Waialua Sugar Mill is established on Oahu.

1868

- Departure of 149 contract workers from Yokohama aboard the Scioto.

1872

- Establishment of Yanaka Cemetery, Sakura Grove.

- Yokohama Union Church is established, serving as one of the oldest Protestant churches in Japan.

1878

- Hawaiian railroads receive authorization to build stations and cross government lands.

1882

- Iolani Palace is built in Hawaii.

1885

- Arrival of 950 contract laborers in Hawaii under an immigration treaty with Japan, marking significant Japanese immigration.

1895

- Daily Bulletin evolves into the Evening Bulletin, advocating for Hawaiian annexation.

1897

- Arrival of the Shinshu Maru in Oahu with 670 Japanese immigrants; most are sent back due to insufficient funds.

1898

- Formation of the Waialua Agricultural Company by Castle & Cooke and purchase of a plantation.

- Establishment of the National Guard of Hawaii.

1908

- Schofield Barracks is established in Oahu for defense purposes.

1916

- Commissioning of the USS Arizona, later memorialized at Pearl Harbor.

1918

- Influenza pandemic affects millions worldwide, including significant casualties in Hawaii.

1926

- Meiji Jingu Stadium, a significant sports venue, is built in Tokyo, representing Japan's modernization and international engagement in sports.

1928

- Construction of the old Waikiki Tavern and Inn.

1932

- The backdrop of the Great Depression.

1934

- Formation of the "Greater Japan Tokyo Baseball Club," the precursor to the Japanese Professional Baseball League.

1935

- Opening of Smith's Union Bar in Chinatown, Honolulu.

1939-1945

- World War II involves Japan as one of the Axis powers.

1940

- The Aloha Café in Honolulu becomes known for its live shows and music.

December 7, 1941

- Attack on Pearl Harbor by Japan, leading to U.S. entry into World War II.

- Sinking of the USS Arizona.

- Establishment of Sand Island internment camp.

- Internment and suspicion of Japanese Americans begin.

December 8, 1941

- President Franklin D. Roosevelt's famous "Day of Infamy" speech and U.S. declaration of war.

1942

- Formation of the Varsity Victory Volunteers (Triple-V) by University of Hawai'i students.

- Evacuation of Japanese Americans from the Pacific Coast.

- War Relocation Authority is created to manage internment camps.

1943

- Activation of the 442nd Regimental Combat Team composed of Nisei soldiers.

- President Roosevelt's approval for the formation of a combat team of Japanese-American soldiers.

- Fort McCoy (Camp McCoy), Wisconsin becomes the largest permanent POW camp for Japanese prisoners.

- March 28: Enlistment march and farewell ceremony for Japanese-American soldiers in Honolulu at Iolani Palace.

1944

- Japanese American soldiers begin combat operations in Europe under the 442nd Regimental Combat Team.

- October 14: The battle for Bruyères and Biffontaine in France during WWII.

- Rescue of the Lost Battalion in the Vosges Mountains, France.

Late 1940s-1950s

- Post-war rebuilding efforts in Japan, with assistance

from the U.S. and efforts from the Japanese diaspora.

1968

- Byodo-in Buddhist Temple, Kahaluʻu, Hawaii is built to honor Japanese culture and heritage in Hawaii.

1990s and Beyond

- Beiju (88th birthday celebration), a traditional Japanese milestone birthday symbolizing longevity and prosperity.

Notable Locations and Establishments

- **Aloha Tower** – Honolulu, a significant location for departures and arrivals by sea.

- **Aloha Café** – Popular restaurant in Honolulu.

- **Chinatown, Honolulu** – Historic area known for nightlife and culture.

- **Hotel Street, Honolulu** – A famous entertainment district.

- **Kalakaua Avenue** – A major thoroughfare in Honolulu.

- **Queen's Hospital, Honolulu** – Established in 1859 and active during WWII.

- **Schofield Barracks** – A military base in Wahiawa, Oahu.

- **Smith's Union Bar** – A popular bar in Chinatown, frequented by locals and servicemen.

- **Waialua** – A plantation town on Oahu.

- **Waikiki Tavern** – A popular social venue in Honolulu.

Cultural and Social Contributions

- **Japanese American Plantation Baseball Teams (Pre-WWII)** – Organized sports teams formed within Hawaiian plantation communities, providing recreational and social opportunities for Japanese immigrants and their families.

- **New Year's Celebrations in Hawaii (Pre-WWII)** – A blend of Japanese and Hawaiian traditions, reflecting the cultural fusion among immigrant communities in Hawaii.

- **Traditional Japanese Tea Ceremony (Pre-WWII)** – A cultural practice emphasizing harmony, respect, purity, and tranquility, often performed during important gatherings and milestones.

- **"Go For Broke" Motto (WWII Era)** – A phrase encapsulating the 442nd Regimental Combat Team's determination to give everything in battle, now an enduring symbol of their bravery and sacrifice.

Pronunciation Guide

A

- A hui hou – Till next time *(ah hoo-ee ho)*

- Aiea – Another location with a plantation hospital *(eye-ay-ah)*

- Aiko – A Japanese name *(eye-ko)*

- Akiko – A Japanese name *(ah-kee-ko)*

- Aloha – Love, affection, peace *(ah-loh-ha)*

- Arigato – Thank you *(ah-ree-gah-toh)*

- Arigato gozaimasu – Thank you very much *(ah-ree-gah-toh goh-zai-mahs)*

B

- Beiju – 88th birthday celebration *(bay-joo)*

- Bonzai – A cheer, meaning "Victory" or "Long life." *(bahn-zai)*

- Byodo-in – A Buddhist temple *(byo-doh-een)*

C

- Char siu – Chinese-style BBQ, popular in Hawaiian cuisine *(char shoo)*

- Chiyoko – Peter's mother *(chee-yoh-koh)*

D

- Dashi – A Japanese soup base commonly used in cooking *(dah-shee)*

- Domo arigato gozaimasu – Thank you very much *(doh-moh ah-ree-gah-toh goh-zai-mahs)*

- Douzo genki de – Take care of yourself *(doh-zoh gen-kee deh)*

E

- Emi – A Japanese name *(eh-mee)*

- Ewa – A location with a plantation hospital *(eh-vah)*

F

- Futon – A Japanese-style mattress *(foo-tawn)*

G

- Ganbatte – Go for it or Do your best *(gahn-baht-teh)*

- Genki desu ka – How are you? *(gen-kee dehs kah)*

- Guava – A fruit commonly grown in Hawaii *(gwah-vah)*

H

- Hachimaki – A headband symbolizing perseverance *(hah-chee-mah-kee)*

- Hai – Yes *(hi or hah-ee)*

- Hanai – Informal Hawaiian adoption *(hah-nai)*

- Hanafuda – Japanese card game *(hah-nah-foo-dah)*

- Hashi – Chopsticks *(hah-shee)*

- Haole – Hawaiian term for a foreigner *(how-lee)*

- Hibachi – Japanese cooking technique *(hee-bah-chee)*

- Huhu – Irritated *(hoo-hoo)*

I

- Ie – No *(ee-eh)*

- Ikeda – A Japanese name *(ee-keh-dah)*

- Iolani – A Hawaiian name *(ee-oh-lah-nee)*

- Ishikawa – A Japanese surname *(ee-shee-kah-wah)*

K

- Kahaluʻu – Location in Hawaii *(kah-hah-loo-oo)*

- Kailua – Town in Hawaii *(kai-loo-ah)*

- Kalakaua – A major thoroughfare in Honolulu, Hawaii *(kah-lah-kow-ah)*

- Kanji – Japanese characters used in writing *(kahn-jee)*

- Keiki – Child in Hawaiian *(kay-kee)*

- Kimiko (Kimi) – A girl's name *(kee-mee-koh)*

- Kimono – A traditional Japanese garment *(kee-moh-noh)*

- Kon'nichiwa – Hello *(kohn-nee-chee-wah)*

- Kosuke – Peter's father *(koh-soo-keh)*

- Koshiki – A type of container or storage method *(koh-shee-kee)*

- Kupuna – Elder or Grandparent *(koo-poo-nah)*

L

- Lei – A traditional Hawaiian garland or wreath *(lay)*

- Lo'i – Hawaiian wet taro patch *(loh-ee)*

- Lyn – Kimi's younger sister *(lin)*

- Lychee – A tropical fruit grown in Hawaii *(lie-chee)*

M

- Mae – Jason's mother *(my)*

- Mahalo – Thank you *(mah-hah-loh)*

- Maika'i – Great or Good *(mai-kah-ee)*

- Makai – Toward the ocean *(mah-kai)*

- Makiki – Valley in Hawaii *(mah-kee-kee)*

- Manoa – A valley and residential neighborhood in Honolulu *(mah-noh-ah)*

- Matsuda – A Japanese name *(maht-soo-dah)*

- Mauka – Toward the mountains *(mow-kah)*

N

- Namio – Kimi and Lyn's father *(nah-mee-oh)*

- Nieele – Nosey *(nee-eh-leh)*

- Nisei – Second generation of Japanese-Americans *(nee-say)*

- Nobu – Uncle, guardian to Kimi and Lyn *(noh-boo)*

- Nobu Takahashi – Full name of Kimi and Lyn's uncle *(noh-boo tah-kah-hah-shee)*

O

- Oama – A type of small fish in Hawaiian waters *(oh-ah-mah)*

- Ohayo – Morning *(oh-hah-yoh)*

- Ohayo gozaimasu – Good morning *(oh-hah-yoh goh-zai-mahs)*

- Okazuya – A Hawaii Japanese restaurant *(oh-kah-zoo-yah)*

- Okaasan – Mother *(oh-kah-ah-sahn)*

- Omedetou – Congratulations *(oh-meh-deh-toh)*

- Omiyage – Gifts *(oh-mee-yah-geh)*

- Onbuhimo – Traditional Japanese baby sling *(ohn-boo-hee-moh)*

- Onsen – Japanese hot spring or bathhouse *(ohn-sen)*

- Ofuro – Japanese soaking tub *(oh-foo-roh)*

- Otosan – Father *(oh-toh-sahn)*

- Ozoni – Traditional Japanese New Year's soup *(oh-zoh-nee)*

R

- Ren – A Japanese/Hawaiian name *(ren)*

- Ryotei – A type of expensive, traditional Japanese restaurant *(ryoh-tay)*

S

- Sake – Japanese rice wine *(sah-keh)*

- Sakura – Cherry blossom, symbolic of transient life *(sah-koo-rah)*

- Sendagi – A location or name in Japan *(sen-dah-gee)*

- Shinto – Japanese religion *(sheen-toh)*

- Sumimasen – Excuse me *(soo-mee-mah-sen)*

T

- Tadashi – A Japanese name *(tah-dah-shee)*

- Tanaka – A common Japanese surname *(tah-nah-kah)*

- Tutu – Hawaiian term for grandmother *(too-too)*

W

- Waialua – The hometown of the main characters *(why-ah-loo-ah)*

- Waikiki – A well-known area in Honolulu, Hawaii *(why-kee-kee)*

- Wahine – Woman *(wah-hee-nay)*

- Wailua – Place in Hawaii *(why-loo-ah)*

Y

- Yanaka – A place in Japan *(yah-nah-kah)*

- Yokohama – A place in Japan *(yoh-koh-hah-mah)*

- Yukie – A Japanese name, Namio's wife *(yoo-kee-eh)*

Bibliography

Books

- Duus, Masayo. *Unlikely Liberators: The Men of the 100th and the 442nd.* University of Hawaii Press, 1987.

- Gordon, Andrew. *A Modern History of Japan: From Tokugawa Times to the Present.* Oxford University Press, 2020.

- Jansen, Marius B. *The Making of Modern Japan.* Harvard University Press, 2002.

- McNaughton, James C. *Nisei Linguists: Japanese Americans in the Military Intelligence Service during World War II.* Department of the Army, 2006.

- Murray, Alice Yang. *Historical Memories of the Japanese American Internment and the Struggle for Redress.* Stanford University Press, 2008.

- "Emigrants to Hawaii in the Meiji Era, Part 2." *Cruise Ferry and Ocean Liner History.* Accessed June 15, 2024. https://cruise-ferry.main.jp/wp-content/uploads/2020/06/ch-2-Hawaii-part-2.pdf.

Government and Military History Sources

- "442nd Infantry Regiment History and Heroism." *U.S. Army Center of Military History.* Accessed July 9, 2024. https://history.army.mil/brochures/nisei/nisei.htm.

- "The Battle of Bruyères and Biffontaine." *U.S. Army Center of Military History.* Accessed May 3, 2024. https://history.army.mil.

- "Go for Broke: The Story of the 442nd RCT." *Densho Encyclopedia.* Accessed August 2, 2024. https://encyclopedia.densho.org/442nd_Regimental_Combat_Team.

- "Honoring the 442nd: Nisei Soldiers in WWII." *National Museum of American History, Smithsonian In-

stitution. Accessed April 22, 2024. https://american history.si.edu.

- "Rescue of the Lost Battalion: A Heroic Effort." *Texas Military Forces Museum*. Accessed January 15, 2024. https://texasmilitaryforcesmuseum.org.

- "The 442nd Regimental Combat Team: A History of Valor." *National Archives*. Accessed March 27, 2024. https://www.archives.gov/research/milita ry/ww2/442nd.

- "The 442nd Regimental Combat Team: Go For Broke." *Go For Broke National Education Center*. Accessed November 10, 2023. https://www.goforbrok e.org.

- "The Legacy of the 442nd Regimental Combat Team." *Go For Broke National Education Center*. Accessed February 14, 2024. https://www.goforbroke. org/history.

- "Records of the Office of War Information (OWI)." *National Archives*. Accessed December 3, 2023. https://www.archives.gov/research/guide-fed -records/groups/208.html.

- "FDR's 'Day of Infamy' Speech." *National Archives.* Accessed May 19, 2024. https://www.archives.gov/exhibits/american_originals/infamy.html.

- "Varsity Victory Volunteers and Their Legacy." *Densho Encyclopedia.* Accessed June 7, 2024. https://encyclopedia.densho.org.

Japanese and Hawaiian History

- "Historical Timeline of Japan." *National Diet Library of Japan.* Accessed July 1, 2024. https://www.ndl.go.jp.

- "Japan Timeline of Events." *Asia for Educators, Columbia University.* Accessed December 12, 2023. http://afe.easia.columbia.edu.

- "Timeline of Japanese History." *The Japan Times.* Accessed August 9, 2024. https://www.japantimes.co.jp.

- "Tokyo Metropolitan History." *Tokyo Metropolitan Government.* Accessed April 8, 2024. https://www.metro.tokyo.lg.jp.

- "Western Influence and Modernization in Japan."

- *Japan Experience.* Accessed January 25, 2024. https://www.japan-experience.com.

- "History of the Hawaiian Kingdom." *Hawaii History Organization.* Accessed March 10, 2024. https://www.hawaiihistory.org.

- "The Overthrow of the Hawaiian Monarchy." *The Atlantic.* Last modified December 11, 2024. https://www.theatlantic.com.

- "Iolani Palace Official History." *Iolani Palace.* Accessed February 2, 2024. https://www.iolanipalace.org.

- "Schofield Barracks and Its Role in WWII." *U.S. Army Garrison Hawaii.* Accessed November 18, 2023. https://home.army.mil/hawaii.

- "USS Arizona Memorial: Remembering Pearl Harbor." *National Park Service.* Accessed July 24, 2024. https://www.nps.gov.

- "Meiji Jingu Stadium: Historical Significance." *Meiji Jingu Stadium.* Accessed May 1, 2024. https://www.jingu-stadium.com.

Cultural Traditions and Locations

- "Yokohama Union Church History." *Yokohama Union Church.* Accessed November 5, 2023. https://www.yokohamaunionchurch.org.

- "The Queen's Hospital: History and Mission." *The Queen's Health Systems.* Accessed June 27, 2024. https://www.queens.org.

- "Laie, Hawaii: A Historical Overview." *Laie Hawaii.* Accessed January 4, 2024. https://www.laiehawaii.com.

- "Waialua Sugar Mill: Plantation History." *Hawaii Plantation Museum.* Accessed August 5, 2024. https://www.hawaiiplantationmuseum.org.

- "Byodo-In Temple in Hawaii." *Valley of the Temples Memorial Park.* Accessed March 21, 2024. https://www.valley-of-the-temples.com.

- "Beiju: The Celebration of 88 Years." *Nippon.com.* Accessed July 14, 2024. https://www.nippon.com.

- "Japanese American Baseball in Hawaii." *Japanese American National Museum.* Accessed February 18, 2024. https://www.janm.org.

- "New Year's Traditions in Hawaii." *Hawaii Magazine.* Accessed April 28, 2024. https://www.hawaii magazine.com.

- "Traditional Japanese Tea Ceremony Explained." *The Urasenke Foundation.* Accessed May 9, 2024. https://www.urasenke.or.jp.

www.ingramcontent.com/pod-product-compliance
Lightning Source LLC
Chambersburg PA
CBHW030340120726
47901CB00007B/1848